Those who knew Jed Lacey best thought he was merciless. They were wrong. He used his weapon repeatedly before he climbed to the street.

Lacey did not really expect to live through the blast. It drove down the hundreds of kilometers of tunnels like a multi-crowned piston, shattering whatever stood in its way. The Boxcars and everything in it were gone, driven meters or kilometers down the tunnel in a tangle of plastic and splinters and blood; everything but Lacey and the safe that shielded him.

The air was choking, but with dust and not K2—yet. The rebounding shock waves of the blast would suck the stockpiled gas into every cranny of the tunnel system soon, but at least the lethal cargo had not ridden the initial wave front. Lacey rose slowly, sucking air through the hard fabric of his sleeve. Once the ground beside him came into focus, he saw a dropped powergun. He picked it up and began to stagger toward an unblocked staircase.

Those who knew Jed Lacey best thought he was merciless. They were wrong. He used his weapon repeatedly before he climbed to the street. That was the only mercy available to the hideously led at him in agony.

D0957860

mangled forms who mswin he the council tx

DAVID DRAKE

BAEN BOOKS

LACEY AND HIS FRIENDS

This is a work of fiction. All the characters and events portrayed in this book are fictional, and any resemblance to real people or incidents is purely coincidental.

Copyright © 1986 by David Drake

All rights reserved, including the right to reproduce this book or portions thereof in any form.

A Baen Books Original

Baen Publishing Enterprises
260 Fifth Avenue
New York, N.Y. 10001

First printing, October 1986

ISBN: 0-671-65593-0

Cover art by Stephen Hickman

Printed in the United States of America

ACKNOWLEDGMENTS: These stories have appeared previously, as follows: "Nation Without Walls," *Analog Science Fiction/Science Fact*, July 1977, © 1977 by The Conde Nast Publications Inc.; "The Predators," *Destinies* Vol. I No. 5 (Oct.-Dec. 1979), © 1979 by David Drake; "Underground," *Destinies* Vol. 2 No. 1 (Feb.-Mar. 1980), © 1980 by David Drake; "Travellers," *Destinies* Vol. 3 No. 1 (Winter 1981), © 1981 by David Drake; "Time Safari," *Destinies* Vol. 3 No. 2, © 1981 by Charter Communications, Inc.

Distributed by
SIMON & SCHUSTER
TRADE PUBLISHING GROUP
1230 Avenue of the Americas
New York, N.Y. 10020

DEDICATION

For Kirby McCauley

Who has been my agent since I lived in Durham
and he lived in Minneapolis; and who has been a
friend for about as long.

Lacey and His Friends

I   NATION WITHOUT WALLS   3
II THE PREDATORS   45
III UNDERGROUND   85

Plus Two Bonus Stories
"Travellers" *and* "Time Safari"

I wrote "Nation without Walls" during the eight years I spent as Assistant Town Attorney for the Town of Chapel Hill. Considered as protagonists for works of fiction, attorneys are perhaps one stage less boring than writers; I've never used either experience as direct background.

But the job certainly did teach me things about low-level politics, elective and bureaucratic both. It gave me insight into, for example, the maneuverings in Rome in 49 BC.

Chapel Hill had no Julius Caesar, goodness knows. But the rest of the cast was present: the drunks and buffoons; politicians who had power blocks and—on a good day—the ability to spell their own names; people who were more pompous than they were well-meaning; people who were more determined to keep their jobs than they were pompous or well-meaning; well-meaning people who didn't understand the system; and well-meaning people who learned the system and promptly left it in disgust.

My job also taught me a great deal about frustration.

So I wrote about a fellow named Jed Lacey in a future that looked more likely in 1977 than it does today (when it's become fashionable again to fear nuclear war instead). It was an important story for me, the first time I grappled with monsters wearing human faces—or, more accurately, monsters wearing the face of humanity. It was Analog's cover story for the month, a piece of ego-boo whose value far outweighed the few hundred bucks I was paid in cash.

And perhaps most important, "Nation without Walls" gave me a socially acceptable way to deal with matters that are best dealt with on paper.

NATION WITHOUT WALLS

The blast echoed much farther and faster than the sound waves alone could have.

Level 17 was to State Standard Floorplan, a sixty-meter circle crammed with almost five hundred desks. The computer was guided by psychiatric profiles and performance analyses to the same instant decision a human director would have made by gut reaction: Lacey's mastoid implant rang him to alert.

This one was too big to be dropped.

"Ready," Lacey said by reflex, swinging away the counterweighted scanner helmet under which he had been hunched at his desk. He was a squat man and as grim as a wolf, dark except for a jagged scar from his right ear to his collarbone. His expression was that of a hunter who had seen much of the world and found little humor in it. Over his net jumpsuit he wore a jacket, opaque and slightly unfashionable; it pouted to hide the needle stunner holstered high on his right hip.

3

"Bomb explosion in the Follard Tower," said the voice behind Lacey's jawbone. "A car and driver are assigned to you. There are currently three dead." After a pause that would have been meaningful in a human, the computer added, "One of the dead has been identified as Loysius Follard."

Lacey was already moving in a quick shuffle that took him around other U-shaped desks and their occupants, men and women sexless under their enveloping scanner helmets or staring blank-eyed beyond the circular confines of the room. A few chatted low-voiced with their neighbors. Few took notice of Lacey's haste: to these investigators, "private" business was no more interesting than naked skin to a Turkish bath attendant.

Over the door to the pad a light panel was flashing the number of the car assigned to Lacey. He ignored the six-digit display, knowing that on a priority run the car would already be swinging toward the doorway to pick him up.

It was, lift fans shrieking as it hopped a row of stationary vehicles to get to him. The driver was a blob of orange in a crash suit, loose fabric that would inflate at a 10-g impact, and a polarized face shield. The passenger compartment behind him was an open box with low bulkheads, a bench, and a scanner helmet for the occupant. The vehicle's own single camera was on a meter-high pole above the nose, a vantage that caught both driver and passenger and was legally adequate so long as they faced it except when grounded and thus in the field of other scanners.

Lacey leaped aboard, slapping the driver on the shoulder as he hit the seat. The car's quick acceleration urged the agent back as, helmet already settled over him, he willed an upward twitch of his ring finger. The nerve had been cut and rerouted to trigger his implant for his commands to the Crime Service data net.

"Explosion site," Lacey directed. In his helmet screen smoke eddied in what had been a ten-meter cubicle before the explosion had blown out the two partitions separating it from the greater office of which it had been one corner. Two of the dead were victims of a wall fragment which had cartwheeled through the banks of desks in the main office. The third corpse lay across the cubicle's own gleaming console of polished mahogany. Incredibly, the dead man had been the only occupant of the smaller room despite the fact that it had the full complement of three scanning cameras and the heavy tax burden that went with them. Lacey realized why the computer had singled out the third man. "Loysius Follard," he told his implant, "Economic highlights."

Instead of an immediate answer, the link made a faint clicking noise like lock tumblers clearing and asked, "Access code, please."

"Access code" from the computer because Lacey had just requested information proscribed even to Crime Service personnel unless they had a particular need. The data were available in a special bank, probably that of the Security Police, to which outside access was rigidly controlled. And the computer had added "Please" because it is easier to program in politeness than it is to defend its absence to people of the stature that sometimes queried the Sepo net.

Blocks like that were unusual, though Lacey had suspected power when he saw Follard's office. Flipping the helmet away from his eyes, Lacey punched his code, B-D-Q, M-E-Z, O-P, on the plate built into the driver's seat back. It was the one portion of the car deliberately hidden from the scanner, just as desk code plates were shrouded from room cameras—one secret in a State dedicated to eradication of all others.

Another faint clicking. Then, "Loysius Follard, controls Kongo Holding Corporation, controls—"

"Cancel," Lacey said. Kongo Holding was, for all practical purposes, the nation of Argentina. He had hoped knowledge of the primary victim's business would be a line on the assassin. Business at Follard's eminence opened, literally, the whole of Earth's seventeen billion people as potential enemies.

It also explained why economic data were on the Sepo list. The omnipresent scanners recorded every act and cut through the sham of straw men and proxy voting. Even a man of Follard's power could not avoid them, but he could arrange that availability of the data be sharply restricted. There would always be friends, contacts, favors. The Thirty-first Amendment and the Open Truth Act implementing it had not been what many saw them to be, an abandonment of the fight for individual privacy against the flood of technological intrusion. Rather, they were an attempt to utilize and control the information-gathering which eighty years of unsuccessful prohibition had proved to be an ineradicable part of American life. When everything became open to a few, much could be forbidden to the generality.

Lacey dropped the helmet over his eyes again. His blocky face was tightening with concentration and the scar had tensed to a line of white fire. On the internal screen appeared the private office at the moment of explosion, images recorded by the scanning cameras and recalled for Lacey from the huge electronic vaults beneath Atlanta. Follard was sprawled across the smooth intarsia of his desk top. His eyes were open and the lighter skin of his right palm was visible through his half-clenched fingers. The bubble of flame which wrecked the room burst from a ventilator duct just as the louvers began to quiver to signal that the fan had switched on.

Lacey requested the scanner on the outer wall, three minutes before the explosion. Follard was slumped even then, a message capsule visible beneath his shoulder from the new angle.

"Give me the third scanner," Lacey said, "explosion minus four." The camera behind Follard's desk should have displayed the capsule's contents when it was opened; instead there was nothing. The camera was out of order, had been out of order minutes before the blast might have damaged it. No object is eternal, but scanning cameras were Man's nearest present approach to that ideal. Lacey switched to the first scanner and a sight of Follard speaking a quick affirmative into a wall microphone—sound simulacra could be developed by the net, but no investigator of Lacey's experience needed them when the subjects' lips were visible. The desktop burped the thin 10-cm-square container, examined in the bowels of the Tower for concealed dangers after a courier service had delivered it. Follard touched the tab of the stiff foil capsule with his signet. The radioactive key within the ring caused the tab to roll back without incinerating the contents as any other means of opening would have done. Then Follard collapsed across his desk.

Lacey's face spread in a grin that bared his prominent eyeteeth. "Technical request," he directed his implant. "I want a desk print-out on lethal gases, instantly fatal and explosive in low concentration."

"Define 'low concentration'," croaked the computer link.

"Bloody hell!" Lacey spat, then considered. "However much an unreinforced 50 cc message capsule could hold, distributed in a . . . twenty-five cubic-meter office."

The driver's hand touched Lacey's forearm, "Sir, we've got the site—but there's a Sepo on the pad and—"

Lacey cocked up the scanner helmet, glaring past the half-turned driver to the roof pad of the Follard Tower. The massive block of concrete and vitril was of standard design, a landing pad on the roof for the top executives—those with air cars—and fifteen floors beneath linked by open stairs. Rank among chiefs would go with altitude, an inversion of that among the lower orders who entered at ground level and climbed stairs to their desks. Follard's top-floor window gaped emptily instead of reflecting from a polarized surface. Seven private cars with closed cabins and luxurious appointments were ranked about the open stairhead. There, one hand on the stair rail and the other holding a modulated-laser communicator, stood a drab, weedy man who had pulled the blue skull-cap of the Security Police from his pocket to assert his authority.

Three news-company cars were in sight but keeping a respectful five-hundred-meter distance from the Sepo. Lacey snorted, knowing that if only Crime Service had been present the reporters would have been swarming over the site. He had once knocked a pair of them down with his stunner when they ignored his demand to keep clear. The microscopic needles and their nerve-scrambling charges had done no permanent harm to the newsmen, but Lacey had been threatened with the Psycomp if he ever did it again. It was surprising that the Sepos were already at the scene. It was almost as if—

The security man raised his communicator and aimed it at the pickup cone on the nose of Lacey's car. The microphone shroud covered the Sepo's lips and the beam itself had too little scatter to be intercepted. The message rumbled out of the car's loudspeaker perfectly audibly: "Shear off, you! This area is under Security control."

The vehicle hesitated in the air, ten meters from the Sepo and slightly above him. The driver was balancing his fans as best he could, but the frail craft still wobbled as Lacey leaned forward with no attempt at secrecy and shouted, "Keep your pants on, friend, I'm from Crime Service and a murder site damned well isn't closed to me."

The Sepo lowered the communicator from his

convulsing face and snarled, "I said shear off, bead brain! Don't you know what 'Security' means?"

"Set me down," said Lacey tightly to his driver. His face was gray and dreadful. Without hesitation the driver canted forward his twin joy sticks. The Sepo's communicator fell as his right hand slashed down to his belt holster. Lacey's driver tramped the foot feed, sending the car howling straight at the blue skullcap. The Sepo shouted and ducked as the screaming lift fans plucked away a bit of his jacket which billowed into their arc. The car hit the pad. It bounced from excess velocity but Lacey had timed the impact to leap clear at the instant steel scraped concrete. The Sepo was on his knees, scrabbling for the weapon he had dropped. Lacey took a half step forward and kicked. The gun was a silvery glitter that spun far over the roof edge and away.

"Oh dear Lord," the security man blurted, sitting back and in his nervousness wiping his face with his skullcap. "If some civilian g-gets that—don't you know what it was? That was a powergun!"

"No it wasn't, friend," said Lacey, satisfaction beginning to melt his face back into human lines. "Powerguns are approved for military use in war zones; not for police, not even for Sepos. And I sort of doubt that anybody's going to use your toy after it fell thirty meters, anyway." Then, with the same precision as before, Lacey's toe caught the Sepo in the temple.

The stairs were open-work which scarcely interfered with the cameras in the big room below. The three hundred workers, mostly clerks and minor supervisors, were crowded into the western half of it while two technicians and the Tower's medical unit worked hastily on the score of living casualties. The line of demarcation was not chance but another blue-capped Sepo whose nervousness evaporated when he saw Lacey and mistook him for a superior in the same organization. "I'm Agent Siemans, sir," he announced with a flat-handed salute. "Kadel and I took over right away and kept everybody off the—him."

Sieman's gestures indicated the desk and body visible through the torn partition. Lacey nodded crisply, quite certain that "everybody" in the Sepo's mind had included Crime Service investigators too. Sieman's cross-draw holster was visible through his unclipped jacket. It held a fat-barrelled powergun.

Lacey quickly covered the private office with his hand scanner. The blast had seared everything in it so that the synthetic fibers of Follard's suit had shrunk over his limbs and left the uncovered skin of his face and hands crinkled. The routing slip on the message capsule was clear, however, protected by the body which had fallen across it. Lacey flicked it upright to record the sender-recipient information. The name of the former—Lyall Mitchelsen, within Richmond Subregion—meant nothing to Lacey. Presumably it had meant a great deal to Follard or the magnate would not have opened the message out of sight of even his personal staff.

Out of sight of the scanning cameras, too—but that had to be a chance malfunction.

Heavy shoes clattered behind Lacey. As he turned, a savage voice cried, "Freeze!" His scar again beginning to flame but a quizzical smirk on his face, the investigator rotated only his head toward the newcomers. Two of them were big men capped with Sepo blue and crouching over automatic powerguns. The third, stepping daintily across a flattened wall-panel, was slim and glittered in a suit like cloth of gold. His hair was white or blond, a determination which the smooth pallor of his skin did nothing to aid. Skin like that meant wealth as often as it did youth, and the slim man radiated wealth.

There was another aura as well: he was unarmed, but he was deadly in a way neither of the gunmen flanking him could equal.

"Good morning, Field Agent Lacey," he said with a smile. His delicate fingers—the nails perfectly matched the sheen and color of his wrist-to-ankle suit—raised the needle gun far enough from Lacey's holster to be sure it was no more than it seemed, then slid it back disdainfully. "I am Sig Hanse, Agent Lacey. I am of the Security Police."

Hanse's tone, his smile, both implied a great deal more than the words alone said.

"You're in the presence of a major Security offense," Lacey said. At Hanse's quick blink he added, "Lethal weapons in non-military hands."

The Sepo's fingers trembled. "Get out of here, Lacey," he said softly. "You've been recalled. This isn't a wife-stabbing, a drunk with a chair-leg bludgeon. It's a Security matter; and if you aren't too stupid to grasp this concept, try to realize that you aren't cleared at a high enough level to be told exactly why. I might add that there is now a Security block over all the records of this crime.

No data will be released without my code—just to remind you of your duty to the State."

"I can be expected to do my duty under the Constitution and the Code, Citizen Hanse," Lacey said. He took an easy, unconcerned step between the two gunmen and then glanced back at their leader. "And you? The powerguns?"

"A needle can bounce from a stud, can fail to discharge when it hits—can just not stun a man instantly unless it gets a ganglion," Hanse snapped. "Our targets are too dangerous—to the State!—to allow that."

"Good hunting," Lacey murmured as he walked out of the room. His shoes whispering on the stair treads were the only other sound his exit made. His eyes were as empty as those of the Sepo now lying among the blast casualties as the technicians and their computer worked to repair the skull fractured by Lacey's foot.

Two new vehicles squatted on the roof: an open car like Lacey's with a blue-capped Sepo on the driver's saddle, and an older but luxurious closed car of a quality equal to that of the private ones already parked there. Lacey jerked a thumb at the Sepo. "Hanse says take your car down and block the front entrance, friend."

The Sepo blinked. "Hey, but how about the roof?" he demanded.

Lacey climbed into his own car. "Well, what about it?" he mimicked. "He's your bleeding boss—you go grill him about it."

The Sepo grunted as though punched in the stomach. He booted his fans to life and sailed over the parapet as soon as their double whine had begun to lift the car. "Hold it," Lacey said to his own driver. He jumped back out and crossed to the superb car beside it. Hanse's vehicle seated three, but he had taken his bodyguards down with him to confront Lacey. There were no loose objects within the cabin. Its design was unusual for a police vehicle in that the scanner helmet was pivoted for use only by the front seat passenger, not for the one on the soft leather bench on which Hanse himself surely rode. That was ostentation of a sort which Lacey, who viewed the helmet as a tool and not a symbol of punishing drudgery, honestly could not understand.

There was a code panel, too, built flush with the seat back. Lacey's hand scanner recorded the banks of letters from several angles. Then he swung quickly back aboard his own assigned craft.

"What're your orders, anyway?" he asked his driver's back.

"Just to remain at your disposal, sir. This was a first-priority call."

"Bleeding right it is," Lacey said. He tried to blank the rage from his voice before he added, "Look, find an empty pad somewhere—an office building too run down to get air traffic, something like that. Set down there and let me think."

As the car rose smoothly, Lacey said to his implant, "Run me life stats on Lyall Mitchelsen, Richmond Subregion."

There was a pause, followed by a crunch of static and a metallic voice stating, "The information you have requested is under Security block. Please punch your access code."

"Cancel," Lacey said so sharply that the syllables clicked. He paused a moment, then said, "Technical request."

"Ready," replied the implant.

"I ran a code board on my hand scanner two minutes ago. Retrieve that and analyze the buttons for wear patterns by group." Using the alphabet rather than Arabic numerals gave more than 2×10^{11} possibilities in an 8-digit figure, hopelessly beyond the realm of chance discovery; however, the buttons would wear with use. If the board was used only by one man, that left 64 combinations to eliminate. Assuming, of course, that the Technical Section had not been programmed to alert Security when a request like Lacey's was received. It was the first time Lacey had tried to break a Security code, but he had gotten where he was by his total unwillingness to stop when he had started something. He wasn't going to back off now.

"Degree of wear is as follows. First group, S. Second group, A-E-G-H-I-N. Third group, remaining buttons, with no significant wear."

"Now—" Lacey began. He planned to set up a dummy query through the CS net to insulate his identity from Security when he began running his potentially 63 incorrect access codes. The pattern of the seven letters—S doubled—struck him suddenly. Barking a laugh of vicious triumph, he keyed his implant and repeated, "Run me life stats on Lyall Mitchelsen, Richmond Subregion."

Crunch. "The information you have requested is under Security block. Please punch your access code."

Lacey's index finger picked out S-I-G-H-A-N-S-E. It would not have been ease of recall that pos-

sessed the Sepo to pick that code—no one with
trouble remembering eight letters would have risen
to Hanse's level. But it could well have been the
silent joke of arrogance between Hanse and the
computer; proving that he, alone among the .8
billion people of Southern Region, the State-ruling
Sun Belt, had not lost his identity.

"Lyall Mitchelsen, 56, industrialist, murdered
4-28-02 in Greater—"

Yesterday. "Method of murder?"

"Air car crash. Controls locked at 500 meters
when a rogue circuit was triggered by a tight-
beam radio signal."

"Bleeding martyrs! How did a circuit like that
get into Mitchelsen's car?"

"The circuit was designed into all 01 and 02
Phaeton Specials. Investigation has as yet failed to
identify the member of the design team actually
responsible. There is an increasing possibility that
it was somehow imported from beyond the team."

The computer had halted, but it added as a
seeming afterthought, "The murder technique was
discovered through analysis of seven identical accidents yesterday within a 21-minute period. The
other victims were . . ."

With the scanner helmet down, using it and his
implant simultaneously, Lacey continued to run
his data oblivious to his external surroundings.
The Security computer had already linked eighteen assassinations in the Southern Region during
the past day and a half, Follard's being the most
recent of them. Aside from their style of death,
the only known factor unifying all eighteen was
their enormous private power. None had been in

government directly—bureaucrats and elected officials both could be scanned at public booths by any citizen at any time—but the wealth of these men and women had given them influence beyond that of all but a handful of those in open authority. Their lives were open to licensed reporters, but reporters—or their superiors—were amenable to pressure unless an incident was too striking to ignore.

And of course, even the most powerful of men could be scanned from all angles by investigators like Lacey, except when a camera went out.

"Give me office scanner repair records for all victims," Lacey demanded with a non-flick of his ring finger.

"The information you have requested is under Security block. Please punch your access code."

Lacey paused, shocked for the first time in the investigation. That the Security terminal had again come on the line meant that the data was covered by a block not associated with the assassinations—which would have seemed absurd, had he not already begun to realize that Security—at least for the Southern Region—had been involved in something very strange which the deaths had begun to make public. Lacey lifted his helmet in order to punch the unfamiliar letters of Hanse's name. He caught the eyes of his driver on him.

"Bleeding idiots!" Lacey screamed, "They know I can't work with women!" He fell back against his seat, his body trembling and his complexion a sudden yellow-green. She had touched him, hadn't she? Though her sexlessness beneath crash suit and mirrored visor had kept the act from immediate impact, memory now sifted nausea through Lacey's body. He leaned over the side of the halted car. After a minute he got his blurring vision focused on the asphalt of the landing pad without having had to vomit first.

"Will you please put your visor down?" Lacey asked in a small voice. A thump indicated that he had been obeyed. It had been an attractive face in many ways, high cheekbones and blue eyes framed by jet hair. His mind still superimposed it on the hard plastic of the helmet.

"Why?" the driver asked. Her throaty voice was slightly camouflaged by the shield, but Lacey could no longer understand how he had imagined it to be masculine.

He turned to the now-blank visor. "I want you out of the car, please. I'll have them send another with a male driver and you can switch with him."

"No, I'm your driver and the people who determined that won't be overruled," she said calmly. "But why does it matter?"

"Why?" whispered Lacey, his face as hard as a headsman's axe. "Because my brain got wet-scrubbed, friend. Because I was frozen in a nutrient bath for three months while a Psycomp made sure that I never raped another woman. Never willingly touched another woman, as a matter of fact, though that may have been a little farther than the computer meant to go." He had the trembling of his hands under control and the bright sun was baking the sweat off his face now.

The driver considered him silently. After a moment she said, "I'm the best in your section, you know. I can do things with a car that none of the others can. Or would try to."

"You dropped us on that Sepo like you were reading my mind," Lacey agreed. "But I still don't want to share a car with you."

"Look, you don't have to touch me, you know." There was an odd tension in her voice, a need that went beyond anything the situation seemed to call for. "Can you work with a driver who drives and who takes orders like nobody else you'll find?"

He looked away, up at a sky that had become blue and pleasant again. Belatedly he punched Hanse's access code. "Do you have a name," he asked, "or do I just call you Fireball?"

"You can call me anything you please," the girl said quietly, "but my name is Tamara Damien."

The data began to fire out of Lacey's implant and he let it carry him out of his personal situation. Of the fifty-four cameras in the victims' offices, only one had ever malfunctioned up to five years before. After that, one after another, brief failures began to show up in the maintenance records. Two to five minutes at a time, ten or a dozen times a year. Long enough to read and memorize a note, enough even to scribble one off. Three victims had no scanner failures at all until Lacey followed up with records of their vehicle units.

"Okay, what other scanners have similar malfunction records?" Lacey asked, his voice still a flat purr with only a trace of hoarseness.

"Vehicle unit, Southern Regional Pool Car 138814; vehicle unit, Southern Regional Pool Car

759541; vehicle unit, Southern Regional Pool Car, 294773. No other units."

Lacey touched his tongue to his lips. "Who were the cars checked to at times of malfunction?" he asked.

"Alvin Hormadz, Director for Security, Atlanta Subregion; Willa Perhabis, Director for Security, Richmond Subregion; Sig Hanse, Security Coordinator, Southern Region."

Which by that time was no surprise.

"Uh-hmm," Lacey sighed, showing his teeth like a satisfied tomcat. He blinked, seeing Tamara for the first time since the data had begun coming in. She was as tense as he had been when he faced the guns of Hanse's bodyguards. "Oh, hell," he said. "Take your helmet off. We're going to be here a while."

She unsnapped the chin strap and slid the gear away from hair that sweat had stuck to her cheeks. It fluffed in the breeze as she freed it. Lacey's stomach roiled but he grinned wider. If he had not been able to laugh at the irony of the situation, he would have committed suicide within days of his psychic remake.

"Can I ask you a personal question?" Tamara said, her eyes on the helmet as she placed it on the seat beside her.

"Sure," Lacey agreed unconcernedly.

"Why did you commit rape? You aren't . . . you aren't cool, but you seem to act as though you were. How did you come to lose control like that?"

"Oh, my," said Lacey, kneading the back of his neck with his eyes closed. "The people *I* pick up talk about losing control, as if that could make me feel sorry for them. I raped the bitch because it was the only way I could punish her as much as I thought she deserved. For this—" he touched his scar—"for a lot of things. I had to find an empty, unfinished dwelling unit with doors I could wedge against the Red Team that was going to come as soon as the scanners picked up what I was doing. You aren't going to successfully rape anybody nowadays if you just lose control, my friend."

Tamara's face was blank. "And you kept your job as an investigator?"

"No, that's not quite what happened," Lacey explained. His grin interrupted him by turning into an open chuckle. "I sold insurance before they got into my mind. The Psycomp seems to have decided that single-mindedness and an ability to plan could be useful to the State—in the right channels, that is."

He nodded at the scanner helmet. "Trouble is, it's not something I can turn off because somebody decided to change the rules. I think I've already gotten deeper in this channel than some folks are going to like, both Hanse and his bunch and the folks who are knocking them off."

"I don't see why the Sepos haven't already arrested you this morning," the girl said. She was facing Lacey, the scanner staring over the top of her head like a one-eyed crow. The sky beyond was empty: Tamara had set them on an older building, designed for elevators and individual offices. When power for the elevators became prohibitive, the upper floors were left untenanted. The view from the room was clear and had be-

cause of its stability an emotional impact unequaled
by that of an air car at the same height.

"Would you rather I didn't ask—?" the girl said
awkwardly.

Lacey blinked. "Sorry, I was drifting," he said
with a nicer smile than before. He scratched his
ribs where his jumpsuit clung to them. "No, I can
explain it. Hanse wasn't going to arrest me for
disarming his thug, he had too much to explain on
that one himself. What he was doing here in person, for instance. Given the timing and the fact his
office is in Atlanta, I'd bet that he was on his way
to warn Follard that somebody had gotten onto
whatever game they were playing. . . ." The smile
broadened, then faded. "There was a chance that he
might have had me shot, of course. That would
have been a little easier to clear."

"But you searched his car, you broke his access
code," Tamara blurted. She was using both hands
to gesture toward Lacey, too agitated to notice
that he slid back away from them. "I saw you, the
car scanner saw you, the three roof scanners saw
you. Why are you still loose?"

"Maybe when Hanse gets around to checking
me, I won't be," Lacey said, motioning the girl to
calmness. "But the things you're talking about don't
flag the computer automatically, friend Tamara.
Certain patterns will be kicked up to a human
observer by the circuit that watch-dogs all scanner
inputs—a room exploding, a CS investigator kicking an armed Sepo in the head—that sort of thing.
But Loysius Follard falling asleep at his desk didn't
set any lights flashing, and neither did a fellow
opening the door of a car, then closing it and

walking away. The data's there in the vaults under Atlanta; but until somebody retrieves it, I'll still be walking free.

"Riding free," he corrected with another smile. "And I think I'm ready, now, to ride back to the State Building. There's some data there for me, and I've had my dose of open space for the day."

He had lied about his purpose. He walked into Level 17 from the landing pad but glanced at the print-out without great interest. The lethal agent had almost certainly been PDT, a volatile liquid explosive/toxin supposedly in military hands only. Anything that exists can be had by a man who knows what to offer the right people.

"Support request," Lacey said to his implant.

"Ready."

"I want a check on PDT stockpiles. Track down any losses and report the results to me."

"Accepted at third priority."

Lacey unlocked the lowest drawer of his desk and took a cylindrical package from it. His face was set but looked ready to explode like a Prince Rupert drop if touched by anyone's glance.

17 was the roof level—government offices were built a little higher, on the average, than new private ones (complaints about "the hogs at the public trough" continued to be useful campaign rhetoric) and Crime Service had to be alongside the pad. Lacey walked the sixteen flights to the ground through offices of identical size and equal crowding. The stairs were a broad helix, thin-railed and with treads which were almost free-standing. They were supposed to deaden sound,

but the material creaked. In late afternoon, Lacey was alone on the staircase and drew occasional eyes. None of them remained on him long.

He had over a kilometer to go but he did not take a bus. It was easier to feel that he was anonymous, stepping into a doorway from a sidewalk—there one moment, then gone—than it would have been when getting off a bus at an address that other passengers might recognize.

Ground floor of the old building which was his destination held a food bazaar that smelled frowsty and sweet. It was unpartitioned with its internal load-bearing pillars replaced by transparent myrmillon, but a greasy coating had opaqued them and no one seemed to care. The second through eighth levels were housing of poor and successively-degenerated quality. The ground plan was marked off into eighty dwelling units by waist-height vitril panels on the lower floors, rusted hog-fencing on the upper ones. The center of the big room was a bank of coin-operated hot plates. Other furniture depended on the whim and wealth of the units' occupiers: chairs and frequently a table, beds on floor-spread mattresses, and occasionally an electric light to supplement the dozen glow-strips in the ceiling. These would go on at sunset and out promptly three hours later, rain or shine. The only sight barriers in the room were the sheets fronting the latrines at either end, so placed that the stools were shielded from viewers in the belly of the room but were swept by one of the three scanners. Need for the law to make that concession to privacy was thrown in doubt by the unrepaired damage to several of the screens, ignored both by users of the latrines and the others in the room. Lacey climbed through the wretched dwelling levels without expression and, just possibly, without notice.

The ninth floor was empty save for a browned, youngish man on a stool at the base of the winding stairs. "Hey, back already?" he cackled, his grin combining cameraderie and condescension. A woman and three men, one of them well-dressed and very drunk, clattered down the stairs together.

Lacey moved aside. He held out three large bills to the doorman. "Which stall?" he asked.

"One a these days you'll want the Honeymoon Suite and I'll fall right off this chair," the seated man chuckled.

"Which stall?"

The doorman blinked up at dark eyes and a neck bright with scarred lightning. His hand twitched toward the length of pipe behind him, but wisely he controlled the motion and took the proffered money instead. "Sixty-one's empty," he said, looking away. "I'll mark you down for it."

Lacey turned without nodding and began to climb the last flight of steps. Under his breath the doorman muttered, "Bet I don't see *you* many more times, buddy. Ones like you they don't let walk around very long."

The tenth floor was sweaty, stinking bedlam, far darker than the lower levels because the canvas cubicles spaced around the walls blocked most of the windows. Studding the ceiling at two-meter intervals were 150 separately-controlled scanner units. They stood like the sprinkler heads of an earlier day in which fire had been thought a greater danger to society than privacy. Beneath them, divided by narrow aisles, were arrayed the cribs that bumped and swayed to the activities of their occupants which the cameras impassively recorded. The accommodation house catered to those who did not want their neighbors in their own dwelling units to learn what they were doing, or who they were doing it with.

In Lacey's case, *what* he was doing it with.

"What stall?" boomed the floor boss, a huge albino with Negroid features who stood in front of a control panel.

"Sixty-one."

"Right, sixty-one," the albino echoed, checking the panel. "Two hours of scanner time. You want company?" His doughy fingers indicated the north wall, the Mourners' Bench, along which waited apathetically a score of haggard prostitutes of both sexes.

"No."

"S'okay, sixty-one," the bigger man repeated. "We rent you four walls and a private scanner. What you do with them's between you and the data bank."

Lacey strode down the jostling aisle to the crib marked 61 in red numerals on the tile floor. He stepped inside and drew the curtain shut. The scanner above him beeped and an orange telltale came on, indicating the unit was in operation. The cubicle was dim enough that the supplementary infra-red system was probably on. Without haste, Lacey stripped off his coveralls and folded them, laying his pistol on top of the garment. He opened the package he had brought and removed the arti-

ficial vagina from its foam nest. He switched it on,
sat down on the cot, and affixed it to himself.

Lacey's eyes were as empty as the lens of the
scanner they stared up toward as his body shuddered. Beneath the emptiness was a rage that
bubbled like lava-filled calderas.

He walked back to the State Building, this time
from a desire for walking rather than from shame. The
shame had drained out of him along with some of
the other emotions he was trying to void. Lacey's
mind was working again, using the rhythm of his
feet to shuffle patterns in the information he had
collected. The dusky street was quiet enough and
as clean as is only possible in a society in which all
litter has value to someone. At alternate blocks
stood uniformed police with gas guns and banana-
clipped stunners, ready for their computer links to
direct them to trouble. For the most part they
appeared as bored and logy as the vagrants with
whom they shared the evening. There was infra-
red for the omnipresent scanners, but no power
was wasted for men to see by. The night is an
irksome companion.

The squad at the gate of the building passed
Lacey without hesitation. Several of the red-hatted
men recognized him, while the rest ignored him
because their implants told them it was safe to do
so. On several floors only the stairway was lighted
by glow strips, since government offices tended to
close at nightfall like everything else. Level 16,
where uniformed monitors wore helmets to direct
squads to trouble spots, was a bright exception;
and Level 17 was about a quarter occupied also.

An investigator could run his subject at any time—
the data bank would wait—but many of the hunters were like Lacey. They stuck to the unusual
criminal who had eluded the first rush of a Red
Team; stuck with him until they had drunk his
blood.

Lacey sat at his desk and pulled down the scanner helmet to begin checking back the message
capsule. In all likelihood the assassin had not believed that would be possible. In general his as-
sumption would have been correct; but this case
had been handed to Lacey. The capsule had popped
onto Follard's desk from the Tower's security system, hidden from the scanners as it ran past a
battery of useless fluoroscopes and radiation tes-
ters. For his own reasons, Follard had not allowed
a subordinate to open the capsule; he had paid for
secrecy with his life. Lacey picked up the capsule
where it had entered the system, delivered ten
minutes before then with a mass of others like it in
the hold of an air car. Lacey switched to a roof
camera showing two bored guards with batons and
the green uniforms of a private message service
standing around while the white-haired driver
dumped armloads of capsules into the chute. Lacey
magnified by ten, then by a hundred, as he focused the image on the tumbling rectangles.

And then the computer took over. With time
and even greater magnification, Lacey might himself have been able to catch the routing slip on the
metal and identify the death capsule. The precise
machinery of the police net scanned the object for
tiny imperfections and for details of the routing
slip so slight that even the corner of a letter in a

camera field would be an identification. Lacking
that, the capsule's albedo alone could identify it
where the light intensity was known. Technology
made practical a job that was otherwise only a
theoretical possibility. It was like giving a blood-
hound an escapee's sock to sniff.

The capsule had been in the morning's delivery.
Had it not been, Lacey would have traced through
the Tower looking for the point at which an insider
had slipped it into the normal flow. He gave quick
directions to his implant and the delivery car jerked
backward across the city in a series of ten-second
jumps in the helmet. They stopped when it had
run back to its loading point, the internal dock of a
regional distribution center.

All but three floors of the huge granite building
were lifeless, filled with sorting machinery and
endless belts studded with hundreds of thousands
of capsules of identical shape and size. Odd-sized
packages were handled by humans on the two
lowest floors, and the charge for such service was
enough to guarantee its use only in cases of necessity. The third level received packages by dumb-
waiter and capsules by chute, integrating them
into the bins from which the delivery cars were
loaded.

The computer needed further guidance at that
point, for the chutes themselves were inaccessible
to men and thus unscanned. The conveyors on
each floor, however, with their complex system of
shunts, feeds, and crossfeeds that sorted each capsule toward its proper drop chute, were as open to
cameras as any other room. Lacey moved floor by
floor, focusing each time on the aperture which

dropped capsules into the Follard Tower bin. His voice had grown husky with giving directions and his fingers stiff from flexing on his chair arms, but if anyone could have seen his face behind the helmet they would have cringed back from a smile more fitted to a tiger than a man. Even a man like Lacey.

Mail to the Follard Tower was delivered at twelve-hour intervals. Lacey ran each floor back to the time the previous load had gone out, then switched up one level. The speeded up, reversed flow of images would have driven mad anyone less used to it than he was; and perhaps—a possibility that Lacey had never denied to himself—he withstood it only because he was already mad.

On the eighth floor he picked up the capsule again, part of a shipment brought from Richmond Subregion by high-altitude airliner. It was not too long afterward that Lacey's helmet focused on a Petersburg street and a man, slim and fiftyish with tight-rolled hair and a skin so black it looked purple, who dropped the capsule into a collection box and then thumbed in coins until the postage light glowed green.

"Name and data," Lacey croaked to his implant.

"William Anton Merritt, age 54, on dole for past thirty-seven months. Eight years Chief of Operations, Security, for Southern Region. Previously—"

Lacey cut off the flow and returned to his man. It was without surprise that he back-tracked Merritt to a counter in the General Delivery room of the Petersburg mail depot where he had peeled off a routing slip addressed to him and replaced it with the one that would carry the toxin to Follard.

There was no reason, after all, that the murder device should have been prepared in the subregion from which it had to be mailed in order to pass as coming from the conspirator Mitchelsen. Back a step further, then; Merritt punching his I.D. on a code board and waiting the few seconds for the capsule to drop into the delivery slot. From there back through a mirror image of the previous routings—no less arduous, but no less possible to follow—for they led straight back to Greensboro Subregion in which sat Lacey hunched under his helmet and the body of Loysius Follard lay on a teak slab with a thousand torchlit mourners howling around it like the damned.

This time, Lacey did not need the data bank to identify the girl who jumped from an air car to mail the capsule to Merritt in Petersburg.

For the moment he did not trace the capsule to the point at which it was filled with explosive and sealed, or back even earlier when the PDT had been removed from some government stockpile. That information was safe in the data bank until he chose to retrieve it, and the people concerned— the scores of perhaps hundreds it had taken to bring off so many simultaneous assassinations— would be just as easy to find a few hours or days later. Only death had ever saved a target from Lacey. Instead of searching for other names now, he twitched the finger no wedding ring would ever grace and said, "Give me a current location on William Anton Merritt."

Information that far-reaching required a delay for computer time to check literally hundreds of thousands of scanner images in a pattern of concentric probabilities; but for Lacey it was only seconds before the data squeaked back into his mastoid. He grunted as he considered it. "Estimated time of arrival?" he asked.

"Forty-three minutes."

How does an ex-bureaucrat, supposedly on State Subsistence Allowance, come to be piloting a private stratosphere craft from Toronto to Greensboro? Friends, doubtless, like everything else Merritt had arranged. Lacey gave a few specific instructions, then asked, "My driver from yesterday—Tamara Damien. Is she on duty?"

"She will report at 0700. Do you wish another driver assigned or should she be given an emergency summons?"

"Hmm. What time is it?" The windows were, Lacey noticed as he swung up the scanner helmet, beginning to pale.

"0637."

"Fine, I'll be in the target range. Tell me when she gets in."

The range was a quadrant of Level 15, separated by opaque partitions despite the added scanner cost. Experience had proven that peripheral images of men raising guns destroyed the efficiency of the clerical unit sharing the floor, even though a myrmillon divider would have been more than adequate to stop the tiny needles.

There were already a dozen shooters using the 20-meter range, standing with their backs to the outside windows and firing inward toward the point of the wedge where the target screen stood. Jacket open, Lacey took a vacant station. His stance comfortable and his fingers curved loosely on his thighs, he announced, "Ready."

A target image visible only from his station flashed, a tawny woman raising what might have been either a length of pipe or a shotgun. Lacey's weapon was in his right hand, then locked with his left as he crouched and fired three shots so sudden they appeared to have been fully automatic.

The target disappeared and a silhouette of it formed on the spotting screen just above Lacey's head, red dots at right wrist, right elbow, and right shoulder identifying his shots. His implant said, "Time, point three six seconds. That is exceptionally good. However, your accuracy continues marginal with no hits in the central body mass"—the silhouette's torso pulsed red for emphasis. "In a true firefight, you may not be lucky enough to get limb hits if you are so far outside your aiming point. Speed is less critical than accuracy."

Computers have no sense of humor, so Lacey avoided even the edge of a smile when he heard it refer to what it imagined had been his aiming point. He had raped, openly and with deliberation, and had forever lost his capacity for a similar act. He would not make the same boastful error if he ever found it necessary to kill: *that* must look to be an accident.

He was a violent man in a world of arrogance—of Sig Hanse and his Sepos, of the sneering Red Team which had taken him into custody years before, of the myriad counterclerks and bureaucrats taking their frustrations out on the nearest target. Lacey avoided an actual explosion only because he knew his hand had the power of life and death over every one of them individually. If the Psycomp had noticed that murderous streak, it had weighed it against Lacey's depth of control and usefulness—then passed him as acceptable to the State.

Targets continued to flash. He sprayed the edges of five more—on one he hit a swinging medallion three times and got zero credit since, of course, a real medallion would have deflected the needles which grounded themselves only after penetration. Finally his implant announced, "Chauffeur 5 Damien has reported to her car."

"Patch me through to her," Lacey said, slapping a fresh magazine into his gun before he holstered it. He turned to the nearest window. For cleaning purposes the whole two-meter vitril panel pivoted inward.

"Ready."

"Morning, Tamara. I'm in the target range, Level 15. Drop down and pick me up, will you?"

The girl's voice was deepened by the car microphone and Lacey's implant. "No landing stage on fifteen, sir."

"Sure, but the windows open."

"On the way."

Lacey swung the vitril off its catch. The gush of air as the car dropped past it, then rose and steadied, brought a startled protest from the shooter beside Lacey. He ignored the other man, set his left foot on the sill and stepped into the back of the car. The slightest queasiness in the vehicle would have catapulted Lacey thirty meters to the pavement. Tamara kept it rock solid until he was seated, then moved off a few meters to where she did not have to fight the eddies around the building.

"You didn't do that to save yourself a walk," she chided. "Trying to prove something to me?"

"That's right," he agreed. "That I can safely trust you with my life." He leaned forward, grinned up at the scanner, and said, "We're going to the airport, friend Tamara, to arrest a man named William Anton Merritt for multiple counts of murder. He wasn't in it alone, Lord knows, but it'll be simpler for a Psycomp to dig out his accomplices than it would be for me and a scanner."

She moved the car off smoothly without apparent emotion, gaining speed and altitude as she headed west. There were no lane markers in the sky, but cars were few and almost all drivers professionals. On balance it was safer than street traffic had been fifty years before.

"You are good, aren't you?" Tamara said at last in a jerky voice. Lacey made no reply. "Don't you even wonder why a, a *citizen* like Bill Merritt would start a p-plot like this?"

"Wonder?" Lacey repeated. "Not really. He was, is, a very damned able man himself. The killings, the planning for them, proved that. Hanse could and did shunt him out of the service, of course, but Merritt's own contacts must have been nearly as good. As Chief of Operations he could have . . . not seen it, I think, because Hanse's a sharp boy too . . . but felt it when some members of his own organization got together with rich men, men with connections outside the country where arms could be stockpiled and soldiers trained. You could take over this State, I think, with a few men in the right place and not too many more scattered around to look menacing. You could do it because damned few of the rest of them care. Of us care."

"Bill cares. He found—a lot of us who do."

"Sure he did, friend Tamara. And he killed not just eighteen people but likely two or three others standing too close to each of the ones he aimed at, too. I won't arrest him for caring, just for the murders; because it's my job and I'm better at it than he hoped."

She turned toward Lacey at last, her eyes full of tears and fire. "Do you know how many thousand they'd have killed if they took over? How many Hanse *will* kill if he gets away to Argentina this morning? Do you call *that* justice?"

"Justice? What's that?" Lacey demanded. "But they pay me to enforce the law, and yes, that's damned well the law!" He took a deep breath. "Now, mind your flying. If we go down, there'll be a Red Team around Merritt before the echoes of the crash have died. Believe me, he'd rather I take him than those animals in uniform. . . . Believe me, I've been there."

She obeyed but the tears gurgled in her voice. "Don't you think you owe anything to society?" she asked.

"This society?" Lacey repeated with savage incredulity. "The society that made me what *I* am?"

Tamara said nothing more for a minute, concentrating on the thickening traffic as they approached the huge concrete slab of the port.

"We've got a priority clearance," Lacey said. "You can set us down on the terminal building."

"We couldn't get close to Hanse," the girl said,

as much to herself as to her companion. "When he
flew it was in his own CT-19, and he always carried his own car with him. He didn't trust anyone,
anything. We delayed, hoping he would slip up;
but we waited too long. And so their plans were so
close to ready that if Hanse gets to Parana now, he
may be able to bring it all off even with Follard
and the others dead."

A heavy cargo aircraft lumbered aloft a hundred
and fifty meters from its painted bay on the great
field. Three seconds later a private supersonic,
incredibly expensive to own or operate, streaked
skyward with its wings folding even as it climbed.
Short takeoff and landing requirements made full
runways a thing of the past, but the congestion
and varied speeds near the port still demanded
rigid control.

Lacey had noticed the girl start as the supersonic shrieked away. "Merritt's in one like that?"
he asked. "Don't get excited, it wasn't his that
time. I've put a hold on him, blocked his controls
through the port computer. He'll be waiting for
us."

Tamara angled for a slot on the crowded roof of
the terminal building. A closed car sped up to
reach the same parking space, then spun away as
Tamara hammered it with the draft of her fans.
Lacey, gripping the bulkhead tightly, grinned over
at the furious red face visible through the cabin
window of the other craft.

Tamara cut the drive and they ghosted to a halt.
She looked back at Lacey. He said, a trifle awkwardly, "It'll be ten, twelve hours before they
start dragging actual names out of Merritt. Some-

body who'd gotten out of the State before then—
used Sig Hanse's access code to fake exit privileges
to Munich, say—would be gone for good."

The girl stared at him, her eyes an acid blue and
her hair springing up like a cobra's hood as she
doffed her helmet. "Bill had me assigned driver to
whoever got tapped to investigate Follard. He
pulled a few strings, nothing major for somebody
who has as many friends as Bill Merritt does.
There was a chance that by giving him a nudge in
the right direction, we could get a CS agent interested in what Hanse was doing. You didn't need
the nudge—or care about what you learned without it.

"But I'm not going to use the position Bill put
me in to, to save myself."

"It's your life," Lacey said, breaking eye contact
as he climbed out of the car. "The Lord knows I'm
not the one to tell you what to do with it."

"I'm coming along," Tamara insisted, swinging
into the narrow aisle between their car and the
next one over. Lacey shrugged and walked toward
the stair head.

Hanse too would be somewhere in the port.
Lacey had said he did not care about the Sepo
conspiracy, and in a way that was true; but the
scar on his neck throbbed like molten steel at the
thought. He jostled his way down the crowded
stairs, Tamara an orange shadow behind him. At
the ground floor he followed the directional arrows
toward a balding fat man serving one stall of the
console marked TRANSPORTATION TO AIRCRAFT. There
was a line but the investigator stepped to the front
of it with a gruff, "Excuse me."

To the clerk he said, "Priority. I need a car to Slip 318," and he cocked his ring finger. The fat man's display obediently lit red in response to an authenticating signal from the CS net.

"Door 12, then," the clerk said with a nervous shrug. "But look, buddy, we're short today, there won't be a driver for seven, eight minutes."

"I didn't ask for a driver." Lacey turned, took the twenty long strides to the indicated portal without speaking. Half a dozen ground cars were lined up on the concrete beyond; nearly a hundred would-be passengers stood beside them docilely, waiting to be taken to their flights.

A big man, one of the pair of guards with Hanse the day before, stepped out of the crowd. It rippled away from him like sheep from a wolf in their midst. He had dropped the poncho which had cloaked the weapon along his right thigh, an automatic powergun with a drum magazine and a flask of liquid nitrogen under the barrel for cooling and ejection. "That's far enough, Lacey," he said with a smile. "You must have known we'd check what you were doing yesterday. So. . . ."

The bodyguard swung up the muzzle of his weapon. Lacey drew without hesitation, shot the Sepo twice in the trigger hand. A fist-sized chunk of concrete blew from the field as the Sepo spasmed off a shot, but his paralyzed body was already twisting into the ground.

"Lacey!" the girl screamed. He spun, his gun leading his body around in a glittering arc—too slowly. Tamara was leaping for the second guard, his eye as black as the bore of the powergun it stared over. Lacey heard the sudden grunt of the shots, saw the cyan glare catch Tamara in mid air and use her own exploding fluids to fling her backward with her chest a slush of blood and charred bone. A cloud of ice crystals hung at the Sepo's side and his plastic empties were still spinning in the air when Lacey shot him in the right eye.

The charge that would have stunned elsewhere blasted the optic nerve and ripped down that straight path to the brain. The Sepo arched in a tetanic convulsion that broke his neck and back in three places. The powergun spun into the building, cracking the vitril and ricochetting to the pavement.

Lacey did not look again at the girl, but he had seen her face as the burst slashed across her. Holstering his needle gun, he mounted the driver's seat of a twelve-passenger crawler and threw it into gear. The numbers on the empty slips were hard to read, scorched and abraded by the lift fans, but Lacey had his implant to guide him across the baking concrete. Once a huge CT-19 freighter staggered aloft just after he had passed its bow, but either luck or the watchful Terminal Control preserved Lacey while his quarry, a spike of silver fire, grew in front of him.

"Status on Merritt?" Lacey asked his implant.

"Three minutes ago requested permission to lift, destination Buenos Aires. Placed on safety hold by Terminal Control on orders of the Crime Service net."

"Umm. Status on Sig Hanse?"

"Cleared for Parana in a CT-19 with five crew and seven passengers, one air car declared as cargo. Estimated lift-off is three minutes thirty."

"And it'll have a battalion aboard when it and a thousand others come back," Lacey muttered, but he did not trigger his implant.

Close up, the craft that looked so slender among the cargo haulers was a study in brutal, wasteful power. Its turbines were spinning fast enough to raise a whine but not dust from the concrete. Lacey pulled in close to the port side, in between two of the ducted intakes. As he did so the cockpit canopy three meters above sprang open. The aging black man Lacey had seen only on the scanner before began to climb down the rungs which had extended from the ship's side.

"Citizen Lacey?" Merritt said as he reached the ground. He stretched out his hand, as dry and unyielding as a cypress knee. "Now I understand why Terminal Control froze me for a circuitry check. I don't suppose they were going to isolate the problem quickly, were they?"

"No, not till I gave the word," Lacey agreed disinterestedly.

Merritt shook his head with a faint smile. "Of course, of course. You're a very able man. And I can almost admire your singlemindedness, since after all that's the way I am. Well, shall we go back and meet your team of brain-wreckers?"

Lacey ran a hand along the stress-rippled skin of the aircraft. "What would you have done if Control hadn't held you?" he asked. "Lifted off in a few minutes?"

"Something like that."

"And you'd have laid your throttle wide open wouldn't you? Put it right through the middle of Hanse's CT-19. Wouldn't that be pretty? You and twelve other people falling out of the sky like shaved meat? You know, I don't ever remember meeting anybody who liked to kill as much as you seem to."

Merritt bit his lip. "Citizen Lacey," he said, "I've lived in this democracy 54 years, worked toward its safety for 31. I would be less than a man if I weren't at least willing to die for it; and to keep it and the world out of the hands of Sig Hanse and his sort—yes, I'll kill."

The emotion behind Lacey's smile was not humor. "Must be nice to know what's best for the world," he said. "I've got enough problems deciding what's best for Jed Lacey, and that's the only thing I've tried to worry about. Figured it was mostly me I had to live with."

"No doubt," Merritt said flatly. "Then if you have nothing further to say, shall we get on?"

"Sure," Lacey agreed. He triggered his implant. "Release the hold on William Anton Merritt," he ordered. "Clear him for immediate lift-off." He stepped back to the ground car alone, waving a casual hand back at the older man. "Have a good flight, Citizen Merritt."

Lacey's car was half a kilometer away when he heard Merritt's turbines shriek up to full power. From further across the concrete came the deep thunder and subsonic trembling of a CT-19's beginning effort to stagger skyward. Lacey's implant cut out both sounds when it announced, "Reply to support request, theft from PDT stockpiles."

"Ready."

"Four hundred liters removed from Redcliffe Arsenal, Toronto Subregion, on 4-23-02. Currently believed being transported in reserve fuel tank of private aircraft number—"

Lacey had anticipated the next words, so he was out of his seat and diving toward the concrete when the concrete rose to meet him. Twenty meters above the field, Merritt's aircraft had collided with Hanse's. The supersonic caught the CT-19 abaft the starboard wing, stabbing through the bulbous cargo hauler like a swordsman seeking the heart. The first microsecond of rending metal was lost in the bellow of the engines; then the PDT went off.

All sound ended as an orange fireball devoured the merged aircraft. The blast that followed was like nothing heard since the end of nuclear testing.

Alive but uncaring, stripped by the winds and hammered by the bucking concrete, Lacey lay on the field. He could let the tears come now.

In his mind, back-lighted by the afterimage of the fireball, was the vision of a girl with blue eyes, jet hair, and a smile of love and triumph.

My wife told me that "The Predators" was written by a man with a deep hatred of house plants. That is untrue; though I may on occasion have spoken harsh words when I met hanging pots which cleared my wife's head by six inches.

I've long been fascinated by Fortean phenomena—red rain, sea monsters, spontaneous human combustion, and similar things of the sort that Charles Fort collected in his four non-fiction books. (I stopped calling myself a Fortean when a newspaper reporter transcribed the word as "Freudian," causing no end of hilarity among my psychiatrist friends.)

At a Fortean convention, I learned that there is some evidence that human thought can act as a stimulus on plants. That strikes me as reasonable, so I used the notion in "The Predators" . . . though stories, at least when I write them, are about people rather than plants.

Incidentally, at the same convention I heard a lengthy exposition of the way Nazis had built a flying saucer base in the Antarctic. That doesn't strike me as even remotely reasonable.

But there was a story in that one, too.

THE PREDATORS

Above the buildings slid air cars. A single private vehicle as luxurious as any of them shared the street below with the wheeled trucks and buses. The closed rear cabin was empty but the chauffeur, a youth whose uniform matched the landeau's smoke-blue paint, drove with the arrogance of one conducting a prince.

In front of the Coeltrans Building he nudged his wheel to the right, edging up over the curb between a pair of trucks unloading yard goods. Pedestrians leaped to avoid the blunt prow. Smiling, the chauffeur set the brake, cut the alcohol flame to idle under the boiler, and tilted a wing mirror to check his appearance. Shoulder-length black hair framed a face whose complexion was as unnaturally brilliant as the best parchment. His lips were red and well-shaped and cruel.

Satisfied, he slid from the ground car's saddle and entered the building, leaving his vehicle for the cameras to watch. They scanned this street as they did every street, every room, in the State; and at the first sign of someone tampering with the car, a monitoring computer would alert the police.

Within the large, single room, narrow aisles separated booths selling fabric and garments. Even during daylight the inner tables were lighted by glow strips to bring out the colors of their merchandise. Eyes turned toward the chauffeur as he passed, some drawn by his iridescent livery but many by his carriage and frame. The body beneath his tight uniform would have done credit to a *kouros* of ancient Athens. He acknowledged the glances only by hooking the left corner of his mouth into a more pronounced sneer.

At the spidery framework of the elevator in the center of the room he halted. Four slim, chromed vertical rods rose from the floor here all the way to the roof of the building. The chauffeur touched the call plate with his ID bracelet; the radio-cesium key imbedded in its silver threw a switch invisibly and the cage began to whine down from the fifteenth level.

Shop owners in the Coeltrans Building were used to the activity, but there was a stir among their customers. Many of them had never seen a working elevator before. The cost of power to run elevators made them rich men's toys—and rich men had air cars to get them between the top-floor suites of their fellows. Supported by the four thin columns, the cage sank through one-meter circles cut through each level. Little more itself than a floor with a waist-high rail plated to match the verticals, the cage appeared shockingly frail. A

more substantial construct would have sometimes
blocked the fields of the three scanning cameras
covering each floor. No citizen, no matter how
rich and powerful, could be granted that potential
for secrecy.

The chauffeur stepped aboard and the cage began to rise. He lounged back against the guard
rail, whistling as his fingers beat time against the
chrome. On each identical level, banks of clerks
looked up from their desks as the cage rose past
them. The motor in the elevator's floor raised it
effortlessly past stairs which were theirs to climb
every time they reported to work. The elevator
was for Citizen Wilhoit alone—and for this youth.

Only on Level 15 was there a break in the vistas
of desks crammed into 60-meter circular floor plans.
Here the outside walls were pierced not by windows but rather by translucent panels cast in various pastels. The room was actually brighter than
those below it, however, because of the sheets of
sunlight-balanced glow strips in its ceiling. Underlings sat in ordinary desks around the level's outer
perimeter, but the central twenty meters were
held by a jungle of potted plants and a single huge
mahogany desk no less impressive for the litter of
papers and instruments on its surface.

The cage stopped. The chauffeur continued to
whistle, his back to the mahogany desk and the
gray-faced man beginning to stand behind it. Then
the current surged through the elevator's handrail
and snapped the chauffeur into a screaming arc.

Alternating current of over 600 volts tends to
fling away those who touch it, saving lives that
lower voltages might have taken. DC instead clamps

and holds and kills; and to avoid inductance losses, Greater Greensboro and most other cities now ran on direct current. The charge ripping through the chauffeur's body broke his ribs with unrelieved muscle contraction, and the screaming stopped only when there was no more air to be forced through the lifeless throat. Seconds later the flow cut off as suddenly as it had begun, and the charred body slumped to the floor of the cage.

The cameras on Level 15 recorded every visible nuance of the death.

Lacey gave the final command to the Crime Service computer. It would send a Red Team after the airport smuggler he had identified following a week of studying the operation from every angle. He swung the scanner helmet up against its counterweight and grinned his wolf's grin of accomplishment. His hand was massaging the old scar on his neck and holding the glow inside him when Billings, the investigator at the desk to his right, got up. "You knocking off too?" Billings asked. He was a blond man with a round face and a quick smile.

Lacey came out of his reverie. He looked at his neighbor, then at the clock across the circular room. 15:40. For the past three nights he had caught cat naps at his desk as leads branched and twined and he wanted thirty hours a day to study scanner images. "Might, yeah," he agreed. There were five hundred desks and investigators on Level 17 of the State Building. Lacey knew and cared as little about Billings as he did about any other of his co-workers.

Billings was straightening the pleats of his collar. "I put in for two hours in the target range," he confided to Lacey's disinterest, "but really I got a date. *Love*-ly girl, lives in the section next to ours. We're going to a time house and buy an hour of privacy. It'll cost a bundle, but it's worth it to keep my wife from learning."

Before Lacey could make his noncommittal reply, the light on Billing's desk blinked orange and the blond man stiffened as information came through his mastoid implant. He swore with frustrated bitterness, punching his left palm with his other hand. "She'll *never* believe this," he said. "They've cancelled my range time and given me an accidental death to check out. An accident!"

"Maybe the computer's a secret puritan," Lacey said, more of a smile on his mouth than in his eyes.

"I always get the leftovers," Billings whined. "You think they'd give me a murder where I could get a little recognition? Hell no! But let some clod touch a hot wire and fry, they drop it in my lap and expect me to work every bleeding hour till I prove it's an accident. And you *can't* prove something didn't happen!" Billings thudded his hands together again. "That tight-assed bitch Sutter's had her thumb on me ever since I offered to give her the time back when I was first on the unit. She won't let the Net give me any decent assignments!"

Billings face suddenly smoothed and he looked at the close-coupled man still listening with bare politeness. "Look, Jed"—Lacey had never called Billings by his first name, did not even remember it—"look, for me this damn thing'll take forever, checking out the number of times each electrician burped for the past year before the Net'll take a negative report from me. But if you took the call, hell, you know how they'll pass just about anything on your say-so. You do five minutes' scan and report 'no crime', they'll clear it, and we both get the afternoon off."

The younger agent saw and misinterpreted the chill in Lacey's eyes. "Ah, say . . . Marie's got, I mean, she's got friends and . . . I think maybe we could—"

"I'll pass on that," Lacey said very softly. The scar on his neck stood out in relief against the veins pulsing there. He caressed it with his stubby, gentle fingers. "But I'll take the call, yeah. I didn't have much on for the afternoon."

"You're a champ, Jed," Billings said, squeezing Lacey's biceps and then striding quickly toward the stairway. He was toying with his collar ruff again, a beefy man who would always be alloted bottom-priority calls and would never understand why.

Lacey sighed and pulled his scanner helmet back down to cover his head like a fat, black artillery shell. Quirking his left ring finger to activate his implanted link with the Crime Service Net, Lacey said, "You just routed a call to station four-three-seven. Transfer it to me and give me a current scan."

"Accepted," said the computer voice from Lacey's mastoid, and the Net tapped his helmet into the output of one of the cameras on Level 15 of the Coeltrans Building. The screen showed emergency technicians who were laying a body on their medicomp, a dull-finished unit that looked like a coffin on casters. God knew why the men bothered, because the charred corpse was clearly beyond repair by any human means. There would be little enough of the victim to send to the Reclamation Depot after Lacey had cleared it for processing.

The rest of the level was normal enough, eccentrically furnished but in the fashion that executive levels of powerful corporations could be expected to be eccentric. Part of the work force was still at its desks, following routine as though that would deny the ghastly incident in the center of the room. The remainder were divided between those elbowing for a closer look at the body and those forcing toward the staircase, waiting to be passed by the bored Red Team securing the death site. No one sat at the broad mahogany desk which stood like an island in a green sea of carefully-tended plants.

Lacey triggered his implant. "Section six," he called, naming the imaginary sixteenth portion of the scanner's view which showed the guard rail of the elevator. "Twenty magnifications." The image zoomed and Lacey could see that what appeared to be a single gleaming circuit was actually divided by four thin insulators, so that each of the verticals of the shaft was insulated from the others. The victim's carbonized skin lumped two quadrants of the ring. Since the rods had to hold the power cables for the elevator's motor, stripped insulation was the obvious cause of the death. As Billings had said, a five-minute job.

Suppressing a yawn under his helmet, Lacey

ordered, "Okay, give me camera two at the time the line shorted."

Obediently the Crime Service computer switched to data stored in the vaults that extended for miles under Greater Atlanta. In Lacey's helmet screen the chauffeur stiffened as the jolt crossed him. A blue nimbus threw his screaming face into high relief. Behind him, rising from the big desk, was a man in conservative clothing with a face as transfigured by horror as that of the victim himself.

"Bloody hell," Lacey whispered. He recognized both men. "Bloody *hell*," he repeated. Then he flicked awake his computer link. "What's the priority on this call?" he demanded.

"Tenth," replied the computer. Its programming did not allow it to add, "Of course."

"Well, better raise it," Lacey said. "You've handed me a murder to clear, and I may need a hell of a lot of help to prove it."

The car was waiting when Lacey swung through the outside door. On his mere statement the Net had rerated the assignment to Priority Two, a comment as to where his stock stood with the computer on the basis of his past performance. The new rating included use of a State vehicle and driver, which Lacey took immediately to the scene of the death. He loved the scanner helmets and did most of his work seated under one; but he could not use them to question witnesses, and he had some questions he needed answered.

Transit time between the pad and the Coeltrans Building was four minutes. Lacey did not waste them, using his implant to get an ID and economic data on the victim and the man behind the mahogany desk. The first was easy. "Terrence Oscar Silvers, age 23; licensed ground vehicle driver employed by the Company for Electrical Transmission for five years, nine months," stated Lacey's mastoid. There was a pause. "Robert Sawney Wilhoit, age 47," the computer voice resumed. It halted. In a different timbre it requested, "Access code, please."

Without surprise or concern, Lacey punched his 8-letter code on the panel set into the back of the driver's seat. Wilhoit's wealth and authority had been obvious from the setting of his office; it would have been unusual if he had not used his power to see that idle thrusts into his personal life should be turned aside. Lacey on a murder call did nothing idly, and he could be as difficult to turn aside as Juggernaut's carriage.

Assured of Lacey's authority, the data bank continued, "President and Chairman of the Board of the Company for Electrical Transmission. Developed and holds patents on three basic processes in DC voltage step-down technology. Extensive holdings in various corporations, primarily in the field of electronic components and design.

Lacey's driver was tapping him on the knee and calling, "Coeltrans Buildings, sir." They were twenty meters above the roof pad of a modern cylindrical structure. One of the vehicles already parked on the roof was a ten-seater with leg shackles and wristlets on several benches: the van that had brought the uniformed police in response to a howl from the computer.

"Fine, set us down," Lacey said. They stuttered

to a halt at the stairhead. "Crime Service," he muttered as he brushed past the uniformed man stationed there.

"Hey, why didn't you just turn us loose through the Net?" the patrolman asked. "You didn't have to show up yourself." Lacey ignored him and stepped down the stairs into the greasy stench of the room below.

In the nervous chaos of the fifteenth level was a woman who had not been there when Lacey had scanned it minutes before. She was tall and fat, wearing stained coveralls. She sat on a wheeled toolbox and shouted angrily into a phone clipped to it, "You stupid son of a bitch, there *can't* be a short. We were *touching* the bleeding line thirty seconds before this beggar fried!" Sweat was bright on her forehead and heavy jowls, and her knuckles were white with her grip on the phone.

The electrician's shout had quieted the room so that her partner's voice from the speaker was clear as he replied, "Look, Margie, the meters show the juice came from the emergency generator. Nobody could've gimmicked'em with us working here, so it *was* a short. And for god's sake, what else could've done it? Bloody lightning?"

"Crime Service," Lacey said to the woman. "I need to ask you some questions."

"Oh, god," she murmured. Her flesh had lost all resiliency and gone gray in the blaze of the glow strips above. "Oh. . . ." Everyone in the room was staring at her and the investigator. "Will they—" she began and choked back her own words. Looking up at Lacey with a sudden fatalistic calm she

started over. "Will you put Jim and me under the
Psycomp for this? Will you wipe us?"

"You'd better tell me what happend," Lacey
said neutrally.

She shrugged and stood, towering over him.
The hand phone made a premonitory squawk and
she cut it off. "They hired Jim and me—Coeltrans
did—hired us to cross-connect the elevator. It—"
almost without pausing, she drew a rubber glove
onto her right hand and gestured with two fingers—
"runs up cog rails in the verticals, these rods. Two
of the rails are hot, insulated from the outer surface of the pole but feeding juice through the
gears themselves to the motor in the cage floor."

Lacey leaned forward for a better look at the
slots in the inner faces of the chrome supports.
"Get back from there!" the woman snapped. "I got
one deader on my conscience already today!"

Lacey blinked at her without emotion. "Go on,"
he said.

"We were supposed to set up a current path in
the other two rails, too," she said, wiping her face
with a sleeve. "Separate service from an emergency generator, a failsafe in case something went
wrong with city power. We punched the lines
through by section but we kept the circuit shut
down except for testing at night after the building
closed. There were bubbles in the insulation, so
until we got'em out we couldn't charge the line
when anybody was around. In case, in case. . . ."
She nodded toward the corpse though she refused
to look at it again. The technicians were now fit-
ting the body into a pressure-sealed bag to be
carried down to the street. "We'd got all the shorts

out of it, we thought, but we weren't quite done testing. Guess I left the switch on last night but it seemed safe—we were touching the posts, *touching* them, Jim and me just before this guy . . . went."

"Why run a generator circuit to an elevator?" Lacey asked. He was watching the electrician's face.

"Why does anybody want an elevator at all?" she replied. The fear was gone, replaced by a dawning curiosity. "It was for the boss himself, Wilhoit. You know, he's a regular guy? Last night he—*oh god!*"

All of the fat woman's confidence suddenly disappeared. If she had been gray when Lacey first spoke, she was white now with memory. "He was watching us last night when we ran the tests, moving the cage up and down. Talked to us some— hell, he was the boss, we couldn't tell him he couldn't hang around when we were working. Nice guy. But when we were packing up, he grabbed rails three and four—the new circuit, you see? Took one in each hand and I thought, 'Thank god we've got all the bugs out'. But we hadn't, you see? Just for some reason the line didn't short then, waited till this afternoon and got this stiff instead of, instead of. . . ."

"I want you to find that short for me," Lacey said, "you and your partner. He's in the building too?"

"Down in the basement," the woman said with a nod. "We were redding up when the floor manager called and said somebody'd died." Her open face suddenly coalesced into a frown. "Look, you trust *us* to check this out?"

"I don't need a Psycomp to tell if somebody's lying to me," Lacey said. "You stay straight with me, like you've been so far, and you'll come out of it all right."

"All right," she echoed. "All right, then wait thirty seconds and I may have an answer for you." She knelt at the base of an elevator support with a multi-windowed instrument in her hands. Holding it against the pole, she ran a dial across its scale and then used a pair of insulated pliers to bridge the two segments of handrail the victim had been holding when he died. The spark was fat and blue and snapped like a pistol shot.

"One'll get you ten that's it," the electrician said matter of factly. She began to put her tools away. The current had eaten a chip out of the nose of the pliers. "Inside the chrome plate, each rod's filled with Dorafeen. It's easy stuff to use, you inject it like grease and let it set. It's hard, it's strong, and it's a hell of a good insulator usually. But if you trip a block of Dorafeen with a magnetic field of whatever the block's loading frequency is, you can get it to conduct like so much copper."

She gestured with her chin. "That's where the whole company started—Citizen Wilhoit came up with a process using Dorafeen to chop high-current DC into AC to run through transformers to step it down. Anyhow, we bored the columns for our power lines, then ran a bare aluminum cable through them. No need to insulate since there was a centimeter of Dorafeen all around the wire. Except we never thought that if the right—wrong—frequency magnetic field was generated right alongside it . . . well, you saw what it did to the pliers when I'd primed it with my tester."

"But it's just a temporary conductor?" Lacey asked.

"Sure, depends on the mass and a lot of other things," the woman said with a shrug. "A couple seconds for this block, milliseconds for the wafers they use in power stations. I wouldn't have believed that a microgauss field could trip that whole rod, but . . . that's the only way the accident could've happened. Some coil with just the right number of windings, laid against the column and switched on while the elevator was being used."

Lacey's tongue touched his lips. "I'll call you if I need anything more," he said to the fat woman, dismissing her. Her face smoothed in relief and she began to roll her tool chest toward the stairs. Raising his voice to cut through the whispering, Lacey addressed the whole room: "All right, who's the highest official on this floor right now?" Answering murmurs were too confused to be intelligible, but a hundred faces turned and triangulated on a plump little man, one of those still seated at his desk.

Lacey grinned so that his teeth glinted. His neck scar was tense and stiff and crawled beneath his skin. "Let the rest of'em go, Corporal," he called to the chief of the uniformed patrol. "You and your boys can blast too. I'll just talk to this citizen a moment about what happened."

The red-capped police stepped aside and began filing up to their car, precipitating a rush of civilians down the single staircase lest the agent change his mind. The seated man watched Lacey approach with the intentness of a rabbit awaiting a black-snake. Like Lacey, he was dressed in gray, but in a muted solid instead of the tiger stripes that blurred the agent's outline. His beard matched his suit in color, a short, smooth arc that seemed a little incongruous beneath the baldly pink skull.

"Good afternoon, Citizen," Lacey said. "Your name and position, please?" He could have gotten the information as quickly through his computer link, but the opening question, the first thrust into his subject's persona, was a needed part of this interrogation.

"I'm Lewis Ashby and I, I assure you that I have far more to do than concern myself with, ah, drivers," the plump man said. His voice was generally steady, his tones rotund—but his eyes would not meet Lacey's.

"You knew Silvers, then?" Lacey prodded gently. "Knew he was a driver?" He and Ashby were about of a height, but the investigator was standing and dominating the clerk physically. He had let his overblouse fall open so that the holstered needle stunner was visible at the level of the civilian's face.

"I didn't say I knew him!" Ashby blurted. "You don't have any right—I don't care who you are, you can't put words in a person's mouth!"

"Did he always use the elevator when he visited Level 15?" Lacey asked, his voice still smooth but his muscles hardening slightly.

"I don't know."

"Umm, well . . . do you know how a Psycomp works, Citizen Ashby?" Ashby's face tilted up at the question, the mouth in a grimace or snarl, the eyes open. He said nothing. Lacey reached down, took a handful of fabric at the other man's throat and guided rather than jerked Ashby erect. "Maybe I'd better tell you, then, because it could be you'll be spending a long time in one yourself. You see, they give you a short-term anesthetic and slip you into a nutrient bath loaded with oxygen. Filling your lungs with it takes the anesthetic, but your body adapts to the system just fine.

"And you lose a little muscle tone, sure, but they won't really atrophy. The techs, though, they've run leads into your brain and as you lie there fed and filtered and breathing without being able to blink, a computer starts playing games in your head. It feeds in signals and sees what your brain does with them. Pretty soon it knows your head better than god himself does. It gets the answers to any questions it's been programmed to ask, and it goes around correcting any things that it's been programmed to correct. So long as it's in there anyway, you see."

Lacey's voice was the husky purring of a cat about to feed. His face was close to Ashby's and he was speaking with great distinctness. The clerk's eyes were bright with panic, and only the touch of Lacey's hand on his garments kept him from bolting. "It's not . . . comfortable," Lacey said, "lying there while a machine turns over every rock in your mind. And sometimes something goes wrong. Sometimes the computer goofs and a fellow comes out normal enough to look at but ready to kill at the slightest provocation, the least little thing that doesn't go his way. . . .

"Oh—I forgot to tell you where they sink the

leads into your skull, didn't I?" Lacey added. He tossed his head so that his brown-blond hair flew back from his forehead. With his free hand he touched two fingers to the white dimples at the hairline. "They go here. At least they did on me." He dropped Ashby and the softer man sagged into his chair like a scarecrow with half the stuffing gone.

"Now do you want to tell me about the driver?" Lacey asked; and through his sobs, Ashby told him.

Robert Wilhoit was afraid of heights. Not to an incapacitating degree, but enough that when he made it big he had begun to travel by ground vehicle despite the awkwardness of not being able to skim over the commercial traffic. For at least the past year, Silvers had been Wilhoit's driver.

The first time Ashby had seen them together was a day that the clerk had arrived early. Wilhoit had left his car and purred up the elevator while Ashby trudged the fourteen flights of stairs to which his position made him subject: no one but Wilhoit ever used the elevator. Three weeks later, the chauffeur had shared the cage with his employer, his haughty smoke-blue livery pressed tight against Wilhoit in the narrow space; and soon after that, the young man had his own key to the device and frequently rode it alone.

"I've worked for Coeltrans for twenty-three years," Ashby explained. Once started, the year of anger that had built up in the clerk spewed out like pus from a squeezed boil. "That's from the day, the very *day* that Citizen Wilhoit incorporated. Did he ever let me ride his elevator? Did he even speak to me, say, 'You're doing good work, Ashby'? Ha! But this little, *greasy* child. . . ."

Ashby raised his face and cupped hands to Lacey, pleading for the agent to understand something that he could not articulate. "He would ride up the elevator, get off at one floor or another. He didn't have any business in the building, he was just a driver. He talked to the younger clerks and the senior people, the floor managers—yes, me! —couldn't stop him. We were . . . we were afraid."

"Did Citizen Wilhoit ever, ah, threaten anyone for trying to get Silvers out of their work area?" Lacey asked.

The clerk grimaced, unwilling to answer the question but unable to avoid it even in his own mind. "Nobody tried to. We were afraid. The whole thing was . . . wrong. Citizen Wilhoit was ignoring it all, pretending that nothing was going on. Except that when this *person* went up to the Citizen's desk and whispered to him, they would leave together. Again and again. . . ."

Lacey looked over at the slab of oiled mahogany. Most top executives would have placed their desks on whatever part of the outer wall gave them the best view. Because Wilhoit disliked heights, his desk was central. The ceiling lights pooled brightly around the desk and the serpentine rings of foliage about it.

Lacey stepped over to the plants where the outermost circle of them lapped against the elevator. Festoons of tubing to carry water and nutrients linked the individual pots. He touched a squat plant whose leaves were like narrow fingers streaked with yellow and green. "Really likes plants, hmm? Don't any of them have flowers?"

"They're Citizen Wilhoit's hobby, not mine. If you want to learn about them, you'll have to ask his gardener."

"Even a gardener?" Lacey said mildly. There was a flower, after all; a pink geranium in a pot beside the elevator. Part of what snaked from its foliage was not plastic tubing but wire.

"Of course a gardener," Ashby was saying, but Lacey was no longer listening to him. The agent had unsheathed his hand scanner and was recording every detail of the apparatus connected to the geranium. The room's three integral scanners covered it in the sense that if it had been empty, at least two lenses would have born on every centimeter of surface. In practice, although opaque objects over 80 cm high were strictly controlled, there were blind angles near the floor which only spot checks by human operatives would record. By chance or otherwise, the geranium was in such an angle. Two short loops of wire were clipped to the leaves. At the other end they disappeared into a sealed, fist-sized box tacked to the nearest post of the elevator.

"What's this?" Lacey called back over his shoulder.

Ashby looked startled. He stood and peered over at where the agent knelt. "No, I told you I don't know anything about plants."

"Not the plant, for god's sake, the box!" Lacey snapped. "You know about electronics, don't you?"

"Certainly not. I'm an accountant, not a, a technician."

Lacey's expression went briefly flat and his scar

stood out. Then he began to chuckle. He was laughing fully, open-mouthed, as he walked past the cringing clerk and up the stairs to where his car and driver waited.

Level 17 was lighted and busy when Lacey got back to the State Building, though it was technically after quitting time and most of the floors below had emptied. Seventeen belonged to the hunters, and the good ones were lonely people. You couldn't take a companion under a scanner helmet with you. Some investigators worked long hours for the thrill of the chase, some because they tracked criminals by rote and had by now no other way to order their time. Lacey worked like a slave at an oar bench, driven by an overseer no one else could see. No one, at least, besides the Psycomp which had shunted his profile to the attention of Crime Service recruiters at the same time it carved away Lacey's ability ever to rape another woman.

His Unit Chief was waiting for him, seated on Billings' chair with her legs crossed at the knees and a glass of something sparkling in her hand. She set the drink down and smiled as the agent approached.

"Hello, Ruby," Lacey said, sitting on the edge of his own desk. "Slumming or hiding?"

The Crime Service Net was a huge computer complex that directed its agents with more than mechanical skill, but it could not interface them with the world. That job took humans—not hunters themselves, but humans who could understand the terrible loneliness and exhilaration of the hunters, who could cushion them against the realities of housing and economics and sex. Ruby Sutter was one of them, and she was one of the best. Tall for a woman, taller than Lacey's own meter seventy, she looked slim and fragile until one noted the muscles knotting close beneath the skin; then she looked only slim. Her hair was darker than brunette, and though her normal work did not require her to use the scanners, she wore it in the tight ringlets that would be comfortable beneath a helmet.

"Working, Jed—got your example to follow, you know." Sutter's station was on the fourth level, not the seventeenth. "Had a citizen complaint about you, as a matter of fact, and I was asked to take care of the problem. Asked from pretty high up."

Her face was bland. Lacey frowned in genuine surprise and asked, "Since when do the high-ups care what citizens think, for god's sake?"

"When the citizen looks a good bet to develop a matter transmitter in the next couple years, they manage to get interested."

Lacey slid down into his chair. "Umm. Sure. Wilhoit wasn't around, but he probably had access to scanner inputs from his own building, huh? Not really supposed to, but. . . . And I don't guess he liked what he saw, either." The squat man chuckled. "That's real freedom of information, isn't it? A murderer using a scanner to track the cops?"

Sutter took a sip of her drink. "The Net says it's an accidental death. Ninety-nine plus probability."

"Going to pull me off it, then?"

"Not if you say it's murder."

Lacey felt his muscles loosen. He had not realized until then how tense he had been. "That's good," he said, running a hand across his forehead. "I was going to nail him anyway. Though I guess you knew that already."

"You do your job, Lacey, and leave me to mine," Sutter replied. The smile left her face and she leaned forward, careful not to touch the agent or even threaten to. "But be careful, Jed. You can't push Wilhoit the way you did Ashby. Even with your past record and everything I can do for you, it'll be your ass if you go one step beyond the law with somebody with Wilhoit's clout."

She leaned back and grinned again. "But just between us and the data banks, that was a lovely bluff you ran on Ashby. Pretending the Psycomp had scrambled your brains and you were going to tear him open unless he talked."

"Bluff?" Lacey repeated. "Oh. Well, he was going to talk. He was the kind who would."

Sutter reached out a hand to brush the air inches short of Lacey's arm, a caress in intent but not in execution. Ever since the Psycomp had gotten through with him, physical contact with a woman threw Lacey into vomiting and convulsions. Sutter knew that and knew why, as she knew everything necessary to the well-being of her agents. It did not keep her from caring. "You're not going to lose control of yourself, Jed," she said. "Not over Ashby. Or anybody."

She stood and walked away.

Lacey was humming to himself very softly as he pulled down his scanner helmet and began running data on the victim. Silvers had spent four non-descript years driving Coeltrans delivery trucks before being picked as Wilhoit's personal chauffeur after the suicide of the previous driver. The data bank showed no reluctance to release information on the boy. Unlike the electronics magnate, Silvers was one more out of billions and his file was open to anyone with access to the computer. There was not even need to show cause.

But the life stats were as uninteresting as they were open. So, with a careful precision that combined years of practice with a knack beyond any experience, Lacey began to dig into the scanner records which stored Silvers' whole life.

"Death site minus 30 seconds," he ordered, using his mastoid implant to control the scanner helmet. Silvers' lounging beauty flashed up obediently, one hand on each of two quarter-circlets of railing that would soon be lethal. Lacey flicked the CS Net to attention again. "Tracer request."

"Go ahead," the computer link said.

"Terrence Oscar Silvers. Template as currently on screen."

"Ready." In a microsecond the Net had analyzed Silvers as he appeared moments before death, taking into account not only externals but details of height and bone structure subject to change only by trauma or the most extensive surgery.

"Same camera, same template—scan to death minus one week," Lacey ordered.

Using the analysis it had made on the victim during life, the Crime Service computer ran the past week's input from the Coeltrans scanner Lacey had made his vantage point. It quickly found and marked congruent subjects. A man could have made the same check—but only if he had a week to spend. Computer review was labor saving, though

in the same sense that a power drill saves labor—
per hole. It does not mean that a miner at the rock
face works less hard than his grandfather did, only
that he cuts out more ore.

"Two samples," the implant reported.

"Run the latest," said Lacey.

The scene in the scanner was visual proof of the
story Ashby had told. Silvers was arriving in his
blue and smoke livery, a stim stick between his
gum and cheek to diffuse its alkaloids into his
bloodstream. His walk missed being a swagger
only by its fluidity. Wilhoit was aware of him as
of nothing else in the room, but he kept his head
bent down and only the tension of his hand on the
desk edge was a communication.

The chauffeur sidled between desks, watching
with bored superiority as clerks tapped figures
into the displays across their desktops. Some stumbled under his gaze. Once Silvers spoke to an
employee, a blond boy whose bones must have
been translucent to give him so ethereal an air.
Lacey switched to another camera for a view of
Silvers' lips, but the words were a bland question
about how long the other had worked for Coeltrans.
The embarrassed clerk only muttered, "Sir, a week
is all," but his eyes followed Silvers until the driver
left, alone, as suddenly and inexplicably as he had
come.

Lacey sent his left ring finger the message to
curl. The rerouted nerve triggered his implant.
"What's Silvers' home address?" he asked.

"Suite 12, Level 3, 184 West Mangum Street."

'Suite' sounded plush, 'Level 3' sounded plush—a
low walk-up but high enough to be clear of the

noise and odors of the inevitable stores on the ground floor—and the street address was in the middle of a very good neighborhood indeed. "Same template, same scan frame, Level 3, 184 West Mangum Street," Lacey directed.

"Five samples."

"Run the latest."

By law and in practice, every room in the State of over five cubic meters was covered by the inter-locked fields of three scanning cameras. The law did not regulate minimum size or occupancy for rooms, but the staggering use-tax linked to every required camera guaranteed that space—and the scanners covering it—would be efficiently used. Silvers' rent was indicated by the fact that his apartment level was planned into fifty suites when many middle-class levels would have held five times as many units in the same area. Lacey's helmet showed him a late-evening scene: Silvers entering from the lower staircase and sauntering along a serpentine corridor to his own suite. He was out of livery, wearing instead a cape and jumpsuit cut conservatively but from lustrous material that flowed through a range of colors. Because the scanners worked on infra-red in the darkness, the precise shades were doubtful; the cost of the garment was not.

The corridors and suites were divided by double floor-to-ceiling sheets of vitril, sound-deadening but kept visually transparent by an expensive static cleaning system. Silvers palmed his lock plate, entered, and began fixing a meal in the kitchen.

"Who's paying for this?" Lacey asked.

The CS Net cleared its throat with a click, then

said, "All charges are paid through Personnel Accounting, Coeltrans."

"On whose request?"

"That information is not available."

A written or verbal order, than, not one punched directly into the corporation's accounts from a high level. Available to Lacey when he began running scanner images and questioning clerks. He didn't need the knowledge yet, and it would still be waiting for him when he did.

Lacey swung away his helmet and rubbed his eyes. The level was almost empty and the sky beyond the windows was black. "Late," he thought, then glanced at the clock hands illuminated over the doorway and realized that instead it was early— and not all that early. He did not feel tired, only light and insubstantial and happy in a way that drugs could never leave him. There was one more matter he could clear up through the helmet while it was still dark outside.

"Same template, same scan frame—Level 9, 304 Corcoran Street," Lacey ordered, shrouding himself with his helmet again.

"One sample."

"Run it."

On the screen flashed a moving image of the anteroom of Hell. In a nation without privacy there can be few statutory crimes. This is neither altruism nor liberality, simply economics. Since every human activity was scanned and the inputs monitored by computers which would ring alerts on every instance of activity they were programmed to find unlawful, there had to be sharp limits to make actual enforcement possible by a police force of acceptable size. In earlier decades, patrolmen could be writing parking tickets within twenty feet of a mugging or rape in progress. Now no crime was ignored and, without the lubricant of ignorance which made the old system work, the statute book itself had to be streamlined into the realm of possibility by a ruthless paring of minor offenses and victimless crimes.

To the State, no form of consensual sexual activity was a crime. Society, however, had a separate opinion.

When poverty becomes the norm, everything is for sale somewhere; but ascetic religion becomes the only real anodyne for the masses. If present squalor is only God's furnace to purify men for posthumous glory, what matter the lack of food and energy, the endemic diseases and the evidence that all over the world Man was staggering down a slope which he was unlikely to rescale. Purity is not a physical fact but a religious state of mind.

Level 9 was the entrance to the accommodation house, the time house, on the floor above. Clients paid for use of one of the hundreds of canvas-walled cribs, each with a single scanner unit mounted in the ceiling above it. You could not shut out the cameras, but the cameras did not care what—consensually—you did or to whom.

In the helmet screen, on the next to the top level of the sleazy residence building, Terry Silvers stood hipshot as his date, a wizened, balding man in a suit of natural silk, paid the attendant to be allowed to climb to the cribs.

"Cancel," Lacey said. He did not need or want

to follow Silvers into the accommodation house.
No law of the State had been broken there. If
Society wished to stigmatize homosexuals as bru-
tally as had Victorian England, if riot squads not
infrequently were called to put down the spontaneous violence offered by mobs of the upright to
uncovered paederasts, it was no business of Lacey's.

No one in an accommodation house is upright.

"Death site minus 30 seconds," Lacey ordered.
Silvers' doomed, smiling face appeared with Wilhoit
and the rest of the room beyond it. "Tracer
request."

"Go ahead."

"Robert Sawney Wilhoit, template as currently
on helmet screen."

"Ready."

"Level 9, 304 Corcoran Street. All samples in
the past six months."

"Twenty-seven samples."

"Run the latest."

Another night on the screen but the same guard
and Silvers with the same haughty expression as
he waited. This time Citizen Robert Wilhoit, inventor and executive, was paying for the crib. He
had the rigid look of a man whose legs were being
amputated without anesthetic. There were other
customers coming down the stairs, a middle-aged
man and a woman too plainly garbed to be a
prostitute. They avoided looking at Wilhoit just as
he did them.

No one was upright in an accommodation house.

"Cancel," Lacey repeated and swung the helmet away. Wilhoit had, perhaps, enough power to
escape the Mob's censure, but he could not have

escaped his own upbringing. A self-made man rather than an aristocrat raised to believe in the propriety of whatever he chose to do, public exposure of his homosexuality would have horrified Wilhoit as surely as it would have the clerks in his office. And he had been willing to kill to keep it . . . not secret, but unproven. The scanner image was evidence of motive for the computer. Lacey had already known it, of course, because he had a sharp memory for faces. He had remembered Wilhoit and the victim from a night some months previous when he had seen them together, leaving the accommodation house as Lacey entered it for his own private needs.

Morning was bright in the windows and the room had begun to fill with returning agents. It remained to learn where Wilhoit was at the moment. Using the scanner helmet once more, Lacey checked the magnate's office and found him seated at his desk speaking into a face-covering hush phone.

Lacey stood. "Ready me a car," he ordered the computer. "I'm going to visit an apartment while its owner's away."

The palm lock set in the clear panel of the suite's door was impossible to pick by conventional means. The flat pouch over Lacey's left hip, balancing his needle stunner, held an electronic pick that was by no means conventional. Itself a terminal to the Crime Service Net, its face was a mesh of microscopic beads that raised, lowered, and changed their conductivity under the direction of the computer. If a pattern was on file, the pick duplicated it instantly. If not, the computer ran a random search certain to open any palm lock within a minute.

It took Lacey a little longer than that to get in, because instead of picking the lock he summoned Wilhoit's live-in house staff to admit him.

There were two of them, both men in their forties. One wore the livery Silvers had died in, a burly, smooth-stepping man, obviously a human watchdog and obviously angry. Lacey had announced his presence by having the CS Net override every sound unit in the suite, ordering the occupants to unlock immediately or face arrest. As the door swung open the guard snarled a quick curse, but he backed off from Lacey's lifted brow and the threat in the eyes beneath it.

The other man was the one Lacey had come to see. He had thin hair and a worn tunic whose loops and pockets held a score of scrupulously clean tools. The light reflected from the myriad plants filling the suite gave the man's pale complexion a greenish cast, and it seemed to fit. He blinked at Lacey with the same mild interest that he might have displayed toward a cafeteria server.

"You're Charles Dornier, Citizen Wilhoit's gardener?" Lacey asked, as an opening rather than because the matter was in doubt.

"Why yes, do you have a delivery for us?" the wispy man responded.

Lacey grinned with something close to humor. "Not exactly," he said. "I'd like to see Citizen Wilhoit's plants, but I'm a Crime Service agent." He turned back to the guard. "You can wait outside in the hall," he said. "And I mean wait. Take

three steps away from the door and there'll be a
Red Team on you."

Dornier had ignored the words, ignored also the
glowering and slammed door with which his companion exited. "It's really a splendid collection,"
he was saying, "and though I must admit it lacks a
certain . . . focus, I suppose, I think the variety
makes it far more interesting. Don't you?"

Lacey had already found what interested him.
Amid the waist-high rows of foliage were six geraniums with gray boxes like the one in the Coeltrans
Building clipped to them. "What're these?" he
asked.

Dornier knelt beside Lacey, warming with pride.
He traced a circuit with his index finger. "It was
my own idea," he said, "but Robert has gotten very
deep in it himself and that's—well, he's a very
brilliant man, you know, very brilliant. I've attached electrodes to different portions of the same
plant to measure the resistance across the current
path. That depends on the number of ions in the
veins and the volume of fluid—and *that* can depend on outside stimuli, including thoughts the
plant's owner directs at it."

"Oh, god have mercy!" Lacey spat. It had been
a rough search already and he didn't need a load of
silly dreck to fuzz the edges further. "You're telling me that plants *think*?"

"No, I'm not telling you that, Citizen, and you're
not listening to what I *am* saying," Dornier snapped
back. The gardener's eyes flashed with anger and
an affronted dignity that Lacey could appreciate.
He suddenly realized that there was a core of
ability in Dornier as real as that within him—that

there had to be, or Wilhoit would never have hired him in so personal a capacity.

"I'm sorry," Lacey apologized. "Please explain." He squatted, his rump just above the floor and his face close to the geraniums. The blooms were odorless but the leaves themselves had a bitter, unexpected tang.

"I've never heard anyone insist that encephalographs think," Dornier said, not wholly mollified, "just because they register brain waves."

"But not thoughts."

"Well, Psycomps then; though perhaps you'll say they do think?" The gardener shrugged, then continued, "But machinery is Robert's field, not mine. And mind you, I'm not saying that my friends here"—he stroked the furry edge of a leaf with a finger that was stained, calloused, and very gentle—"don't think. It doesn't particularly matter to me at the moment. What does matter is that I can make any of these six raise or lower the resistance of their leaves, just by thinking at them from across the room."

For a moment the suite was so still that the drip of moisture from the plant-watering conduits was audible. Lacey rested like a mottled gray stone until he asked, "What would happen then?"

"Anything, anything," the gardener said with a trace of sharpness directed at what he saw as a silly question. "What happens when you flip any switch? The lights go on, the door opens, the, the rocket ignites. It's a control you can touch at a distance and through walls, that's what it is. What happens here is that the recorder, that's the box the electrodes hook to, marks the peak."

"Umm. And does a little coil energize when that happens?" Lacey's voice was as soft as the fur on a cat's belly.

"You'd have to ask Robert about that, of course. He built the system for me. For us, now—he's been testing a plant himself at his office for the past several weeks."

Lacey looked up at one of the level's scanning cameras. It stared straight at him and Dornier and recorded their every movement. But not their thoughts: that would have to wait for a further improvement in the machinery. "And anybody can do it?" he asked.

"I think so, at least," said Dornier cheerfully, again tracing a leaf with his fingernail. "Of course, it takes a little preparation, a, a tuning of yourself and the plant. Watering it, talking to it"—he broke off quickly and added in response to a comment that had not been made, "I'm not saying that it understands what you say any more than a chameleon understands that bricks are red and leaves are green. It's just a matter of tuning, that's all."

Lacey stood. "You've been a lot of help," he said, "and I appreciate it. And I really believe you've found something here." He walked to the door, looked out at the guard scowling through the vitril. "I'll tell you, though," he added over his shoulder before palming the latch, "I think you'll have one hell of a hard time convincing anybody else."

"Well, with Robert's backing, you know . . . ," Dornier said.

"Yeah, well. Good luck, anyway."

Lacey whistled between his teeth as he walked

to the aircar and ordered his driver to take him back to the State Building and wait. Still whistling, he washed his hands in the male lavatory on Level 14, returned to his desk, and made a quick check with the scanner helmet and the Net.

He was back in the air car ten minutes after he had left it, giving the driver a new destination.

Ruby Sutter found Lacey drowsing at his desk in the late afternoon. He awakened at her approach and his smile was a spreading contrast to the grim set of the woman's face. Billings had quickly ducked under his helmet at sight of his superior. Sutter sneered at his back. With a concern she tried to hide, she asked Lacey, "How close to a kill are you, Jed?"

"As close as I can come without putting Wilhoit under a Psycomp. I know why he did it and how; but to prove it, I'd have to get into his mind."

She slashed her hands and turned away. "Then it's over. There's no way to get him under a 'Comp. No way."

"Sure, that's what I thought too."

Sutter cursed, bitterly and at length. She poised her hips on the edge of the desk and looked Lacey in the eyes. "Jed, I'll be very lucky to save your job as it is. I had another talk with . . . well, several officials. They want you off this Wilhoit thing. If there was a chance you could close it, I'd . . . but if you can't. . . ."

Lacey's smile changed as all his muscles tautened. His voice burred, like a saw on hard wood as he said, "They could come to me directly, these

officials. Do they think I might—might take offense at them?"

He laughed suddenly and stood, his laughter
genuine—that of a cynic who sees his worst fore-
bodings proven true. "Look," he said, "I know you'd
go to the gallows with me, for me, Ruby. That
wouldn't do a bit of good. So I *am* going to drop
the investigation, mark it as an industrial accident—
but I'm going to see Wilhoit one time before I do
that."

"I'll come along."

"To hold my hand?" Lacey asked with a grin.
"No, you can watch here just as well."

Sutter bit her lower lip. "Look, just let me run
down to my desk and I'll be right back."

"Ruby, you wouldn't need a gun for this anyway—
and I really don't want you to come. You'd threaten
Wilhoit in the wrong way."

"I'm supposed to trust *your* judgment?" she
asked, but she bent a smile around the question.
She was watching his back as he walked through
the door to the landing pad; then she covered her
head with his scanner helmet.

As Lacey entered the top level of the Coeltrans
Building, eyes all around the room turned toward
him like filings aligned by a magnet. The man in
the center of the pool of plants was no exception.
He stared over the mahogany desk and the litter
of charts and tools and components upon it. Paying
no attention to the employees, Lacey picked his
way through the snaky aisles of plants leading to
Wilhoit. The silence was uncanny. Only the hiss of
his clothing on the leaves seemed to mar it. "Good

afternoon, Citizen Wilhoit," the agent said. "I'm Lacey."

The executive nodded. "You were here this morning, too, while I was in a board meeting. I would have expected you to check through your—cameras to see if I was here before you came."

"I did." Lacey poised the fingers of his left hand on the desk for support. He looked at ease but the scar on his neck burned like a magnesium flare. "I've been investigating your murder of Terry Silvers—but that's not news either, is it?"

Wilhoit picked up a delicate construct of glass and etched metal. His short, capable fingers turned it over for his inspection. Without looking away from his hands, he said, "I didn't kill Terry Silvers. Or anybody."

"But there's evidence, isn't there?" Lacey pressed. "There's all the records you could ask for that he was blackmailing you—"

"Citizen," Wilhoit said, now staring in the agent's face. His voice was no less vibrant for being pitched too low to pass beyond the circles of plants surrounding him. "You can prove my—orientation, if you want. And you can prove that Silvers was using the threat of exposing it to extort things from me that he would not have been granted otherwise. He was an animal, yes, a predator more interested in the fact that he could ruin a powerful man than in any real benefits the fact brought him, but yes. . . . What you don't have proof of, because it doesn't exist, not in any form the Justice computers could accept, is that I killed him. And so you can't arrest me, and you may as well leave."

"Oh, I can arrest you, all right," chuckled Lacey.

"If you're right, of course, you'd be released as soon as you had your preliminary hearing at the State Building."

"And you would be fired, perhaps even prosecuted under the circumstances."

Lacey ignored the comment. "You gave Silvers a key to the elevator," he said. "You knew how the support rods were constructed—you're the sort who would—but I'll bet you checked the working drawings anyway before you ordered the work done on the elevator. That I could prove."

"It wouldn't mean anything." Wilhoit had set his electronic tracery back on his desk.

"Then you rigged the recorder for your geranium experiment," Lacey went on, "so that it had a coil of the right frequency to trip the Dorafeen in the column. You could have used an electronic trigger instead of the plant, but computers understand electronics. Sure, the coil'd do something reasonable as well, move a stylus or the like—but you're used to thinking about multi-use components, aren't you? And then you waited for the right time and . . . conducted your experiment. Quite a job of planning." He looked sidelong at Wilhoit. "What, ah, formula did you use to send the plant off? I think I'd try something like, 'You are life; I am life; we are one in the universe', since the idea is to blend with the plant."

"You too," Wilhoit said. His breath was hissing as he rose to his feet, his flesh gone sallow and trembling. "Just like Terry, aren't you? The lust for a chance to bring down someone who really can do something important in this wretched world. But you won't do it, either—if your scanners don't show a damned thing, you can't prove a damned thing. Now get out!"

Lacey straightened. His face was a mask. "Robert Sawney Wilhoit," he said, "by virtue of the authority vested in me by the State of North America, I hereby direct you to accompany me in order to be formally charged in connection with the murder of Terrence Oscar Silvers."

Wilhoit slammed the desk with his fist. "You're going to play this farce to the end? I'll be released as soon as your Receiving Unit processes the charges. Do you think that people of the level who *could* override the computer's decisions are going to *want* to, to destroy me just so that you could win your game?"

"It's not a game, Citizen," said the agent with a smile as stark as a naked skull's. "It's my life. Winning, beating people like you, is about the only thing I've got left since they put me under the Psycomp. I can't lose. I can't afford to lose." He took a breath that shuddered like the wind in a loose-braced sail. "Come up to the air car."

"No!" Wilhoit shouted. He looked around, saw the open mouths of his staff gaping at him. "No," he repeated in a lower voice, "I'll meet you at the State Building if you must, but I won't ride in an air car. You'll have to shoot me to get me in one."

"Suit yourself," the agent shrugged as if it did not matter. "I'm not worried that you'll try to run. Go on down to your own vehicle, then."

Feet clattered on the stairs from the roof pad— Ruby Sutter, wearing a high-necked sheath of red and orange and a death mask in place of a normal expression. Lacey moved to her swiftly while Wilhoit, still standing, began to poke buttons recessed into his desk and speak soft commands to the microphones they activated.

"I was watching you," Sutter said. They were in the middle of hundreds of clerks, all straining to hear but afraid to look up at the two intruders. "You know that Receiving can't hold him. Jed, for god's sake don't throw yourself away! There's still time—"

"There's no time." Lacey looked back at Wilhoit who, his conversation with attorney or politician finished, had shrugged on an outer jacket and stepped to his elevator. Lacey took from his side pocket an empty plastic bag with a sealable edge and the glitter of a few drops of water within. His fingers toyed with it as he concentrated on something else.

Sutter bore his silence briefly, then demanded, "What've you got there?"

"Oh, I washed my hands this morning and saved the water to pour in that geranium," Lacey said, pointing to the recorder-linked plant by the elevator shaft. Wilhoit's head had just sunk below floor level. "It struck me that wash water might be a faster way of getting in tune with a plant than what Wilhoit's gardener was mentioning."

His unit chief blinked in puzzlement. "I don't understand," she said.

"Wilhoit would," said Lacey.

A scream burst from the elevator shaft, cutting through even the roar of a high-voltage arc. It hung over the blank faces of the clerks as smoke and the stench of burned meat began to bubble out of the shaft.

"I can't afford to lose," repeated Lacey.

Sutter looked at his face and shuddered. After a time, the screaming stopped.

When your fictional postulate is a world in which no crime goes unreported, the fun lies in exploring the limits of the postulate. The first two Lacey stories involved criminals trying to finesse the system. "Underground" deals with the brute force approach . . . which, in my opinion and experience, is more likely to produce a desired end than is subtlety. (It's also more likely to produce undesirable side-effects: you pays your money and you takes your choice.)

The background and several of the major characters in the story were drawn directly from New York City before the Civil War. Like Armageddon, the world which Law-and-Order advocates fear has already come and gone. (Which isn't to say that it couldn't come again: people keep fighting over the Hill of Megiddo on a regular basis.)

Another Lacey story was vaguely planned. I didn't write it (nor have I written anything else in the series) because my head is no longer in the place where Jed Lacey is. Lacey wasn't a happy man, and he didn't see any way out.

As for me—I stopped working as an attorney and instead drove a bus for a year. The world is what you make it.

UNDERGROUND

Two sections of floor collapsed and armed figures began to leap upward into the electronics emporium above. Two of the three Commissioners scowled as they watched the projection sphere, though they knew that the scene had actually occurred more than a year before. Lemba, the Chief Commissioner, was fat and black and too experienced to show emotion except as a ploy. He gestured toward the sudden chaos in the sphere. "At the start, no one was killed. Knocked around, threatened if they got in the way of the looters, but—"

A red-capped policeman burst through the outside door, carrying his heavy-duty stunner at high port. The projection brightened as a dazzling crossfire cut the patrolman in half.

Arcadio, the other male Commissioner, swore under his breath. "Powerguns, when we can't get them ourselves."

Lemba nodded.

Except for the Commissioners themselves, the

sixty-meter room was empty of its usual crowd. Further, though scanning cameras recorded the events of the room as they did the events of all other rooms in the State, the data of this meeting were restricted to the Security Police alone. Newshawks could appeal the Interdict to the courts, but even if they were successful, the delay of several months would kill news value in a society that lived from day to day.

Chains of pale, ragged looters were shifting equipment down through the gaps in the floor. Others guarded the hundreds of frightened hostages and the outside doors. The raiders were armed with a variety of weapons, including the powerguns which were supposedly only in the hands of the military. A stocky, red-haired woman raised her pistol and fired. One of the scanning cameras exploded into gobbets of burning plastic. The looter turned and blew apart a second camera. The scene in the projection sphere lost much of its precision, but the computer directing the simulacrum still managed to import an illusion of three-dimensionality.

The woman turned to face the remaining scanner. What looked like a bead necklace trembled on her bare bosom. As she leveled her powergun she grinned and extended the middle finger of her left hand. The whole screen spurted cyan, then went transparent.

"At the end of it there were five dead," Lemba said to his colleagues. "The one you saw, and a patrol car that exploded in the air. Red Teams were dispatched automatically, of course, and they weren't equipped to deal with powerguns."

"It isn't just the dead, though," objected Arcadio.

"That's right," agreed Kuhn, whose hair today matched the giraffe-patterned brown-on-blond polygons of her suit. She slapped the data print-out in front of her. "Of the 212 persons inside when the raid began, 27 are missing. Some—most—can be presumed to have been abducted for reasons one can guess. But there were several others, men and women who nobody'd have grabbed for a brothel or ransom. They were just ordinary people who opted to go Underground when they found the way clear. And *that's* the frightening thing."

"Not in comparison to the reason for this particular raid," Lemba replied equably. "Perhaps you thought this incident"—he waved at the vanished projection—"merely underscores the fact that Underground is organized and controlled by persons who are utterly ruthless?"

Arcadio and Kuhn stared at the fat man. Their expressions were compounded of disgust and irritation. "If you've requested an Interdict merely to play games—" Arcadio began.

"What's really frightening," Lemba went on, tapping his own data sheet with a callused index finger, "is that this raid provided all the necessary control components for a fusion powerplant. Coupled with other recent raids and . . . various other sources of information, Central has determined that Underground *has* a fusion unit in operation now. Beneath the City, where it will kill ten or twenty million people when it fails. And it's up to the three of us to decide how to shut that plant down before the disaster."

The hard faces of the subordinate Commissioners went blank. After a moment, Lemba continued, "Since I had a little advance notice of this—"

"Something this critical should have been routed to all of us, immediately!" Kuhn interrupted.

"—I was able to get a possible answer from Central Records. The data bank states that while a full-scale assault would almost certainly fail, an individual infiltrator might be able to eliminate the plant . . . and its personnel. It's probable that we will get only one opportunity, so we need to choose the most effective person for the task. The man the data bank recommends is a Crime Service employee in Southern Region. His name is—"

"Field Agent Jed Lacey?" queried a young man in a crisp yellow uniform. The legend printed on his cap band read, "TAKE PRIDE IN OUR CITY".

Lacey looked up abruptly. His mastoid implant was useless out of Greater Greensboro Subregion. He felt naked without it, his link to all the knowledge in the State. For that matter, Lacey missed the needle stunner which normally rode high on his hip. "Right, I'm Lacey," he said when he had identified the speaker from among the throng filling the airport terminal. "You my driver?"

"Well, I'm your guide, citizen," the City employee said with a false smile. "My name is Theron Barbee. We'll be taking public transit to the Commission offices. We don't approve of the waste of air cars here, you see."

"Right, I see," Lacey said sourly. He nodded toward the sky. Air cars streamed among the buildings like foam on a rocky strand.

"Well, of course that's private sector," the guide

said with a sniff as he led Lacey toward the long queue for the buses.

"Sure," agreed Lacey. "Well, if they won't give their people tools to do their jobs right, they needn't be surprised when the jobs get done half-assed. But it's not my City."

The sprawling crowds were an emotional shock to Lacey, though intellectually he had known what to expect and had tried to prepare for it. His suit of red-orange covered him throat to digits in high style. He liked the color, though it was too blatant for him to have worn it while working. Lacey had stopped working the moment he boarded the airliner in Greater Greensboro, answering a summons relayed through his superiors.

But more than the color, Lacey liked the fact that the suit left only his face bare to a woman's touch. For fifteen years, physical contact with a woman was all that it took to crumple Lacey as effectively as a kidney punch could; and in the crowded City, he knew he could not avoid such contact.

When the third bus hissed up to their stop, Barbee called, "Quick now!" and swung aboard without further warning. Lacey followed the yellow-clad man, using his locked fists as a prow to split the would-be passengers who had pushed ahead of him. He ignored the yelps, the elbows chopping at his ribs and the boot-spikes gouging his shin armor. He had tried to ignore the other people, because half of them were women; and if he even let himself think of that for a moment, he would collapse in uncontrollable nausea. Though his suit kept him from actual contact, Lacey's real problem was a psychic one: a repulsion implanted in his mind by a Psycomp after his conviction for rape.

The bus moved off slowly. A dozen people gripped the door jambs with all but their fingers and toes outside the vehicle. "It's an express," the guide shouted to Lacey over the babble. The powerplant itself keened through a hole in its condenser tubing. "It'll take us straight to the City Complex."

Lacey muttered something under his breath.

Actually, they were still a kilometer from the Complex when the bus halted in a traffic jam the like of which Lacey had never imagined. "Well," Barbee said with a bright smile, "I guess we'll just walk from here."

"This happen often?" Lacey asked as he jumped to the sidewalk. The buildings glowered down at him. They had been too massive to demolish and rebuild at heights which could be served by stairs. Though the cost of power for elevators was almost prohibitive, there were people who would pay it for the privilege of living and working in this giant replica of a termite colony.

"Well, it happens," the guide replied ambiguously. He set off at a rapid pace.

They climbed over and scraped between the vehicles which had mounted the sidewalks in vain attempts to clear the jam. At last Lacey saw what the trouble was. An entire block was covered, building-front to building-front, by a roiling party of more than 5,000 people. They were dressed and undressed in a multiplicity of styles. Banners shaded the gathering with slogans which were meaningless to the Southerner. As he began to thread his

way through the celebrants, Lacey realized that
they were homosexuals.

The squat field agent bumped a man whose
nude body was tattooed in a pair of polychromatic
starbursts. The man turned and raised a cup of
something amber and alcoholic. "Join us, love," he
offered.

"Thanks anyway, friend," Lacey said and moved
on by. When he had caught up with Barbee—the
local was far more adept at slipping through the
dense crowd—Lacey demanded, "Where the hell
are your cops?"

The guide looked back with distaste. "You'd
better get rid of your provincial sexual attitudes
fast," he said with a sniff.

Lacey snorted back. "Look, if they're out of *my*
subregion, I don't care what they do to who with
what. I just mean I'd expect your Red Teams to
pay some attention to people blocking a street—in
the middle of town, in the middle of the bleeding
day!"

"Well, they're quiet, they're not hurting anybody," the man in yellow said. Then, with some
embarrassment, he added, "Besides, the patrols
are understrength now. Finances are, well. . . ."

"Sure," Lacey said, glancing over his shoulder
at the party. He was visualizing how twenty men
could clear the street with a tanker of stun gas and
enough trucks to hold the bodies. It wasn't his
city, though; and Lacey was far too intelligent to
believe the State would be a better place if everyone's instincts were like his. Control was the key
. . . but no control was as important as his own
self-control.

Barbee stopped finally in front of one of a line of concrete buildings, new enough to be twenty stories high instead of eighty. The windows were opened in more facets than a beetle's eyes. "Here you are," said the guide, "the Tweed Building. You're to report to Captain Max Nootbaar on Level Twenty. He'll have your instructions."

Lacey looked upward. Yellow-painted air cars burred to and from the landing stage on the building's roof. At least somebody on the City payroll had access to transport that couldn't be mired by block parties. "Crime Service headquarters?" the Southerner queried.

"That's right."

"And no elevators, I'd guess."

"Of course not."

Barbee was already walking away, toward a more distant building of the vast Complex. Lacey let out an inarticulate scream and leaped upon the slimmer man, throwing him to the ground. The Southerner brought a flat tube from under his tunic. It snicked out a 5-cm. blade when he squeezed. "I'll kill you!" he shouted to the guide. "I'll cut your heart out!" Only someone who had seen Lacey in a killing rage before would have noticed that this time his neck scar did not writhe against flushed skin.

The street was straight and broad; a dozen scanning cameras on it recorded the incipient mayhem. Relays tripped, panels glowed red, and a patrol car slowing to land on the Tweed Building instead plunged down toward Lacey. In contrast, the pedestrian traffic surged outward like a creek against an obstructing rock. The passers-by contin-

ued to move as if they were oblivious to the min-
gled screams of victim and assailant.

Lacey suddenly stood, closing and slipping away
his knife. He reached out a hand to help Barbee
up. The guide screamed again and tried to crawl
away. Fear wedged his body against the seam of
building and sidewalk.

The ten-place patrol car slammed to the pavement behind Lacey. "Get'em up!" a hoarse voice
shouted.

Lacey raised his hands and turned with a quizzical expression. The four uniformed policemen had
him covered with needle guns and a stun gas
projector. "Good morning, sergeant, patrolmen,"
Lacey said calmly. "I'm Field Agent Jed Lacey
from Greater Greensboro. I'm due for an appoint-
ment with Captain Nootbaar. My guide here tripped
on that crack in the pavement. Must say I'm a little
surprised to have a Red Team react to that." He
smiled. "I'd have expected Public Works, if anyone."

The sergeant frowned. Barbee saw that Lacey's
back was turned. He began running down the
sidewalk, first in a crouch and then full-tilt. Lacey
glanced at him. "Must be in as much of a hurry as
I am," he remarked disinterestedly.

The patrolmen wore puzzled expressions. Their
sergeant queried his mastoid implant, then waited
for the answer with his hand cocked. When it
came, he spat disgustedly and reslung his gas gun.
"Yeah, Captain Nootbaar says send him up," he
said. "Two bleeding false alarms in one day."

"If you don't mind, I'll ride up with you," Lacey
said, lowering his hands as the Red Team locked

its weapons back on safe. "I was afraid for a moment I'd have to climb twenty flights of stairs."

"Sure, room we got," the sergeant grunted. "Men, no, but we got room." The driver lifted them vertically, faster than they would have dropped in free fall. "First the computer crashes us in on a strangling. That turns out to be two kids screwing under a sheet. Then we're held over our shift 'cause the bloody Streets Department sits around with its thumb up its ass instead of fixing the sidewalks. I swear, a bit more of this and they'll have to look for me Underground too."

Captain Nootbaar had been alerted by the sergeant's call. He waved toward the doorway to attract Lacey's attention. The captain's desk was a little larger than most of the hundreds of others crowding the unpartitioned room, and extensions from the desk supported three scanner helmets instead of just one. Lacey made his way to Nootbaar with practiced care; governmental offices were just as crowded in Southern Region as they were here. At a glance, Lacey assessed the captain as sixty, softly massive, and a better cop than this place had any right to hope for.

"Expected you by the stairs," the big man said as they shook hands. He tapped his scanner helmet. "Interesting replay here of how your guide tripped."

Lacey smiled. "I'm an honored guest of the City," he said. "They could find me a car. Besides, it's been a while since you've climbed any stairs yourself, hasn't it?"

Nootbaar looked down ruefully at his gut. "Well, there's a patrol inbound past my block every morning at 0655. Wouldn't be efficient for me to waste energy walking, would it?" His eyes raised and caught Lacey's. "You know, if I'd realized you weren't just some rube the brass was wasting my time with, there'd have been a car at the airport. Sorry."

Lacey smiled more broadly. "Guess if I'd needed your help, I wouldn't have deserved it, hey?" The smile passed. "Though you *can* help me learn what the hell I'm doing here."

Nootbaar shrugged. "Pull down some headgear," he said as he reached for one of the scanner helmets himself. "I'm supposed to give you background," he went on, his voice muffled by the two helmets. "I don't know quite what they want you to do with it; but if they give you a chance to back out, Lacey, don't wait for them to ask twice."

Lacey's helmet formed a dull image in response to Nootbaar's direction. "I'm picking this pretty much at random," the local man explained obscurely to Lacey. They were watching a sub-surface level of an old building converted to residential occupancy. Sparse glow strips provided less light than would suffice for reading. Transparent panels, waist high, marked off narrow aisles and living units scarcely more spacious. "Do you have a district, a tolerated zone, where you are?" Nootbaar asked.

"You mean, no scanners, no police?" Lacey said. "Enter at your own risk?"

"That sort of thing, yeah. A place all the decent folk kind of ignore, unless they need something that's sold there. Violates State statutes as well as local, but let the State try and enforce it if they think it's so damned important."

"I know the theory," the Southerner replied. "There's places I've been that have them. But not Greensboro. Christ, there's nothing you can't buy legally, unless it'll permanently injure somebody else. And if it's just that you don't want the scanners watching—" Lacey paused, his flesh trembling with the memory of his own needs being satisfied under a scanner's glare— "that's tough."

"We got a district here," Nootbaar said. "It's called Underground."

On the helmet screens a figure rose from out of the floor and began scuttling toward the open staircase. "There's one for sure!" the captain exclaimed. He boosted the magnification. First the scanner focused on the wooden grating that had been shifted to give entry to the level. Then Nootbaar switched to close coverage of the figure itself as it scurried up the stairs. "Probably an old heating duct," Nootbaar said, presumably referring to the access hole. Lacey waited with the silent patience of a sniper who moves only enough to start a bullet toward an opponent's heart.

After walking up three levels of stairs, the figure exited to the outside. Street cameras automatically shunted their data to the watching helmets. The subject was a woman in flowing gray coveralls and a hat whose brim flopped over her eyes. She turned into the doorway of a quality clothing emporium. The floor within was leased on a square-meter basis to scores of individual boutiques.

Without warning, the woman scooped up three dresses awaiting alterations on a counter. The boutique manager shouted and leaped atop the counter. The thief ran for the door as the manager collapsed. A "customer" standing in the next booth had stitched him through the chest with a needle stunner before following the woman out the door.

Thief and guard burst back outside. The light-sensitive fabric of the stolen garments blazed like a sodium flare. There was no patrolman in sight. Heedless of the slow traffic, the pair darted to a pedestrian island in the middle of the six lanes. A metal plate there hinged downward. In the instant before it closed again over the fugitives, Lacey caught a glimpse of stone steps and a dozen other faces.

"Old subway entrance," Nootbaar said with dismal satisfaction. "That's all the show. We may as well look at each other for a while."

Lacey swung up his counterweighted helmet. "You've got a Coventry for *thieves* up here?" he said incredulously. "You just ignore them if they make it to ground before you catch them?"

The bigger man sighed. "Maybe there was a choice once," he said, "but the size of it scared people. The subways'd been closed because they were inefficient and the surface streets were enough without private cars. There were water and sewer mains; some of them forgotten, some operating but big enough to hide in anyhow, to splash through . . . almost all the time at least. Cable vaults and steam ducts and sealed-off sub-basements; parking garages and a thousand other things, a maze twenty levels below you.

"You close one off and somebody breaks into it again before the crew's out of sight. Set up a

scanning camera and in ten minutes it shows you a
man reaching toward it with a crowbar. Send down
a Red Team and nobody comes back." Nootbaar
looked up. "And it's all so easy to say, 'They want
to live like rats, what's that to you or me or the
State?' "

"So it's a separate society?" Lacey offered.

"It's a worm in the guts of the City!" Nootbaar
snapped back. "It's fences who sell goods at a
tenth their surface price; cribs where they hose
the girls off because they're too wasted to clean
themselves. It's a family living in a section of
36-inch pipe, with no water and no light within a
hundred meters. It's slash shops that generally
poison their customers even when they don't mean
to. And Lacey—" the captain leaned across his
narrow desk, his eyes black and burning with furious despair— "it's ten thousand people, or a hundred thousand, or just maybe—and they don't
believe me, Lacey, but I've been down there—just
maybe a million rotting devils and more every day."

Nootbaar shook himself and leaned back in his
chair. "It's called Underground," he repeated.

Lacey traced his neck scar with one stubby finger. "What do they expect me to do?" he asked.

The heavy captain spread his palms. "I don't
know," he said. "I don't think anything can be
done. We can't cut them off from water or electri-
city—they tap the distribution lines. We'd have to
shut the whole City down. We can't close off the
exits from their warrens, because there's at least
one opening in every block in the City. If we
arrested everybody who came out of Underground,
we'd have half the population in the slammer by

Sunday morning. It's a cut that's bleeding us day by day, and some day it'll bleed us out; but there's nothing we can do."

"So take the gloves off," Lacey said. The captain's ironic smile grew broader. Lacey ignored it. "Get the State to send help. Hell, get the military in, it'll be a change from the Cordillera Central. Go in with stun gas, back it with powerguns; and when you've cleared a stretch, seal it for good with a long-term toxin like K2 so nobody'll try moving back in fifty years or so. It'll cost something, cost a lot; but it's still cheap at the price."

"You'd have enjoyed talking to Director Wheil," Nootbaar said reminiscently. "He planned it just that way, ten years ago."

Lacey frowned. "Don't tell me you couldn't shoot your way through a bunch of untrained thugs, even if they were tough," he said.

Nootbaar shook his head. "We were making good headway—not cheap, but like you say cheap at the price—when about a thousand of 'em came outa the ground and took over Stuyvesant Armory." Nootbaar paused and sucked his lips in, his eyes focusing on the close-chewed nails of his left hand. "It wasn't the powerguns they took, though the fighting down below'd been hot enough already," he continued. "And it wasn't just that they got enough explosive to crater the City Complex like an asteroid hit it. The real thing was, they got all the K2 we'd stockpiled to close Underground after we'd cleared it. Used right, there was enough gas in Stuyvesant to wipe out the whole City; and nobody thought the people who'd planned the raid couldn't figure out how to use the goodies they'd taken."

Nootbaar looked at Lacey. "We hadn't figured a counter-attack, you see. Everybody we could trust with a gun had been sent Underground. So they recalled us without waiting for a demonstration; and that was the end of the only chance this city was going to have of getting shut of Underground."

Lacey drummed his left middle and index fingers. "You know pretty much what goes on down there?"

Nootbaar shrugged. "Sure, Intelligence Section runs people in all the time. For that matter, cops get laid and get drunk and buy hot goods too. But any time we've really tried to assassinate the leaders down there—Bill Allen, Butcher Bob Poole, Black May . . . especially Black May—the people we send don't come back. There's lines from here to Underground, and they go a ways up. They've got access to the scanners for sure."

Lacey massaged his short hair with both hands. "What's the drill, then? What am I supposed to do?"

"I'm to send you over to the Fernando Wood Building and the Commissioners'll tell you themselves," Nootbaar said, rising. He grinned, a transfiguring flash. "Wouldn't be real surprised if there was a patrol headed that way about now. After all, it's only a hundred meters—unless you have to go down and up twenty flights of stairs in the mean time."

Lacey laughed and shook the heavy captain's hand. Nootbaar sobered and added, "Look, if there's anything I can do for you. . . ."

"You gave me some good advice at the start of

this," the Southerner assured him. "I'll go listen to what your Commissioners have to say, but I'll bet I'm going to do just like you said. I'll get my ass back South where it belongs."

Nootbaar frowned. "I'm not telling you anything you don't know," he said, "but remember: all you need to get elected Commissioner is a constituency. You don't need brains or ability, and you sure as death don't need ethics. Don't give them anything they haven't paid you cash for."

Save for a narrow anteroom, the City Commissioners' offices filled the whole top level of the Wood Building. The anteroom had its own trio of scanning cameras, along with four clerks and a dozen uniformed guards who checked all would-be visitors before they were allowed into the Commissioners' sanctum.

Lacey bore the questioning with equanimity and even some interest. He had never met the elected powers of his own subregion. The whole business amused him.

When Lacey passed through the inner doorway, an alarm bell rang. Scores of people, both petitioners and functionaries, were already within the larger room. They got up at once and began to stream outside. Many stared at Lacey as they passed.

Puzzled, the Southerner turned to follow the crowd. From the center of the room, a fat, black man in a pneumochair with synchronized desk called, "No, not you, Citizen Lacey. Come over here."

The door closed. Lacey was in a huge chamber,

alone except for the scanners and the three seated
persons: the City Commissioners. Off-hand, Lacey
did not believe he had ever before shared so large
an enclosed space with so few people. Carefully,
fighting an impulse to look over his shoulder, he
walked into the semicircle of desks.

"I've placed an Interdict on this discussion, Citizen Lacey," the fat man said. The woman to his
right glared from under a mass of green hair that
matched her dress. The black grinned and corrected himself, saying, "Pardon, I should have
explained that *we* placed the Interdict. Commissioner Kuhn—" he nodded right; the woman's glare
transferred itself to Lacey— "Commissioner Arcadio—" he nodded left at the man with long, nervous fingers and a nose like an owl's beak— "and I
myself am Chief Commissioner Lemba. I mention
the Interdict only so you realize how important
the matter you are about to learn is considered by
ourselves . . . and by the State."

"All right," Lacey said quietly. There was a
small secretary's console nearby. He slid it over to
him, sitting on the desk rather than the low-slung
seat.

Lemba continued, "You've been given the background on Underground. It's an unfortunate situation, especially since there appears to be a misguided
minority which thinks it better to live in squalor
and anarchy—" his voice swelled— "than as a part
of the greatest city this world has ever known!"

"I've never voted in my life, Citizen Lemba,"
Lacey interjected, hunching a little as he sat. "And
I couldn't vote in this region if I wanted to."

Lemba blinked, Arcadio smiled for the first time,

and even Kuhn's eyes had briefly less of hatred in them than before. She must have seen his life stats, Lacey thought. Couldn't expect her to like them.

"The problem, citizen," Lemba continued in less rounded tones, "is that some of those who have gone Underground are scientists of international reputation. One of them—" a head formed in a projection sphere over the desk on which Lacey was sitting. The Southerner stood and walked back a few steps to where he had a good view of a balding, white-haired man with a look as sour as Kuhn's— "Dr. Jerry Swoboda, seems to have built a fusion powerplant down there."

The Chief Commissioner took a deep breath, more as a rhetorical device than from any onset of emotion. "I don't have to tell you how dangerous fusion power is. Environmental groups and the State Regulatory Board shut off even research on it two decades ago. And I don't have to tell you how many innocent men, women and children would die horribly in the event such a plant failed beneath the City.

"*Will* die. Unless the plant is shut down and destroyed, and Dr. Swoboda and his associates are—" Lemba looked up at one of the room's scanners, still operating even though its output was restricted— "prevented from building another such death machine. Central Records says you are the best man to carry out this crucial mission."

Lacey filled his cheeks, then puffed the air out glumly. "Do the data banks give any reason why I'd want to carry out your 'mission'?" he asked.

"How about ten million lives, citizen?" Commissioner Kuhn snapped. Her irises had been dyed to match her hair and clothing. "Or don't you care about lives?"

Lacey met her glare. It did not bother him—as Lemba's growing smile did. "Look, it's not something we can argue about," the Southerner said in a reasonable voice. "You want to save them, then you go down and save them. Myself, I can live the rest of *my* life without your City. I've lived the past fifteen years without things that were a lot more impor—"

Lacey's voice died. He turned again to face Lemba. "You son of a bitch," he said to the commissioner in awe. "You knew I wouldn't be able to go down there without being able to touch women. . . ."

"What a Psycomp did, a Psycomp can undo," Lemba agreed in satisfaction. "Your psyche, Citizen Lacey, isn't the sort of thing that everyone would care to own. Still, I thought that in exchange for our unblocking it again, you'd be willing to do the City a little service."

Commissioner Kuhn was standing, her face flushed in ugly contrast to her clothes. "It's bad enough a man like this still walks the earth!" she shouted at Lemba. "Did you *see* what he did to get wet-scrubbed? You're *not* going to turn him loose the way he was before!"

Arcadio interrupted for the first time. "What happened fifteen years ago doesn't matter," he said. "What's important is what is going to happen right here if we don't act promptly."

"Citizen Kuhn," Lacey said.

She whirled on him, mouth opening to rasp

insults; but ungoverned behavior had not brought her to a Commissionership. She waited for Lacey to speak.

"I'm not, I won't be, the guy I was before they . . . wet-scrubbed me," the Southerner said. His hands were locked tightly together. "I don't say I'm any better; but I'm not as young. I won't risk my—mind—on another gesture. Unless the gesture is more important than I ever expect anything to be again."

Kuhn looked at Lacey in disgust, then looked back at Lemba. "I won't argue with two votes," she spat. "But if he comes back alive, it's on your consciences. And it's up to you to explain to the female voters of this City."

Kuhn walked out of the meeting room, letting the door bang to behind her. Lemba beamed at the standing agent and said, "Dr. Kabiliak is waiting on Level 3 with a Psycomp team—I rather suspected you were going to volunteer. We'll prepare everything else you'll need during the three days you're in the tank. We need to hurry on with this, you know." The Chief Commissioner chuckled.

Lacey turned and walked toward the door. He was already planning his insertion into Underground. He had as little feeling as he would have had if someone else were wearing his flesh.

Lacey vaulted the stair railing and dropped the eight feet to the floor of the lowest level. His bent knees absorbed the shock, then thrust him down the dim aisle at a run. Boots clattered on the stairs one level up, growing louder.

Two women were gossiping across the aisle as

they would have done over the back fence of earlier ages. They lunged away, calling to their children in high voices. Lacey squirmed through an opening in the floor that had been an 18-inch drain pipe. A few feet down it made a 90° bend. Someone shouted from the stairs and a sheaf of stun needles clicked against the concrete flooring and vitril partitions. Lacey shoved himself forward with an echoing curse, heedless of the nub of ceramic pipe that was gouging his suit and the thigh beneath it.

A pair of needles flicked his boot-sole, minuscule taps like a sparrow's kisses. Then Lacey was through, worming toward a dimness only less black than the tile tube itself. He could have been frozen and dragged back if one of the Red Team in pursuit had simply lowered a needle gun into the drain and fired a burst down its axis; but no one bothered to take that obvious step. Underground was safe, Lacey thought disgustedly; a self-fulfilling prophecy if ever there was one.

When Lacey fell into the sixty-inch pipe under the street, the first thing he noticed was the stench. In part, that was because his eyes had not adjusted to the absence of light. Still, the fetor would have been overpowering under any conditions. Thousands of fans pulled a draft into the tunnels, but tens of thousands of people breathed and sweated and excreted in them.

There were whispers and scrabbling. Lacey tensed for attack from some unseen direction. Fingers traced his throat and down his torso. "Come for a good time, honey?" a voice croaked. Other fingers, arthritic and cold, sought Lacey's hand

and tried to drag it toward their owner's body. "Crystal'll show you a good time, better'n any a' those—"

Lacey shook himself loose. "I didn't come for that," he said. "I just needed to get away."

He crawled toward the main drain. Part of the evidence for a functioning fusion plant Underground had been the suddenly-increased theft and even purchase of lights and glow strips. Power pilfering had, if anything, decreased at the same time. The blackness here emphasized the enormous volume of tunnels which not even epic banditry could illuminate.

Hunched over, Lacey began to walk toward the diffused light twenty meters away. The pipe, sloping upward to either side, made footing tricky. Hands caught him again.

"No!" Lacey shouted.

There was a blur in front of him, another figure or figures. More groping hands at his belt, his pockets, his groin. Lacey blazed with conscious loathing spawned by fifteen years of necessary avoidance. His boots and elbows slashed out. The little knife was in his hand, its blade already smeared with dried blood. The hands dropped away. Cracked voices lifted in a chorus of ecstatic pain.

The light came through a gap hacked without finesse into a subway line. The tracks had been reclaimed for their metal after the system was shut down, leaving an echoing waste of concrete and ballast. Now the axis of the great hollow was lumped with cribs and shanties of every style and construction. At intervals of twenty meters or so, glow strips were spiked to the tunnel ceiling. Their

light would have been called inadequate even in
the cheapest tenements above ground, but here if
formed luxurious pools.

Lacey paused to get his bearings. He tucked
away his knife. A grizzled woman was leaning the
back of her chair against the tunnel wall beside the
opening. She dropped the chair legs to the ground
and whistled toward a seated trio fifty meters away.
Near them a flight of steps led upward to a subway
entrance. The three men rose and began walking
toward Lacey and the woman. Weapons trembled
in their hands.

Lacey glanced at them, then took a step toward
a near-by canvas shanty. Four patrons were drinking from mugs and arguing with the blocky bartender. The woman behind Lacey tapped him on
the shoulder. In the dim light she had seemed to
be carrying a short bamboo cane. It was in fact a
length of steel reinforcing rod.

"Where you going, buddy?" she demanded.

Lacey's tongue touched his lips. "Look, I got in
a little trouble—" he shrugged one shoulder in the
direction he had come— "topside. Thought I'd—"

"Says he's a mole, sure enough, Mooch," the
woman cackled to the leader of the approaching
trio. "He thinks he is." Then, "Watch him, he's
got a knife."

"Does he?" said Mooch. He was taller than
Lacey and his broad shoulders supported arms so
long his hands dangled near his knees. Mooch's
bare torso sagged over his belt. Despite the fat,
the muscles were there as well, and the many
scars suggested how they had been used. "Funny,
I got one too." He caressed the hilt of a long bread

knife thrust bare between his belt and waist-band. Slung across Mooch's back was a gunpowder weapon whose magazine protruded over his right shoulder.

"Let's see your knife, boy," the burly man ordered flatly. The two men with him tensed. Lacey heard a whisper of metal as the woman moved behind him.

The Southerner's tongue touched his lips again. Very carefully, he brought the little weapon from its concealed pocket and handed it to Mooch. The bigger man turned the hilt over as he inspected it, looking for the mechanism. His thumb and forefinger accidently squeezed together on opposite sides near one end. The blade shot out and nicked his palm. Mooch cursed, swapped ends of the knife, and snapped the blade off with a sideways flick of his thumb. He let the pieces clatter to the ground. A drop of his blood splashed on them.

"Cute," the leader said. More to the others than to Lacey, he added, "Bill's coming, I buzzed soon as Angel here whistled . . . but I don't guess he'll mind if we see what this mole's got on him.

"Bet you thought you could just come Underground and nobody'd think twice, hey?" said one of Mooch's henchmen, a twisted black in a caftan.

Lacey felt himself edging backward even though he knew the woman was there with the steel rod. "Christ, there's a million people come down here each week," he stammered.

The black laughed and spun the chain in his hands as if it were a short jump rope. "Sure, but you wanna stay, you wanna be a mole. And we got word to watch out for moles for a while. Well, you may stay at that."

"Turn your pockets out," Mooch said.

Lacey obeyed without protest. He handed the burly man his stylus and his wallet with $32 and a Class IV bank card. Mooch frowned. "Where's the rest?"

"Look, I didn't mean for this to happen," Lacey whined. "I didn't make any plans."

"Strip," Mooch ordered. His right hand was flexing on the hilt of the bread knife.

Again Lacey obeyed, folding his jacket and laying it on his neatly-arranged boots. Mooch snatched it up. He squeezed it into a tight ball to see if anything crinkled or poked within. Nothing did. He dropped the sheer fabric to the ballast and stepped on it.

Lacey swallowed but said nothing. He took off his trousers. The fresh scrape was a scarlet pennon on his thigh. He wore no underclothing. Mooch took the trousers from him, wadded them, and dropped them on the jacket. Then he punched the Southerner in the stomach.

Lacey kept his feet for the first few blows. He knew that however punishing the big hands might seem, the boots would be worse once he was down. His bare buttocks touched the concrete wall. The next side-thrown fist slammed him to the ground.

In his scanner helmet, Lacey had seen every form of mayhem humans could inflict on one another. Years before he had been beaten himself by the experts of the Red Team that arrested him for rape. He kept his fists pressed against his eyes and his knees high up to protect his groin. It wasn't enough, but it was all there was to do. The pain lessened after a boot drove his head back against the concrete. Then all Lacey's nerves seemed to have been coated in honey.

"Here comes Bill," the woman said.

The boots stopped pounding. "Took him long enough," Mooch grumbled.

The guard's chair was where Lacey had marked it as he went down. He reached for it, rolling to his feet in a motion that seemed too smooth for the red pain it brought him.

"Mooch!" one of the guards cried.

Lacey swung the chair horizontally, not in a downward arc that could have been avoided. Mooch had time to turn his head toward Lacey's fury. A corner of the chairseat caught him in the ribs, just below his slung weapon. Mooch yelped as the air was smashed out of his lungs. The impact lifted the leader's feet from the roadbed. He flew forward, stopping only when his skull slammed the wooden frame of the nearest shanty. The structure sagged while its shouting owner tried to brace it with his hands.

Faces turned from either end of the tunnel, interest spreading like ripples in a long pool.

Lacey's body was white except where blood marked it. The scar on his neck was molten steel. He backed against the tunnel wall, waggling the chair. "Who's next?" he wheezed. "Which a' you bleeders is next?"

The chair legs wavered like a forest of spears in the face of the black with the chain. He stepped back, then stared into Lacey's eyes. He took another step backwards.

"Okay, buddy, you made your point," said a

new voice. The speaker was also black and a head taller than anyone else in sight. He wore a power-gun in an Army-issue holster. It was as much a badge of authority as it was a weapon, an authority underlined by his score of armed followers. "Now, put the chair down or I'll blow you in half."

Lacey lowered his makeshift weapon. He leaned on it, breathing hard.

"Bill," said one of Mooch's subordinates, "he—"

"Shut up," ordered Bill, and one of his own men lowered a shotgun in response to the tone. "Next time Mooch works somebody over before I get there, I'll do worse to him myself."

As if in answer, the fallen thug vomited a mass of bright orange blood. His back arched, the shat-tered ribs clicking together like knitting needles. The next instant, Mooch went limp and still.

The black chieftain scratched at the butt of his pistol. "I'm Bill Allen," he said, "and you're in my territory. Who are you, and what do you think you're doing here?"

Lacey swallowed. The pain he had suppressed for a chance at revenge was returning. "I'm Jed Lacey," he said. "From Southern Region . . . Greater Greensboro. I . . . am on the street, a bloody queer . . . with his *prick* out, and he touched me, *touched* me . . . I don't know how people can *live* with slime like—" He looked up, blinking the glaze from his eyes. Bill Allen was frowning. "I cut the bastard," Lacey said. "Every way but loose. So I had to run, and I ran here."

"What did he have with him?" Allen asked at random.

The female guard nodded twice to herself and

said, "His clothes. And a little knife. And his wallet and a stylus. Mooch searched the clothes and that was all."

"Then put your clothes on, buddy," Allen said to Lacey. To the woman he ordered, "Bring me the rest of his gear."

Lacey limped to his clothing. As the Southerner shrugged on the jacket, his hands tangled with the sleeves, Allen drew his pistol. "Now freeze right there, sucker, until you tell me how a stranger knew that pipe would lead to Underground."

Lacey held as still as a poised mantis. "Because I'm a cop," he said. "Because I was being briefed to lead a hundred men from my subregion down here next month. Us, and maybe fifty other subregions, and the Army; *and* every goddam cop in this city. Because they're planning to shut this place down for good and all."

No one within hearing made a sound. Allen's hand tensed on his gunbutt, then relaxed.

In the same wooden voice with which he had made the announcement, Lacey said, "Now can I put my pants on, citizen?"

"Put your pants on," Allen agreed. He knuckled his forehead with his gun hand. To no one in particular, he added, "We'll take this one to see Black May, he can talk to her . . . and god help him if he lies."

They moved fast through the hollow layers beneath the City. The number of people in the dim tunnels was amazing. Even more surprising was the constant traffic up and down passageways to the upper world. Undergound was no less a part of the City than intestines were parts of the body that housed them. Say rather, an intestinal cancer.

At first Lacey thought there was no pretence of sanitation; then the Southerner noticed a gang of persons chained in pairs at the ankles. They were shovelling manure into a cart which two of them pushed along the aisles beside the cribs. The chains made them awkward, but they could not dash up one of the outlets to the surface. They appeared to be unsupervised.

"What're they?" Lacey asked Allen as they squeezed by the wagon.

"Umm?" the big man grunted. "Committee slaves. Those're mine, though I guess May thinks she's the Committee all by herself. They don't carry a full honeywagon down to the Basement, they don't get fed."

"Basement?"

"Where they grow the plants and crap," Allen said. "You know." He looked more sharply at Lacey. "Or if you don't, you don't need to. So shut it off."

Because there were so many entrances to Underground, there had been neither need nor effort to group its pleasures by type or quality. To get from one parlor house to another, a squeamish customer could walk a block on the surface and thus avoid entering a warren of slash shops and dollar cribs.

One huge establishment, The Boxcars, completely blocked a tunnel intersection with walls of transparent sheeting. Girls paraded nude behind the wall when they were not working customers. Passage through the armed guards at either end of the house required purchase of a drink at the bar filling the lowest of the three levels, or a trick with one of the girls. The drinks were slash distilled from anything that would ferment. For additional kick, it was mixed with stolen industrial alcohols of which methanol was one of the least harmful. The whores were cheaper than the slash and, on the average, probably a greater risk to the user's health.

The guards nodded obsequiously when they recognized Bill Allen. "Any calls?" the big chieftain asked.

"Noonan put some messages on your desk," the guard captain said, nodding toward an opaque door at the end of the bar. "Nothing that won't keep."

Allen grunted and lead the way through the far door. Lacey noted that two of the party had dropped off in The Boxcars instead of continuing on with their leader. The organization Underground was beyond anything Lacey could have imagined without seeing it, but the discipline appeared to be something short of a military ideal.

They had walked over two kilometers. There had been at least a single guard at each direct outlet to the surface. Despite the darkness and the maze of passageways, Lacey was sure he could find his way back. It was an ability demanded by his years of service beneath a scanner helmet, tracking subjects by rapid leaps from camera to camera and keeping his orientation at all times.

Allen's entourage turned from a subway spur into a dry 8-foot main of some sort and then to a new opening burned through concrete and bedrock by the most modern mining equipment. Just inside the cutting was another band of guards lounging in a pathetic mixture of squalor and finery.

There were more of them even than accompanied
Allen—and they were better armed. Over half the
men and women carried powerguns. The remainder had gunpowder weapons of one type or another, in addition to an arsenal of edged or blunt
instruments. A small brazier warmed the fetid air.
To Lacey's surprise, a telephone was glued to the
rock wall. Shadows of microwire ran both inside
and out in the direction from which Allen had led
them.

"Got somebody to show to May," Allen announced.

The guards were rising, pocketing their dice
and drawing weapons more for display than out of
apparent need. Their leader was pale as boiled
rice and missing his left arm from the elbow. "Got
the hit man that's s'posed to be coming?" he asked.

Allen shrugged nonchalantly. "Maybe so, maybe
not. We stripped him clean."

The guard chief shrugged in turn. "He goes
down in chains anyway," he said. "You know the
rules." He pointed his powergun at Lacey's mid-
riff. "Get over there by the fire," he ordered, "so
we can fit you for some new jewelry."

Lacey obeyed as humbly as he had Mooch. His
mind was on something else. Nootbaar had warned
him that Underground had a pipeline into the
City administration, but Lacey had not expected
confirmation so quickly or so off-hand. Not that he
was a hit man, exactly. . . . As directed, he rested
his feet one at a time on a stool. A scabby dwarf
tried hinged leg irons for size above his ankles.
When a pair fit, another guard held the halves
together while the smith fitted a hot rivet to the

hole. He peened the ends over against a piece of subway rail. The shackles were locked to both legs with half a meter of chain between them. Lacey could shuffle, but he could not run or even walk normally.

And if the Underground's source of information were good enough, Lacey would not even be able to shuffle for long.

"Zack, Slicer," Allen ordered as soon as the second cuff was riveted home. A pair of husky cut-throats lifted Lacey by his shoulders and ankles. They carried him toward a steep flight of stairs. Allen's party had entered toward the middle of a multi-level parking garage. The two porters, followed by their chief and the rest of his entourage, descended the stone steps at a deliberate pace. As he passed doorways, the Southerner caught glimpses of barracks and equipment filling the large open areas. Each level was guarded by a separate contingent, bored-looking but armed to the teeth.

On the fourth level down, the lowest, no one looked bored. Lacey was momentarily startled that none of the crew of hard-faced guards meeting them carried powerguns. Despite the lack of that symbol, they were clearly an elite group. Lacey took in the pallets standing in floor-to-ceiling blocks. He grunted in disbelief. At least half the level was stacked with gray military containers of high explosive and bright orange tanks of toxic gas. A powergun bolt here would rock the whole city like an earthquake. The Southerner could suddenly appreciate Nootbaar's concern for how Underground could respond to an all-out attack.

In the midst of the aisles of lethal material was a throne room. A dais and a massive arm-chair, both draped with cloth-of-gold, shimmered under a solid sheet of glow strips. On the throne sat the queen—black and perhaps fifty years old, with no hair on the left side of her head. On one arm of her throne lolled a white man less than half her age. He was dressed in tights and a cloak of rich purple.

"May," said Bill Allen in a subdued voice, "I brought a cop who says he's on the run. Says topside's getting ready to shoot their way down here the way they tried before."

The white youth giggled. Black May did not, but she thumbed toward the stacks of Amatex and K2. She said, "They weren't crazy ten years ago, what happened to them since?" She stared at Lacey, her eyes disconcertingly sharp. "Okay, what's *your* story?" she demanded.

"They seconded me from Greater Greensboro," Lacey began. In a few terse sentences he repeated the partial lie he had told Mooch and Bill Allen: the planned attack, the chance contact with a homosexual in the crowded streets; the knifing and escape down one of the routes his command was to have used for the attack. The story was as real as Lacey's foresight and utter ruthlessness could make it.

"Wank, check this out," Black May ordered. The man at an ordinary secretarial console beside the dais began speaking into his telephone. Radio would be useless for contact within the maze of tunnels. While ground-conduction equipment would have worked, it could not have doubled as a link to the normal communications of the City proper.

It was obvious that such links were important to the governance of Underground. Lacey fleetingly wondered whether the Commissioners had any real insight into their counterparts Underground, or whether topside intelligence sources stopped with estimates of bars, whores, and weapons.

"All of a sudden they don't care if everybody on the street at rush hour turns black and dies?" May asked rhetorically. She gestured again at the gas and high explosive ranked about her. The boy laid a proprietary hand on her shoulder, but she shrugged it off impatiently. He drew back with a moue.

Lacey tongued his lips. "They've got an insider," he said. "I never heard the name but I saw him. He's supposed to take you out—and all this—before it drops in the pot."

There was a sudden silence in the big room, marred only by the whisper of the telephone. Black May leaned forward, frozen.

"An old guy, about a meter seventy," Lacey went on. "White hair in a fringe behind his ears. But mostly bald, you know? Very thin, with a nose that's twice as long and half as thick as it ought to be."

"Swoboda!" somebody hissed behind Lacey. May's hand slashed him to silence as she thought.

Wank, bent over the telephone, missed the by-play. "Colosimo checked it on the scanners, May," he said. "Says it's just like the fellow says, a fag turns around and bumps him and this guy cuts the shit out of him. Blade wasn't very long, but it wasn't no fake. The crash crew had to collapse a lung, and if the flit pulls through, he'll do it on one less kidney than God meant him to have. It was real."

The news deepened the tense silence.

Lacey met Black May's eyes for a moment, then blinked. "Look," he said, "I got to take a crap."

The woman chuckled. "Well, don't look at me, sweetie," she said. "You'll have to ease it yourself."

The tension broke in general laughter. Lacey flushed and said, "Look, I mean . . . where?"

Black May waved her hand. "Take your choice," she said. "The honeywagon'll get to it sooner or later."

As if embarrassed, Lacey moved off into the shadow of a stack of explosives. A suspicious thug—courtier was too pretentious a word—peered around the corner a moment later, but she disappeared when she saw the Southerner was squatting with his pants down.

A thirty-gram ball of C-9 plastic explosive had been concealed in Lacey's rectum. He molded it quickly into the seam between the floor and a container of Amatex. Its detonator pellet lay against the stone flooring. If all went well, Lacey would be able to retrieve the charge and place it as intended, at the controls of the fusion plant. If not, it was where it would do some good as soon as somebody sent the right ground-conduction signal. Nature had left Lacey no choice but to remove the tiny bomb from its hiding place soon.

Lacey shuffled back into Black May's presence. The queen broke off in the middle of an order to the lanky red-head captaining her guard. "You!" she snapped, pointing a finger as blunt as a pistol's barrel at the Southerner, "How'd you come to see this traitor?"

Lacey shrugged. "A captain, Nootbaar, was briefing me three weeks ago Thursday when they first brought me up from Greensboro," Lacey lied. He had ordered a computer scan of the data banks to cull out any appearance of Swoboda on the surface during the past year. As the Southerner had expected, the physicist had come topside a score of times. The most recent instance had been three weeks previous; Swoboda had talked to a former faculty colleague in the latter's living area. If the City hierarchy had been alert, they could have arrested Swoboda then without difficulty—but that would have raised questions as to why the physicist was wanted. Besides, the search would have tied up great chunks of computer time in a subregion in which availability was already far below requirements.

For now, all that mattered was that Swoboda could have been doing just what Lacey described. "This bald geezer walked through the room on his way up to twenty. Nootbaar pointed to him and said he was going to zap the big bosses and their goodies just before we dropped in on them."

"Wank?" Black May queried.

The secretary spread his hands. "No way to tell, May; a precinct helmet won't get us into the City Central scanners. Colosimo can follow Swoboda himself, maybe, if he keeps it to short segments and don't get the oversight program in the data bank interested. But Swoboda was topside that day—I met him as he went out and told him to get a tan for me, why didn't he."

"That son of a bitch!" the half-bald woman snarled. "And I trusted him. Bill!"

"May?"

"You and a few of your crew come on with me to the Basement. If this turns out to be straight, Swoboda's gonna get it where the chicken got the axe." May glanced at Lacey. "You come too," she ordered. "And somebody bring extra chains."

Half a dozen of Allen's cut-throats accompanied their leader in the vanguard. May's personal guards jostled after them. Lacey was thrust into the midst of May's entourage, shuffling quickly to avoid the possibility of a knife jabbed with more enthusiasm than care. They moved down an aisle between gray canisters. Lacey's chains clinked discordantly, like the background to a Vietnamese opera. The Southerner pressed his palms together, as close to a prayer as he had made in twenty-nine years.

At the end of the aisle was a steel door, massive and obviously of recent installation. It reminded Lacey of a vault door or of a pressure lock, rather than any lesser type of portal. Allen swung it open; the four locking dogs had not been turned. There was a hint of suction as the door opened out from a meter-by-two-meter slot cut deep in the living rock beyond. Allen and the others began to enter, stepping carefully over the steel sill. It was pitch dark within.

"Keep your hand on one wall," Black May suggested. "There's bends."

"Bends" was not the word for the right angles that broke the narrow tunnel every few meters.

Lacey bumped and cursed. "What the hell is this?" he demanded.

May chuckled behind him. "Anybody who came Underground looking for me was gonna have the devil's own time at this end, especially with all the tunnels full a' K2, hey?" she explained cheerfully. Then her mood changed and she snarled. "Unless some bastard thought he'd cut me off on the outside of this!"

There was another heavy door at the far end. It also pivoted outward from the tunnel. In the pause before Bill Allen shoved it open, Lacey felt an edge of claustrophobia. Then there was light in the tunnel, more light than Lacey had seen since he came Underground. Blinking, Lacey stumbled with the pack of killers out into muggy brightness.

There was a squad of the same ilk guarding the inner door. They nodded respectfully to Allen and his men, then shuffled to their feet when they saw Black May was present as well. "Swoboda and the rest a' the needleheads here?" May asked the squad leader, a stocky redhead. She wore a necklace of what appeared to be dried fingers against her bare breasts.

"Unless they left before our shift started, May," the guard said. She grinned. "Hey, want us along?" she asked, touching the long sheath knife at her belt.

"Just don't let anybody out without I tell you, Minkie," Black May replied grimly. "Maybe nothing's wrong, maybe it is. . . ."

The huge cavern through which they began to stride was incredible to Lacey. Rank after rank of algae tanks marched in all directions. Though stone pillars studded the greenery, there were no walls as far as Lacey could see down any of the aisles they crossed. The roof, three meters above the floor, was bright with daylight-balanced glow strips. "Where the hell did you find *this* place?" Lacey asked in open amazement.

"Find?" May sneered. "Built, sonny, excavated it and sold the rock topside to the outfit filling ocean to build Treasure Isle. Honest business!" she added with a guffaw. "Bought the strips, too; there wasn't any place in the City where we could liberate as much as we needed. No problem, money we got. Only thing we needed then was the power to run them, and I guess we twisted that tail all right too." But the Queen of Underground scowled, and Lacey knew that her mind was on the man who had built her that powerplant.

There were men and women tending the algae tanks. They were as different from the crew surrounding Lacey as rabbits are from weasels, and they eyed the scarred cut-throats with rodent-like concern. May's henchmen, for their part, appeared as ill at ease in the lush surroundings as they were out of place. This orderly Eden had been created for technicians, not blood-letters, and both sides knew it.

"It we depend on topside, they own us," Black May said, as much to herself as to Lacey. "Down here, now, we got synthesizers and enough algae to work from to feed the whole City. We got power, a well four hundred meters down for fresh water, and a pair of ducts into the East River to dump waste heat. If we got to, there's the power and the tools here to punch a line out to the ocean. There's a thousand techs to work it, and I got ten thousand guns I can put topside without emptying the bars." May knuckled Lacey's shoulder to make sure she had his attention as she concluded, "They were too late up there, sonny. I got a base. I own the City. I just haven't gone up to tell'em—yet."

They had finally reached the far side of the artificial cavern. Apartments of opaque sheeting were built against the stone. There was a neatness and order to these dwellings which was missing from what passed for human habitation elsewhere Underground—or topside, for that matter. Some of the buildings appeared to be shops and offices as well.

"Where's your power come from?" Lacey asked idly.

Black May looked at him. "It's here in the Basement," she said. "Don't worry about it, sonny."

A group of nervous techs was drifting out of the nearest building. A few of them carried tools in feigned nonchalance, hammers and hand cultivators. Against May's crew, they were as harmless as dolphins facing killer whales.

"I need to talk to Doc Swoboda," May boomed jovially. The listeners stirred, frowning.

"He's not—" a young black woman began. She broke off when a man stepped out into the bright light. He was old, balding, and knife-nosed.

Lacey pointed at him. "That's the one," he said. "That's the informer."

All but one pair of eyes followed Lacey's gesture. The exception was a squat thug with curling black hair so thick on his arms that it made his pallid skin seem swarthy. His fellows had called him Horn. The girl who had spoken saw where the cut-throat's gaze was focused. Her mahogany skin flushed deeper and she crossed her arms over her breasts, bare in the clean warmth.

"I don't understand," Jerry Swoboda was saying, drumming both forefingers nervously on his sternum. "Is something wrong, May?"

"Hard telling, Doc," the queen said, arms akimbo, "but I need to take you back for a while to see. Put the irons on him, Boxie."

"No!" the black girl shouted. As she leaped forward, Bill Allen blew her head apart with a bolt from his powergun. At the shot, a thug with a submachinegun sprayed a burst into the stone floor and his own feet. The lead splashed and howled. The clot of technicians flew apart screaming. The gunman toppled in silence, too stunned for a moment to feel pain.

"For Chris' *sake!*" Black May stormed. A chip of jacket metal had cut her cheek so that it drooled a fat line of blood down to her jawbone. "Get them chains on and let's get outa here."

There was no question as to where the powerplant was located. A great conduit lined across the rock ceiling. Lacey had seen its exit into Underground proper through its own opening above the air-lock door. Wire tendrils from it fed the thousands of glow strips, and the roots of the conduit were somewhere in or beyond the apartment from which Swoboda had appeared. When the time came, Lacey would have no difficulty in locating his target.

His non-human target. Swoboda's eyes had the glassy stare of a fear-drugged martyr. Two women wearing knives were fastening his shackles. They used small padlocks through the holes in lieu of rivets. The physicist was given twice the length of chain that hobbled Lacey; no one was concerned about what the old man could do with a moment's inattention and a sudden leap.

At Black May's order, her entourage turned back the way they had come—with one exception. Lacey had already noticed Horn and what he was doing. Now Bill Allen noticed also and shouted, "Hey!"

There was no response. The chief's face hardened. He took two steps and kicked his subordinate in the buttocks. Horn leaped up from the tech's corpse. His eyes for the instant were as blank as Swoboda's had become. "You stupid bastard!" Allen shouted. "Save that for later!"

"Aw, Bill," the hairy man muttered. He fell into line shamefacedly behind Lacey.

The returning party's pace was faster than it had been as they entered the uncomfortable caverns. Enthusiasm at leaving made up for the need to carry Swoboda and the wounded gunman. Lacey had learned to throw his own chain forward with short, quick steps. He kept up with the others without being goaded. Rather to his surprise, the Southerner found that his mind was no longer on how best to accomplish his real mission. All the way back to the throne room, he was considering how to kill Horn and Bill Allen.

Black May sat down on her gold-draped chair and stared at the chained men. Her boy stopped pouting and began to massage the bare side of her scalp. Lacey tried to look nonchalant. If May didn't order his release now, he was in trouble.

"Bill," she said, "I want them where they're out a' the way." The bald side of her head was faceted by scar tissue. "Keep'em where you've got prisoners for ransom—or do you have any now?"

"Naw, two got paid off and the woman's working The Boxcars right now."

"Good. Keep this pair there and keep a guard on'em. That one for starters—" she pointed a finger at Horn; she hadn't forgotten either. "I'm going to get 38th Precinct to run Doc here's movements for the last few times he was topside. It'll maybe take a couple days, 'cause it'll have to go in as routine street-sweeps; but if our fink's right, it'll be hard lines for the Doc."

Lacey grinned broadly. It made him look cruel and confident, both of them qualities Black May would appreciate. Besides, it genuinely amused the Southerner that he would soon be unmasked by the very data banks he had served for fifteen years.

As he shuffled toward the steps beside Allen, Lacey suggested, "If you cut these damned chains now, it'll save you having to lug me up these stairs."

The big chieftain snorted. "Sure. I watch you lay out Mooch and I'm supposed to take your chains off when May says not to. Besides, it ain't *my* back you'll ride on. Horn, Ledder—get this bastard up the steps. If you drop him, I'll kick your butts all the way to the bottom myself."

The trip back through the tunnels gave Lacey a charleyhorse in each thigh. Since that came on top of the beating he had taken from Mooch, Lacey was dizzy with pain by the time they stopped. According to his reckoning, they were in a branch tunnel near The Boxcars. Allen unlocked what had probably been an equipment closet. The door was sheet metal and not particularly substantial. Some of the customers in nearby booths watched what was going on. The shills and bartenders did not: they knew Bill Allen, and they knew that his business was none of theirs.

The rock on the other side of the small closet had been cut away recently. Allen shone a hand light within. The new opening gave into what seemed to be a blocked-off elevator well. The area was choked with trash, but in the middle of it stood a massive eyebolt, its base sunk deep into the concrete floor. "Home, simps," Allen said with a chuckle. "Till May gives the word."

A pair of his subordinates had appeared from the direction of The Boxcars, carrying shackles and a glowing brazier. Wank must have summoned them by phone. Allen nodded to the pair and said, "Lock this pair by the wrists, Becky. You can give 'em three meters to be comfortable; but don't knock the leg irons off, hey?"

The smith and her helper riveted a manacle to Lacey's right wrist with a few expert blows, using the eyebolt as an anvil. Then they ran the attached length of chain through the eye itself and manacled the other end to Swoboda.

"Horn," Allen said grimly, "you sit right there at the doorway. Anybody tries to get in or out, you cut 'em apart with your toy there. I'll have a meal sent down in a couple hours. And you do *any* goddam thing but what you're told to, I make a belt of your hide and give the rest of you to May. Understood?"

Horn grunted sullenly. As his colleagues strode off toward drinks and ease, he glared at the prisoners. "You pull any goddam thing," he snarled in unconscious mimickry, "and I cut you apart." He fingered the hilt of the fighting knife in his belt. Then, with his back to the doorframe, he began to throw a pair of dice morosely.

"Why did you lie about me?" Dr. Swoboda asked in a low voice.

Lacey started, but the words were calm and not the prelude to an attack. He could just make out the physicist's form in the light that filtered through the open door. He did not reply.

"You can't just be a boaster who thought he'd denounce somebody important," Swoboda went on. "I don't think anyone in Underground but May herself really thinks that what I've done *is* important." He paused. "Oh," he said, "of course— anyone Underground. But by now the State has probably decided the blackout eight months ago was caused by the load from me starting up a fusion powerplant."

"You've built a fusion plant?" Lacey said, snorting as if incredulous.

"Of course," Swoboda repeated, and it was an instant before Lacey realized that the words were in answer to his question. "It would have been the one hope for the world itself, but that was impossible. Still, there's a self-sufficient colony in the, in the Basement now. Perhaps that will be able to continue, whatever happens to me."

"One hope for this whole island to be blown to

slag," Lacey gibed. He brushed a spot cleared of varied garbage and sat down on the floor. "Go on," he said, "you wouldn't have built a fusion plant down here with all those people living over it. Why, I hear it wouldn't even be possible to shut one down safely if it *was* lit up."

"Nonsense!" the physicist snapped with more spirit than he had shown since being taken into custody. "All that it takes to shut down the plant is to open the fuel feed and chill the reaction. Two turns on a petcock! And the rest of what you're saying is *just* as absurd. People have always wanted to live fifty years in the past, and that was all right . . . but it isn't all right any more, it's suicide! Yesterday's fears are going to *kill* us, kill *all* human civilization."

"Such as it is," Lacey chuckled. He felt a sudden added coldness when he realized that he was no longer merely leading his quarry on, that he was actually becoming involved in the discussion.

"That's the point, you know," Swoboda said, returning to the emotionless delivery with which he had begun the discussion. "I couldn't convince the authorities that what I was offering would be safe. They wouldn't even let me experiment in an unpopulated area. They were afraid the newshawks would watch the scanners. They'd report that the laws were being flouted—and they're *stupid* laws! —and that a 'bomb of unguessable destructiveness' was being built; and every person who'd had anything to do with approving my project would be voted out or fired. Myself, I'd go under a Psycomp to have my brain cleaned. But *whatever* the risk—without power for growth, what will this

City be in ten years? What will the world itself be like in fifty? What kind of death would be worse?"

Lacey shrugged. "You're talking to the wrong guy," he said.

The physicist sighed. "No doubt, no doubt; but there isn't anyone else to talk to, is there?" He glanced toward Horn, who looked up from his dice to glower back. "No human being, at any rate."

Swoboda started to clear a place on the floor, but he was too nervous to sit. He began walking and turning, a pace in either direction so as not to foul the chain. "I felt like this three years ago," he said, "when I finally realized that I was never going to be allowed to build even a pilot model. The energy source that could save civilization, and it could never be built because the world saw too much and understood too little. That's when Leah Geilblum visited me." The physicist looked at Lacey. The Southerner's eyes had adapted to the dark well enough to catch a sheen of remembered hope in the older man's expression.

"I knew her by reputation, of course," Swoboda continued, "as she knew me. As an anthropologist, she saw even more clearly than I the horror, the irreversible horror, into which the world was slipping; and she saw the hope that my power source could provide.

"Black May had already recruited several biologists, planning her 'base'. It wasn't hard for her, you know. The more intelligent someone is, the more clear the need for a, a bolthole, becomes. And word of mouth moves swiftly in the academic community. Leah—she died only last month—she was 83 and it wasn't at all for herself that the concern lay—she convinced me to try to work with Black May, now that Underground had a single, intelligent leader. And Leah was right. It just seems that that wasn't enough."

There was an interruption from the doorway. Horn scooped up his dice and stood, trying to embrace the lithe woman who carried three meal packets and a canteen. "Rickie, hey, how about a trick, hey?" the guard rasped. "Look, I can pay—"

The woman dropped her burden without ceremony and elbowed Horn in the stomach. "Think I haven't heard, creep? Keep the hell away from me!"

"Look, just a feel, then, Rickie," Horn begged, crouching in desire and extending his hands. Rickie reached behind her back, then extended her right fist wrapped in barbed-wire claws.

"I'll feel the heart right outa your chest, I will!"

Horn's mouth pursed and his hands dropped to his knife. Booth personnel were beginning to view the disruption blackly, and a few customers seemed to be drifting toward other parts of the tunnels. The woman swiped at Horn's eyes. "You try that," she hissed, "and I'll feed it to your asshole. And if I don't, cutie, what d'ye suppose Bill and May'll do?"

Horn cursed and turned and slammed his fist into the open door. It boomed thunderously. The woman walked back the way she had come. Horn saw the food containers and kicked all three of them violently into the closet. One of them sailed through the opening to the elevator shaft. Lacey ducked. The ruptured plastic spewed juices. Its integral heating element stank with only the empty container to absorb its energy.

Lacey smiled. It was as well for Swoboda's peace of mind that the dim light kept him from seeing the hunter's face clearly. Lacey tugged his companion silently toward the eyebolt so that the old man's hand rested on the metal. All the slack in the chain was on Lacey's side of the bolt.

"Hey Horn," he called to the guard, sitting again in the doorway. "There's rats in here."

"Hope they chew your eyes out!"

"No, I mean they're screwing in the corner," Lacey said. "Shine your light so's we can get a better look at 'em, will you?"

Horn bounced to his feet and raised the flashlight Bill Allen had left with him. Then he paused and shifted the light to his left hand. He drew his knife and gestured with it. "Get smart and I'll spread you all over the room," he said.

Lacey nodded and stepped back. Out of the bright disk of the flashlight, he thumbed a chunk of potato into the pile of trash in the far corner. The litter rustled.

Horn stepped through the opening to the shaft. His knife pointed up at Lacey's throat, but his eyes were on the quivering circle of light. "Where—" he began.

Lacey flipped a loop of chain over the guard's head and jerked him backward. Swoboda squealed. Horn could not shout with the chain crushing his throat, but he slashed out with his knife. Lacey threw himself aside, tugging frenziedly at the chain. His body knocked the physicist down.

Horn tried to rise. He cut wildly to the side; his wrist struck the eyebolt. A cry wheezed past the chain and the knife sailed loose in the darkness.

Horn's hand twisted toward the blackjack in his hip pocket, but his fingers would not close.

Lacey moved nearer. The manacle on his right wrist gave him an unbreakable grip on the chain. He planted both feet on the other side of the loop, pinning it to the floor. Then he pulled upward with his whole body. Horn thrashed furiously. Blood flecked his chin and the hairs on his chest. The motions became instinctual, like those of a fish on the sand. He gave a final, back-arching convulsion and lay still.

Lacey tossed the loop of chain free and collapsed beside the body. His gasping breaths came like sobs. "Get me the knife," he whispered to his companion.

"But we're still chained," Swoboda protested.

"Get me the bloody knife!"

Using the light, the physicist located the weapon. Diffidently, he set it beside Lacey's hand. The Southerner picked it up. The knife was of the finest craftsmanship. Its blade was 7 mm across the flats. Both the edge and the false edge had the yellow sheen which indicated they had been treated to triple density after grinding.

"Hold your shackle against the bolt and keep the light on the rivet," Lacey directed. He slipped Horn's blackjack from his pocket and stood.

Swoboda caught at his lower lip with his teeth. Lacey positioned the manacle as he wanted it. He set the knife edge against the peened end of the rivet, then struck the back of the blade sharply with the sap. The 3-mm rivet sheared.

"Why, that's incredible!" Swoboda blurted.

"Nothing incredible," Lacey said sourly. "Just a

hell of a thing to do to a good knife." He pried at the manacle carefully, using the false edge and trying not to cut the physicist's wrist. There was already bleeding from damage the shackle had inflicted during the struggle with Horn.

The iron popped apart. "Now you get mine," Lacey said, handing the tools to Swoboda.

It took repeated blows by the older man before the second rivet parted, but even so it was only the matter of a minute. Lacey struck off their leg irons. He paused, staring into the physicist's eyes. "Can you get back to your Basement and dog the doors shut?" he asked.

Swoboda thought calmly, then nodded. "Probably. It isn't necessary to pass through the throne room, and the guards at the entrance door should have changed shift by now. They're used to me entering and leaving, so that shouldn't cause any comment unless I chance upon someone who saw my . . . arrest."

The older man rubbed his forehead. "As for dogging the inside door, the guards will probably believe me if I say it's necessary for a few days because we're, oh, raising the humidity briefly to enhance growth."

Lacey nodded. "I'll give you half an hour," he said. "That's all; and if it's not enough, that's too bad. Now get moving."

"Why?" Swoboda asked unexpectedly.

"Why the hell do you care?" the hunter blazed. He flung the knife away from him. It clanged and sparked on the concrete. "Mostly I do what I'm told. It doesn't make any difference, you see? *I* know we're all going down the tubes, I'm not blind. So it's easier." Lacey took a deep breath, fingering his scar. "Only maybe this time it makes a difference. To somebody. Now just get out of here."

Swoboda touched Lacey's hand, then squeezed it. As he turned, the hunter called after him, "You'll have to handle the guards inside yourself, afterwards. But I can't do it all."

No one shouted when the physicist slipped out into the tunnels. People Underground minded their own business; and besides, the thin old man was of small interest, even to the whores.

Lacey waited briefly, then strolled out to a bar. It had more pretensions then the blind pigs around it and there was a twenty-four-hour clock on its back wall. Horn had had some money in his pockets. Lacey used part of it to buy a beer. The liquid was thin and bland—and therefore safe from being loaded with knock-out drops.

Lacey smiled as the bartender eyed him. Actually, there was nothing unusual about the Southerner's appearance compared to that of many others Underground. It was just unusual that someone as battered as Lacey was would have enough money left for a drink.

Lacey nursed the beer for the half hour he had promised Swoboda. He ignored the prostitutes who approached him. If the bartender felt he was not drinking fast enough, he had better sense than to push the matter with the scarred man in red.

When the time came, Lacey up-ended his glass and strode out of the stew. As he neared The Boxcars, the hunter began to jog and then run. His face grew wild and he shoved people out of his way. The guards at the entrance to the brothel braced to stop him. Lacey thrust the remainder of Horn's money out with both hands. "Bill Allen," he wheezed. "I gotta talk to Bill!"

The guard chief frowned, then thumbed inside. "He's in his office," she said. "If he sees you or not's his business."

Lacey pushed through the cordon of naked women who tried both to entice him and strip his empty pockets. He flung open the door to Allen's office before a house man could stop him. "Bill, I gotta see you!" he said, slamming the door.

"What the bleedin' hell!" the black chieftain snarled. He was alone in the room, punching buttons on a computer console with one hand while the other held a sandwich. An open floor safe protruded 200 mm from the rock beside him. He banged the heavy lid closed with his foot. "How did you get loose?"

"Bill, Black May's going to kill all of us," Lacey whined. The enclosed privacy of the office was disconcerting to him. "She's going to take her buddy-buddies into the Basement and *gas* us, gas all Underground to keep the topsiders from finding where she's hid!"

Allen was frowning, but he set down his sandwich. Before the chieftain spoke, Lacey blurted, "Look, Bill, I'm afraid your guards'd grab me 'f I tried to go topside alone. You need to get out too—you can take me! Bill, you ever seen what K2 *does* to a guy?"

"Balls," Allen said flatly. "Let's see what May says about this." He began to punch out a phone code, keeping a corner of his eye on Lacey.

The Southerner's face tightened into intersecting planes of despair. "Bill," he pleaded, "Take me topside and I'll give you a gadget you wouldn't believe."

Allen paused, his finger above the last digit of the code. "Talk," he said.

Lacey licked his lips. "Well," he said, "You got the stylus Mooch took off me?"

Allen nodded, his forehead wrinkling. He slid open a drawer in the console and pulled the ivory-colored instrument from the varied truck within.

"It's not just a stylus," the hunter said truthfully. "They learned a trick from Tesla—it's a laser that'll cut forever if you just hold the base against a good ground. The wall behind you'd do. You press the button on the side and it shoots forever."

Allen stared eye to eye at the smaller man. "You're lying," he said. With the beginning of a smile, the leader touched the back of the stylus against the wall and pressed the button. The tip was centered on Lacey's breast.

The ground conduction signal shivered into the rock. Nothing visible occurred in the room.

Lacey relaxed. He smiled like a shark feeding. Bill Allen blinked in surprise, not at the failure of the "weapon," but at the hunter's reaction to his attempted murder. "This far away, there's maybe a ten-second delay," Lacey said. He dropped flat on the floor beside the safe.

"What—" Allen began. He groped for the powergun in his belt. The shock wave from the explosion in Black May's quarters reached him before he could draw. The wave front drove the

mahogany bar at an angle before it, pulping all of
Allen's body between his neck and his diaphragm.

Lacey did not really expect to live through the
blast. It drove down the hundreds of kilometers of
tunnels like a multi-crowned piston, shattering whatever stood in its way. The Boxcars and everything
in it were gone, driven meters or kilometers down
the tunnel in a tangle of plastic and splinters and
blood; everything but Lacey and the safe that
shielded him.

There was no sound, but Lacey found he could
see after the ground stopped quivering like a har-
pooned manta. A hundred meters of tunnel roof
had been lifted by the blast. It collapsed when it
fell back, close enough to Lacey that his feet touched
the concrete morraine when he tried to straighten
from the ball into which instinct had curled him.

The air was choking, but with dust and not
K2—yet. The rebounding shock waves of the blast
would suck the stockpiled gas into every cranny of
the tunnel system soon, but at least the lethal
cargo had not ridden the initial wave front. Even
with the safe to turn it, the blast had pounded
Lacey like a rain of fine lead shot. He rose slowly,
sucking air through the hard fabric of his sleeve.
Once the ground beside him came into focus, he
saw a dropped powergun. Lacey picked it up and
began to stagger toward an unblocked staircase.

Those who knew Jed Lacey best thought he was
merciless. They were wrong. He used his weapon
repeatedly before he climbed to the street. That
was the only mercy desired or available to the
hideously mangled forms who mewled at him in
agony.

*   *   *

The guards at the anteroom of Level 20 were nervous and confused, like everyone else in the City. The lower levels of some buildings had burst upward, killing thousands. Long sections of traffic-laden streets had collapsed, adding their loads to the death tolls. K2 was denser than air, but the swirling currents raised by the explosion had blown tendrils of the gas to the surface in many places. Where the odorless hemotoxin touched, skin blackened and flesh swelled until it sloughed. Red Teams wearing atmosphere suits were patrolling streets that were otherwise deserted by the living.

Lacey pushed through the shouting clot of newshawks. He was gaunt and cold. His suit had been shredded into the garb of a jester mocking the Plague. No one who looked at Lacey stayed in his way.

The door from the Commission Room slid open to pass a uniformed captain in full riot harness. "Max!" Lacey croaked. His fingers brushed the heavy man's wrist to keep him from leveling the slung needle gun.

"Where the hell did you come from, Lacey?" Nootbaar grunted. The guards stood tense and featureless behind their faceplates.

Lacey grinned horribly. "That's right, Max," he said. "Now I need to see the brass—" he thumbed toward the closed door— "bad. I know what happened."

Nootbaar bit a knuckle. "Okay," he said, and he held the door open for Lacey.

Commission staff and uniformed police made the room itself seem alive with their motion. Lacey slipped among them, headed for the three desks in the middle. A projection sphere was relaying the horror of a dwelling unit where three levels had sunk into a pool of K2.

Characteristically, it was Lemba who first noticed Lacey's approach. He spoke silently to his implant. A klaxon hooted and the projection sphere pulsed red for attention. The Chief Commissioner's voice boomed from ceiling speakers, "Clear the room! Clear the room!"

"What the—" Commissioner Kuhn began, but she too saw the ragged figure and understood. "Did he—?"

"Silence!" Lemba growled. "Until the room's cleared." The woman glared but accepted the logic of secrecy. Her gown was a frothy ball of red. It was much the same shade that Lacey's suit had once been.

The door closed behind the last pair of armed guards.

"I've done what you wanted," Lacey lied. But he had done what the world needed instead, protected one seed of civilization against the day when it could sprout . . . "Now give me a pardon for what I did for you. Then you'll never have to see me again."

"Nothing was said about a pardon," Arcadio muttered over tented fingers.

"I did what you wanted!" Lacey repeated. He did not raise his voice, but his eyes were balefires licking the bones of each Commissioner. "Give me a pardon and no one will ever know about it. Even you won't have to learn."

"The explosion, the gas. . . ," Commissioner

Kuhn whispered. "All these people dead in the streets—"

"They died!" Lacey snarled. "It was cheap at the price, do you see? You've got your city back now, because the scum below blew themselves apart. The ones down there were tougher than you and smarter than you worms'll ever be—but they're dead. Don't clear the K2, just seal all the openings. You're safe forever now—from Underground. You're safe from the dead."

"We aren't going to turn that loose, are we?" Kuhn asked slowly. There was nothing rhetorical in her question.

"The alternative is to try to keep it caged," Lemba noted. He shrugged toward Arcadio. "I doubt that would be a profitable undertaking. And we have a great deal else to concern ourselves with at the moment."

"All those dead," Kuhn said. "And we directed. . . ."

The Chief Commissioner coughed. Neither of the others spoke. "Citizen Lacey," Lemba said, "by virtue of the powers civil and criminal vested in me by the Charter of this City, and with the concurrence of my co-commissioners—" he looked at each of them. Arcadio nodded minusculy; Kuhn did not, her cheeks as bright as her garments, but she did not gainsay Lemba— "I do hereby pardon you for all crimes, actual or alleged, which you may have committed within this subregion to the present date."

Lacey nodded. "That pardon's the only thing I'll take with me from this City, then," he said, "besides my mind." He slipped the powergun from beneath his tunic and laid it on the smooth floor. His toes sent it spinning toward the frozen Commissioners. At the door, Lacey called over his shoulder, "Careful of that. There's still one up the spout and two more behind it."

The door closed behind him.

The six-year-old was blind with tears as she ran into his legs. Lacey lifted her one-handed. "Can I help?" he asked.

"The street fell!" she blubbered. "I can't go home because the street fell!"

"Umm. What building?" By now the gas would have seeped back into Underground, but a windrow of blackening bodies kept the thoroughfare empty. The dead did not touch Lacey any more. Only the living mattered.

"Three-oh-three-oh forty-ninth street level ten," the child parroted, her arms locking about Lacey's neck.

"Sure, Level 10, no problem," the Southerner said. He glanced around to get his bearings. "Your parents'll be looking for you, so we better get you home, hey?"

Humming to himself and the girl, Lacey skirted a wrecked truck still lapped with burning alcohol. Lacey was alive, maybe for the first time in fifteen years. It was going to take work, but he thought he liked being a human being again.

THE END

There was a spate of flying-object reports in 1896. Not UFOs, technically, because they were identified as dirigible airships which one inventor or another had built to traverse the country. Perhaps they should be called misidentified flying objects, because none of those airships worked anywhere but in the inventor's mind—or in the minds of reporters even less scrupulous than the majority of their contemporaries.

There were sightings, interviews with pilot/inventors, and circumstantial stories about country folk who were taken aboard for short flights. The similarities to post-1947 UFO data are obvious. The explanation—whatever the hell that is—is probably the same also.

Both my wife and I were born and raised in Dubuque, Iowa—she on a farm at the outskirts of town. That statement involves the human background of "Travellers" as well as the initial setting.

TRAVELLERS

Carl had not seen it coming over the eastern horizon toward the farm.

As the trickle under which he had washed died away, Carl slid the bucket beneath the pump. He worked the handle with three smooth, powerful strokes, the creaking of the cast iron evoking squeals from the piglets in the shed. Over his head the sky was clear enough that stars already flecked it, but the west beyond the farm house was a purple backdrop of cloud. Carl stretched, sighed, and picked up the bucket his mother would need for the dinner dishes.

A spotlight threw his long shadow on the ground before him. Carl turned, the bucket splashing some of the muck from his boots. The light was round and for an instant as harsh as the sun. Prismatic changes flickered across the face of it. The beam spread to either side of Carl in a fan that illuminated but no longer blinded him. The light was hanging above the barn. There was a bulk beyond

it, solider than the sky: an airship such as Carl had
never dreamed he would see.

"Stand by to take a line, lad," called a male
voice. Carl's knees were trembling and the bucket
was forgotten in his hand as the airship drifted
upwind toward him. Something aboard made a
sound like chains rattling, muted where Carl stood
but loud enough to have roused the cows. Their
bawling would bring his father out at any moment,
a part of Carl's mind recognized, but nothing in
the world of a moment before was real any longer.

The airship crawled directly over Carl. It was
huge, blocking most of the hundred feet of sky
separating house from barn. Besides the spotlight,
now diffusing its radiance across most of the farmyard, there were rectangles of yellower light from
the gondola hanging beneath the main hull of the
airship. A hatch opened in the side, silhouetting a
gangling figure. "Here it comes," said the figure in
the voice that had spoken before. A grapnel on a
line thudded to the ground in front of Carl. It
began to dig a double furrow in the dust as the
airship drifted backwards. "Well, set it, lad—set
it!" the voice called. "So that we can land."

Carl came out of his numb surprise. He dropped
the water bucket and ran to the line. It was of
horsehair, supple and strong. Someone played it
out above as Carl carried the grapnelled end to
the pump. He hooked it to the underedge of the
concrete well-cap.

As soon as Carl had set the grapnel, the line
stiffened. There was another rattle from above and
a whine like that of an electric pump. The airship
began to settle. Four jointed, mantis-like legs were

extending from the belly of the gondola. Carl backed
toward the house a step at a time while the great
form sank into the farmyard. The legs touched,
first one and then the four of them together. Their
apparent delicacy was belied by the great plumes
of dust which the contact raised. The whine rose
to a high keening, then shut off entirely. The light
died to a glowing ember in the night.

Behind Carl the screen door banged. "Carl,"
called Mrs. Gudeint, "where are—oh dear Lord
have mercy! Fred! *Fred!*"

The gangling man reappeared at the gondola door.
He swung three metal steps down with a crash.
The stranger wore a brown tweed suit of coarse
weave with a gold watch-guard and a fob of some
sort hanging across the vest. He smiled at Carl,
crinkling the full moustache that looked so incon-
grous beneath his high forehead. Looking back
into the gondola he said, "Oh—if you will snuff
the light, my dear?" A girl appeared in the doorway, turning down the wick of an oil lamp. Carl
stared at her as he had at the airship itself. There
was a bustle behind him as his father and brothers
pushed out of the house with eating utensils still
in their hands.

The girl was beautiful even in the dim light.
Her hair, caught neatly in a bun, was as richly
black as the pelt of a sable. She wore a patterned
percale wrapper, simple but new and of an attractive cut.

"Carl, what have you brought here?" Mr. Gudeint
rumbled from close to his youngest son's shoulder.

"Gentlemen," said the stranger, turning again
with the girl beside him and the airship a vast gray

backdrop beyond, "I am Professor John K. Erlenwanger, and this is my daughter Molly." The girl
curtsied. Erlenwanger caught sight of Carl's mother
beyond the wall of broad-shouldered men. He
made a little bow of his own. "And madam, of
course; my apologies.

"Madam and gentlemen," he continued. "I am,
as you see, an aeronaut. My daughter and I are
travelling from Boston to California, testing my
airship, *The Enterprise*—which, I may say, contains certain advances over all earlier directable
designs. We have stopped here for a safe mooring
during the night and perhaps some assistance in
the morning."

"You're from Boston?" demanded Fred, the eldest of Carl's brothers. "You flew this thing a
thousand miles?"

"We have indeed flown a thousand miles," the
Professor said with a quick nod, "and I expect to
fly twice again that distance before completing my
endeavor. But although we have set out from Boston, I am myself a Californian by birth and
breeding."

"Well, they'll have dinner with us, surely," said
Carl's mother, twisting her hands in the pockets of
her apron. She looked up anxiously at Erlenwanger.
"You will, won't you? We've a roast and—"

The Professor cut her off with another half-bow.
"We would be honored, Mrs. . . ?"

"Gudeint," Carl's father grunted. He wore a
blue work shirt, buttoned at the throat and cuffs as
it had been all day despite the heat of the Indian
Summer sun. His sons wore sleeveless undershirts
or, in Carl's case, only a set of galluses that had

blazed a white cross in his otherwise-sunburned back. Mr. Gudeint extended his hand, broad and as hard as the head of a maul from fifty years of farming. "I'm Fred Gudeint and that's my wife Maxine there—"

"Fred, I'll take the stoneware off and put out the china and the silver since—"

Carl's father turned on her, his red forehead furrowed like a field in springtime. "Maxine, you'll pretend you've got the sense God gave a goose and do no such thing. We've already started eating from the stoneware!"

Mrs. Gudeint bobbed her head and scurried back into the house with a worried look on her face. Carl's father shook his head and said, "Your pardon, Professor, but we're not used to guests dropping out of the sky on us. It upsets the routine." He grinned perfunctorily, as if that would make his statement less true. "That's Fred there, my oldest—" Fred, his father's surrogate in form as well as name shook hands in turn— "George, Danny, and that's Carl, the last by six years. Boy, be sure to fill that bucket before you come in."

"Yes, father," Carl said. Professor Erlenwanger's hand was cool and firm and smooth as a farmer's hands can never be. As Carl's father and brothers led the guests into the house, the Professor's daughter tilted her eyes at Carl and gave him a timid smile. Why, she looks as nervous as I am, Carl thought as he pumped the bucket full again beneath the airship.

Carl entered the house through the side door to leave the bucket beside the sink. His mother had already slipped a third leaf into the table and replaced the checkered oilcloth with her best Irish linen table cover. As Mr. Gudeint had insisted, the stoneware plates still remained with the mashed potatoes and slices of beef with which they had been heaped before the excitement. The two new place settings, to right and left of the head of the table where Carl's father sat, were of the Sunday china. The delicate cups and saucers looked particularly incongruous beside the heavy mugs at the other places. From the front room came the creak of Grandpa Roseliep's rocker; nowadays he always ate before the rest of them.

Carl sat quickly between his mother at the foot of the table and his brother George. He began serving himself. Danny was saying, "I'd read a story about your balloon in the *Register* last week in the barbershop, Professor; but I recall it gave the name as Cox. Sure, Cox."

Professor Erlenwanger ladled gravy onto his mashed potatoes with a liberal hand. "I can't say who Mr. Cox may be, sir; but I assure you that he and I are not the same. I have eschewed all publicity for the Erlenwanger Directable Airship—not balloon, I must protest, any more than your Guernsey milkers are steers—eschewed all publicity, as I say, until I have proven the capacity of my invention in a fashion none can doubt. Unless I am fully satisfied, no one will hear a word from my lips about it. Except, of course, for the good people like yourselves who have acted as hosts to my daughter and myself. Madam," he added, nodding to Mrs. Gudeint, "these fresh peas are magnificent."

Erlenwanger ate like a man who appreciated his food. His bites were gentlemanly and were chewed with the thoroughness demanded by a roast from a superannuated dairy cow, but he cleaned his plate handily despite the constant stream of questions directed at him by the Gudeints. Carl noticed that Molly spoke rarely and then with a distinct Irish brogue at variance with the Professor's cultured accents.

Carl said little himself. The Professor's descriptions—sunlight flaring from cloud tops; tailwinds pressing the airship along faster than a railway magnate's special—were in themselves so fascinating that Carl was unwilling to interject a question. It might break the spell.

At last Fred, speaking through a mouthful of roast and gesturing with his fork, said, "Look here, Professor. You're an educated man. What do you think about all this business about Cuba? Isn't it about time those Dagoes're taught what they can and can't do on Uncle Sam's doorstep?"

Erlenwanger paused, staring across the table. The light reflected from his high forehead. He looked half the bulk of the big farmer, but at that moment the stranger's dominance was no less certain than that of a diamond over the metal of its setting. "I think," he said with neither conciliation nor overt hostility in his firm tones, "that misguided men will fight a foolish war over Cuba very soon. The world as a whole will be none the better for such a war, and many individuals will be very much the worse." He stared around the table as if daring anyone to disagree with him.

In a sudden rush of bitterness, Carl said, "The Army might be better'n the back end of a plow horse, day in and day out."

"There are roads to adventure that are not built on the bodies of your fellow men, lad," Erlenwanger said. He turned back to Fred and added more harshly, "And there are ways of honoring the flag that do not call for 'civilizing' native races with a Krag-Jorgensen rifle. It will take men a long time as a race to learn that; but until we have done so, we have done nothing."

Mr. Gudeint sopped the last of his gravy in a slice of bread, swallowed it, and pushed his chair back from the table. Professor Erlenwanger cleared his throat and said, "You have been so generous to my daughter and myself that I wonder if I might impose on your time for one further moment? You will have noted the cases I brought in with me." Erlenwanger nodded toward the leather grips now standing against the wall next to the curio cabinet. "They contain my camera equipment. I would be most appreciative if you would permit me to photograph your whole family together."

"You mean in the daylight, don't you?" said George, who had his own Kodak. "You can't take one now?"

"On the contrary, the process I am using is so sensitive that what the eye can see, my lens can record," the Professor replied. He turned to Mr. Gudeint. "With your leave, sir?"

Carl's father frowned. "Strikes me that you're wasting your plates; but then, I never saw a fellow fly before, neither. Sure, we'll sit for you. How do you want us?"

"In your front room, I believe," said the Professor, his hands already busy with the contents of one of his cases. "In whatever grouping seems good to you; though with seven subjects to fit into the plate, I trust you'll group yourselves rather tightly."

"Seven?" repeated Fred. "There's only—oh, sure," he broke off, looking at Grandpa Roseliep in his stuffed rocker.

"You will join us, will you not, sir?" Professor Erlenwanger said, looking up at the old man as he fitted his camera onto its collapsible wooden tripod. Beside him, Molly had removed a plate from the other grip and was carefully polishing dust from its surfaces with a soft cloth.

Roseliep was reading *Der Kanarienzüchter*, one of the three bi-weekly issues that had arrived from Leipzig in yesterday's mail. From the shelter of the paper he grunted, "What do you want with me? I know nothing about cows, so I am useless— nein? And with these hands, I am surely no cabinetmaker any more." The paper shook, perhaps in frustration rather than from a deliberate attempt to emphasize the arthritis-twisted fingers which gripped its edges. "Go on, leave me alone."

Professor Erlenwanger stood, the brass and cherry-wood of his camera glinting under the light of the dining room lamp. He spoke in German, briefly and fiercely.

Grandpa Roseliep set down his canary-breeders journal. His full, white beard blazed like a flag. The old man fingered the stem of his pipe on the end table, but he left that sitting as well. In deliberate English he said, "An old man is a man still? Wait till you become old, Professor." The two men stared at one another. Abruptly, Grandpa

Roseliep said, "But I will be in your picture, since you ask."

The old man levered himself out of his chair, stiff-armed. Carl moved to him quickly, holding out an arm for his grandfather to grip. The old man's shoulder brushed the covered canary cage beside his chair. One of the birds within peeped nervously. Absently, Roseliep soothed it with a murmur from deep in his throat.

Carl's parents and brothers were standing by the fireplace, looking a little uncomfortable. The Professor had set up his tripod in front of the staircase across the room. Molly stood beside him, holding out the photographic plate. Carl led his grandfather into the center of the group between his father and Fred. He knelt down in front of them, facing the camera as the Professor loaded it.

Granda Roseliep turned slowly. His foot caught on the edge of the fireplace fender. He stumbled, gripping Mr. Gudeint's arm to keep from falling. The farmer jerked back. He looked down at the knotted fingers with instinctual distaste.

Roseliep followed his son-in-law's glance. "Yes," he said, "but once they were strong, were they they not? Strong enough to build this house for my daughter on her marriage." With his left hand he rapped the carven oak mantlepiece. "And the house gives shelter yet."

Mr. Gudeint bit his lip. He put his arm around his father-in-law, gripping him under the arm and absorbing enough of the weight that the old man's body could stretch back to its full six feet of height. "We're ready for your picture now, Professor," he said.

Across the room the camera lens winked, and the Professor's bright eyes winked above it.

Carl and his father returned from the barn together for breakfast. The three older sons were already at their pancakes, along with Professor Erlenwanger and Molly. Mr. Gudeint called into the front room, "George? Come on in and sit with us, will you? Your birds can take care of themselves for a while. I want to rig a pole and winch to load bales into the barn, and I figure you can help."

Grandpa Roseliep walked slowly into the kitchen on his crutch-headed cane. "You know, Frederick," he said, "I am no longer a woodworker."

Carl's father grunted. "I know you can figure how to make a piece of wood do everything but talk," he said. "We'll do the muscle work, me'n the boys, if you'll tell us what to do. For that matter, we're not talking about fancy work—and I don't know but what swinging a hammer'd loosen your joints up some. But that's up to you."

The big farmer took his usual place at the head of the table and noticed for the first time that all the place settings were china. He poured milk into the wine goblet beside his coffee cup and said with half-humor, "Professor John K. Erlenwanger, hey? From the way Maxine's acting, I'd judge the 'K' must stand for king."

Erlenwanger touched his napkin to his lips. "Kennedy, sir. To my parents, a greater man than any king could ever be." Mr. Gudeint looked puzzled, but before he could speak the Professor added, "Last night you thought it would be possible to take my daughter and me into town to purchase supplies. Is that still the case?"

Carl's father nodded with his mouth full of pancake and molasses. "Sure, the boy can haul you along when he carries the milk into the dairy after breakfast. But I'd have thought you'd just fly?"

"I prefer to avoid built-up areas," Erlenwanger explained. "The appearance of my airship would arouse more interest than I desire at this time, and maneuvering a construct as large as *The Enterprise* becomes a . . . difficult proposition in close quarters." The shadow of the great, gray cylinder darkened the dining room, lending weight to the stranger's shrug.

"Look," said George abruptly, "I'll carry the milk in today instead of the kid."

Carl jumped to his feet, flushing, and cried, "Look, I'm going to take them in. And get off this 'kid' business—I'm eighteen and I'm as much a—"

"Carl, sit down!" Mr. Gudeint snapped. "And George, you be quiet too. I'll decide who's going to do what around here."

"Though I was rather hoping that Carl would drive us to town, as you'd said," Molly interjected unexpectedly. She gave a nervous smile to Mr. Gudeint, who blinked at her. She was wearing a bengaline cotton dress with vertical stripes of green and olive this morning. The silk threads gave it a sheen like that of her black hair.

"The boy'll do it," Carl's father said. "It's his chore." He turned to Carl. "About time you got started, isn't it? The sun's high enough, though you don't see it with that great metal thing out in the yard."

"Yes sir!" said Carl, bolting the last of his breakfast and washing it down with his milk. To the visitors he added, "I'll have the wagon loaded in two flips of a lamb's tail. I'll holler when it's ready."

It was killing work to hand the heavy, tin-plated milk cans up to Danny on the wagon bed. Carl finished the job in record time, however, and without any spillage past the pressure-fitted lids. Erlenwanger and Molly came out of the house just as Danny ran the safety rope across the box of the wagon to keep the cans from oversetting on the bumpy ride. "Just in time," Carl called to them. "I'll get the horses and we're off."

Molly sat between Carl and Erlenwanger as the pair of bays plodded along the familiar trail with only voice commands. A light breeze from the south kept the worst of the road dust from the travellers, but a plume rose behind the wagon like smoke from a grass fire. "It'll be all over us coming back," Carl said.

"And you have to drive this every day?" Molly asked. "There's so much work on a farm."

"Not enough for four sons," Carl said gloomily. He caught himself and added, before anyone could follow up his earlier comment, "I guess you need food, hey?"

"Not at this point, I think," Erlenwanger replied. "What we particularly need is lamp oil."

"Lamp oil?" repeated Carl. "Good Christ, Professor—sorry, miss—we'd have given you lamp oil if you'd spoken. We're not electrified out where we are!"

The older man smiled past Molly's bonnet. "Not a hundred gallons, I think."

"Good Christ—oh Hell, I'm sorry again," Carl blurted. "What on earth do you want with that much lamp oil?"

"It's for our motor," Professor Erlenwanger explained. "Other researchers into directed airship flight are concentrating on petrol-burning motors of the Benz type. This is a serious error, I believe. Compression-ignited kerosine engines built to the design of Herr Rudolph Diesel are far more efficient. In addition, lamp oil is available at even the most out-of-the-way farmstead in a pinch, no small recommendation on a journey which crosses the very continent."

The city limits were marked by a metalled road. It was bright with the rich yellow limestone gravel crushed out of the bluffs on which the city was built. A bicyclist passed the wagon, free-wheeling with the momentum he had picked up coming down a side street. "Darn fool," Carl grunted, noting Molly's attention to the speedster. "In town, a gadget like that's good for nothing but running you under a wagon. Now I've rode'em, but it was at Starways Rink where they belong."

Carl turned onto Central Avenue, letting the horses ease along despite his desire to oblige the Professor. The brick avenue was slippery, and it would be easy to throw a shoe if haste brought nothing worse. Carl pulled around the yellow-brick building of the dairy and backed expertly to the loading dock, clucking to his team. "Won't be a moment," he said to his passengers. He poised on the wagon seat, then vaulted over the milk cans to land on the pine bed with a crash. "Charlie!

Jess," he shouted into the dairy. "Lend me a god damn hand! I'm in a hurry."

Erlenwanger and his daughter watched with silent interest. Carl rolled the heavy cans on their rims up the loading gate to the dock where the two dairymen manhandled them into the building. His muscles rippled, but the familiar effort did not even raise sweat-stains on his shirt. "Christ you guys're slow," Carl grumbled as he rolled the last can onto the dock. "I'll hook out the empties myself." It took him two trips, carrying a pair of the heavy cans in either hand each time. They would be hauled back and refilled the next day. Life was an endless cycle of milk cans and horse butts, Carl thought savagely to himself.

As he settled back onto the wagon seat, Carl noticed for the first time that the Professor's two camera cases were on the shelf beneath. "Frummelt's is just down Central," he said. "Say, you carry that camera most everywhere, don't you?"

"I do indeed," Erlenwanger agreed. "No amount of trouble in carrying the apparatus along is too great to be justified by the capturing of one scene that cannot be duplicated. And compared to the effort of bringing the apparatus . . . to the vicinity . . . any trouble to be endured on the ground, so to speak, is nothing."

Carl pulled in through the gate in the green-painted hoardings, into the yard of Frummelt's Coal and Ice. It was crowded with delivery wagons. Carl locked wheels with one and traded curses with the Irish driver as he angled into a place at the dock.

"We need twenty cans of coal oil," Carl shouted to the squat loading master.

The Frummelt employee cocked an eyebrow at them, lifting the brim of his bowler. "Christ, boy," he said, "I see why you came here steada' the front. If it's charge, you'll have to go up to the front anyhow, though."

"It's cash," said the Professor, balancing his weight carefully as he stepped onto the dock with his camera. He reached into his coat and brought out a purse from which he poured silver dollars into his left palm. One of the coins slipped and rang on the concrete. Carl knelt and handed it back to the older man. It bore an 1890 date stamp, but the finish was as bright and clean as if the coin had just been issued. Carl's eyes narrowed, but the loading master took the payment without comment. He counted a quarter and two dimes from the change-maker on his belt and shouted an order to a pair of dock hands.

"I wonder if I might photograph you and your men at work?" Erlenwanger asked as he watched the load of laquered rectangular cans being rolled out on a hand truck.

"Good God, why?" demanded the loading master, ignoring the driver of an ice wagon waiting for orders.

"Today, this is the petroleum business," the Professor explained obliquely. "If a time comes during which all carts and wagons are replaced by self-powered vehicles, the whole shape of the world will change. You and your men here will be important in the way the first lungfish to scramble onto dry land to snap at an insect was important.

Your feelings, your sense of place in the world—
this will never come again."

The loading master touched the right curl of his
handlebar moustache. "You can't get all that in a
picture," he said.

"What I call my photographs capture more than
one might think," Erlenwanger responded.

"Then go ahead and waste your time," grunted
the squat man as he turned away. "So long as you
stay clear of the wheels and don't waste my time
too."

As the bays plodded back along Bluff Road, Carl
said, "I've thought about what you were saying
back at Frummelt's, Professor."

"And?" the older man prompted.

Carl turned and saw Molly's intent smile instead
of the Professor. He lost his train of thought for
a moment. At last he said, "Well, it won't happen.
The wagons with motors, I mean. Not in Iowa, at
least." He gestured toward the road in front of
them. "When it rains, this's mud. Two, sometimes
three feet deep, up to the bed of a wagon. I've
seen traction engines get stuck in fields in a wet
year and us have to hitch the plow horses, three
teams all told, just to get the milk to town. They'll
never make an engine that'll handle mud like a
good team will."

Professor Erlenwanger nodded seriously. "There's
reason in what you say, Carl. Many men much
older and better educated would say the same
thing. But one of the most important lessons that
people must learn if they are to deal with the
coming age is that nothing, whether good or bad,

cannot happen. If there is something to do with the way humans interact with their world, it probably will happen. It is only when we all recognize that as a fact that we have a chance to guide some of the change that will occur anyway."

The Professor waved as Carl had at the track of rich, black earth pulverized by horse hooves and the iron wheels of wagons. "No one today—or a century hence—will find it conceivable that sane human beings would build roads of concrete a hundred feet wide in place of this. Such roads would be to the benefit of self-moving vehicles and the detriment of everything else, humans in particular. Yet, if it shall have happened, the humans of the Twenty-First Century will have to accept it as true; and the humans of the Nineteenth and Twentieth Centuries will bear the burden of failing to have guided and controlled a development which they thought was impossible—until it became inevitable.

Carl looked at the horses ahead of him. He licked his lips, ignoring from long familiarity the gritty taste of the dust on them. "Professor," he said without turning around, "I want to come with you. On your airship."

"Molly and I can use another hand on *The Enterprise*," Erlenwanger said mildly, "and there is ample room and lifting capacity, to be sure. But have you considered just what leaving home will mean to you?"

Carl risked a glance. Molly was looking straight ahead, twisting her ungloved hands in her lap. The Professor was leaning forward with a bland expression. Carl nodded, his throat tight. "I'm

leaving, that's decided," he explained. "I thought
it was going to be the Navy, is all. You see, it's not
that I don't love my folks . . . or them love me, for
that matter. But I'm the little kid. I'm eighteen
and I'm the little kid. So long as I live and even
one of my brothers lives, I'll be the little kid—if I
don't get out now. Maybe after I've made my own
way for a time, I can come back. Maybe I could
even work the farm again, though I don't guess I'd
want to. But for now, I've got to cut the traces."

"Very well, Carl," said the Professor. "I won't
insult you by questioning your decision. If I did
not think you were capable of soundly assessing a
situation, I would not have considered making you
the offer. You no doubt realize that we will leave
as soon as *The Enterprise* has been refueled?"

"Oh, that's best," breathed Carl in double relief. "I'll bundle my clothes and . . . say what
needs to be said. Then it'll be best all round if I
leave." His eyes sought the Professor's, caught
Molly's instead. They both looked away.

Carl's mother came into the room her two youngest sons shared. Carl was rolling the extra set of
dungarees around the rest of his meager belong-
ings. He tied the bindle off with twine. Mrs. Gudeint
said nothing. Carl glanced at her, saw her tears,
and looked away again very quickly. She was in
the doorway and Carl was finished packing. Looking out the window, he said, "Mom, I brushed
down the horses before I came in. I'm not going to
stay here, I never was—you know that. So just
kiss me and don't . . . all the rest."

Turning very quickly, the boy pecked his mother

on the cheek and tried to swing around her in the same motion. She clung to him, her face pressed against his blue cotton workshirt. At last she said, "You've told your father?"

"I'll be back one day soon and I'll tell him," Carl said. He squeezed his mother closer and, in the instant that she relaxed, disengaged himself from her. "Mom, I love you," he said. He reached the staircase in one stride and was down its ten steps in three great jumps. He did not look back after the screen door banged behind him.

While Carl finished his business with the farm, Professor Erlenwanger had poured the twenty cans of kerosine into the funnel-mouthed nozzle he had extended from the rear of the gondola. Molly was stacking the empty cans up against the wall of the barn for the Gudeints to use or return for credit. She nodded to Carl as she entered the gondola and sat primly at a bank of sixteen levers, each with a gauge above it. The Professor himself stood at a helm like that of a ship. The spokes appeared to have additional control switches built into them. To the right front of the helm, along the glazed forward bulkhead, was a double bank of waist-high levers. The control room was no more spacious than the garret bedrooms Fred and George each had to themselves, but it was only the front third of the gondola.

"Carl, if you'll take a seat at the other console," Erlenwanger said, gesturing to the chair just aft of the gondola's door. "Soon I'll teach you how to operate the motor controls yourself; but now, in the interests of a prompt departure. . . ."

Carl nodded and sat as directed, eying the north

field where his father and eldest brother were
haying. The Professor leaned over him and threw
a switch. "Since we ride on hydrogen," he said
cryptically, "it's no difficulty to bleed some into
the injectors in place of ether for starting. . . ."
He flipped a second switch. Something whined
briefly and the motor grunted to life. It sank quickly
into a hum that was felt but not really heard in the
forward compartment. Erlenwanger listened for a
moment, then said, "Very good." He pointed to a
knob with a milled rim. "When I direct you to,
Carl, please turn this knob a quarter turn clock-
wise. It engages the airscrew, which we don't
want to do until we have a little altitude, do we?"
He smiled brightly at both his crew members.
"Not pointed at the house as we are, that is."

Erlenwanger returned to the helm. "There
doesn't seem to be enough wind today to require
us to make an immediate jump for altitude. I'm
always concerned about that, for fear that a line
stoppage will lift us asymetrically; so Molly, if you
will fill tanks five and eight."

The girl quickly threw two levers. The gauges
above them began to rise as the metal fabric trembled to a mild hissing. The older man said, "Each
of the sixteen tanks is split in two by a movable
partition. The partition acts as a piston when the
pressure on one side of it becomes higher than
that on the other side. One and sixteen, Molly;
then two and fifteen," the Professor continued.

Molly worked the requested pairs of switches,
pausing after the first to make sure the operation
was smooth. She glanced at Carl over her shoulder and said, "What he means is, the gas pushes

air out of the tanks when we want to go up, and the air pushes the gas out when we want to go down."

Erlenwanger turned and blinked. "That's very good, Molly. I'm afraid I often talk more than I communicate. Though air is a gas as well as hydrogen, of course. . . . Still. If you will fill the next three pairs in order, please."

The hiss of gas was a living sound now. The gondola was rocking like a rubber ball on the surface of a lake, not lifting off the ground but responsive to every ripple in the air. "I think we're about ready," said Erlenwanger. "Carl, I'll give you the word in a moment. Molly, fill the central tanks."

The gondola shuddered. The pattern of light through the side windows shifted as they swung beneath the lifting hull. The ship was rising at a walking pace, drifting toward the barn and rotating about 30° in the grip of the mild breeze. "Carl, engage the screw," said the Professor. The boy obeyed, his hand so tight on the knurled brass that it did not slip despite its sweatiness. Erlenwanger rocked his helm forward on its post as he felt the propeller bite. The side-slipping continued but was lost in the greater surge of the airship's forward motion. They were still rising. Looking through the windows beyond Molly, Carl could see the hay-cutting rig at the point of the bright swathe cut from the darker green of the north field. The horses were the size of chihuahuas. The two men in the field shaded their eyes with their hands as they stared at the shimmering oval in their sky. They were too far away for Carl to have recognized them by sight alone. They did not wave. After a moment, as the field and his former life slipped behind at locomotive speed, Carl did.

Professor Erlenwanger released the helm and stepped over to where Molly sat. The airship continued moving smoothly at better than twenty miles an hour. The rolling land was now almost three thousand feet below. "We're a little higher than I care to be without a reason," Erlenwanger said. "Probably because the sun is so bright. Molly, would you care to balance all the tanks at 75%? That should bring us down about a thousand feet. Besides, I prefer to have some pressure in all tanks rather than flying with some voided and others full."

Using the bar that fitted the full length of her panel, Molly slid the fourteen open switches down to three-quarters. Simultaneously, she slid the other pair up to the bar with her free hand. The airship lurched, steadied, and continued to skim through the air. It was dropping noticeably, a sensation less like diving into a pond than it was like a toboggan ride down Indian Mound Hill. Erlenwanger studied the line of silver in the etched glass column above his helm. His lips pursed and he touched another display to the side of the column. "We aren't getting the lift we should out of the forward tanks," he said to no one in particular, "though we seem to have leveled off satisfactorily. Moisture in the tanks, I suppose. We'll have to empty them in the near future."

"Where do you buy your hydrogen, Professor?" Carl asked, staring down through the transparent quarter-panels of the gondola. He had seen fields from atop the sharp bluffs which wrinkled eastern Iowa, but there was something marvelous in watching solid ground flow by below like a river choked with debris.

"I manufacture it from water," the older man said. "Our motor powers an electrical generator. When it is necessary to fill a hydrogen tank, I simply run a current through a container of water and collect the separated hydrogen atoms above the cathode."

Warming to his subject—though little of what he had already stated made sense to Carl—Erlenwanger continued, "You see, that is where some theorists go wrong in asserting that helium is safer than hydrogen because it cannot be ignited. What they ignore is the *cost* of helium. The only way to keep an airship safe over a long period is to clear it of the condensate that otherwise—and inevitably—loads it down to the point that a storm smashes it. And the only sure way to clear the condensate is to vent your tanks and dry them periodically. Helium is rare and far too expensive to be 'wasted' in that fashion—so lives will be wasted instead. Hydrogen is cheap and can be manufactured anywhere, either from acid and iron filings or—much more practically—by electrolysis, as I do."

The Professor shook his head. "It will be a long time, if ever, that men will stop sending other men to their deaths by ignoring the practical realities which make their theories specious. We should not enshrine human realities, my young friends, whether economic or otherwise; but neither should we expect them to disappear because we ignore them."

Erlenwanger caught himself. He smiled wryly at both his companions. Their eyes were focused at about the level of his stick-pin in determined efforts not to look bored. "Well," he said, "I think it's far more important to teach Carl the rudiments of *The Enterprise* than it is for me to go on about things that only time will change. Molly, would you care to show our new recruit how your panel functions? I can listen and make suggestions if it seems useful."

The older man sat in Carl's chair, watching as Carl moved over beside Molly. The airship flew on at a steady pace, over farms and wooded hilltops, water courses in which cattle stood to their bellies, and occasionally a small town in a web of dry, gray roads. Throughout the afternoon, Carl learned the workings of the machine which was less wonderful to him than was the girl at whose side he sat. The levers of the starboard panel controlled the flow of hydrogen between the buoyancy tanks and the storage reservoir in the keel. "It's held in a liquid state," the Professor interjected, "and the insulation of the reservoir is an improvement—a very great improvement—over previous applications of Dewar's principles."

Understanding the technique of raising or lowering the airship was easy, but executing the technique was another matter again. Carl made several attempts to modify the craft's buoyancy at Erlenwanger's direction. Each experiment sent *The Enterprise* staggering through the air at an unexpected angle or altitude. At the end of the session, the boy had a fair grasp of what the duties entailed—and he had enormous respect for the girl who performed them.

"How long have you been practicing this?" asked Carl as Molly brought them back to level flight at two thousand feet following his own series of unintentional aerobatics.

"Well, about four days, now," said the girl, glancing over at the Professor for confirmation. "I've been doing it ever since the Professor—oh dear." She broke off in indecipherable confusion, blushing and looking away from both men. "I'm sorry, I didn't mean to—"

"Nor did you, my dear," Professor Erlenwanger said calmly. "And in any case, I intended to explain the situation to Carl at once anyway. "You see," he continued, turning to the boy, "Molly is no more my daughter than you are my son—which is how I intend to describe you to those whom we meet on our travels. I assure you, there is no improper conduct involved in Molly's accompanying me, any more than there would be had she been a blood relation. However, so as not to offend those persons whom we meet, I determined to tell an untruth—a lie, if you will. I dislike lying, and I will not lie to another's harm; but the truth is less important than the fellowship of many humans meeting without enmity."

Carl licked his lips. "What did your real parents say?" he asked.

Molly looked down. "I haven't real parents," she said softly.

"Molly was a foundling," Erlenwanger said. "She was in service at a house in Boston until she refused a—an improper demand by the master of the house. She was turned out of her place the day before I met her."

"I never told you that!" the girl blurted.

"Nor do I mention it to embarrass you, my dear," Erlenwager said. "We will be together for some days and in close proximity, however, and I think it necessary that Carl understand your situation as clearly as you do his."

They proceeded through the airship's two other stations. The motor-starting drill appeared to be ridiculously simple: depress the hydrogen feed for three or four seconds, release it, and flip the starter switch. Shut-down was even more basic, a third switch that "shut off the injectors," which meant nothing at all to Carl but obviously seemed an adequate explanation to the Professor.

There were a dozen circular gauges above the switch panel. "While the motor is running," Erlenwanger said with a gesture, "the pointers should all be in the green zone. If one of the pointers falls into the red or rises to the white, tell me. Nothing very dreadful is going to happen without our hearing it, though, so don't feel you have to stare at the dials."

"It isn't really very simple, is it?" Carl said thoughtfully.

"Umm?" said Erlenwanger, pausing in mid-step as he moved to the helm.

"You make it look easier than running a feed mill," Carl went on. "Maybe it is, too. But it's not simple, it's just simple to run. Being able to milk a cow don't mean you could build a cow yourself."

"That's true, of course," the older man agreed with a pleased expression. "I'm really delighted to have met you, Carl. One has an emotional tendency to equate ignorance with stupidity, which meeting you—meeting you both—" and his hand spread toward Molly—"has dispelled.

"But to answer your implied question, Carl, *The Enterprise* is unique in the world. However, if she were examined at length by today's finest scientists and engineers, they would find only her workmanship to be exceptional. Others—many others today—have all the 'secrets' I have embodied in the Erlenwanger Directable Airship. I have refined metals to great purity and machined them to—great—tolerances; but all this can be duplicated." The Professor paused and smiled again. "So while I will agree that the construct is not simple, my friend, it is simple enough."

The helm station was another example of the horribly complex overlaid by barnyard basic. Rotating the spokes did not change the direction of travel, as Carl had assumed from analogy to a steamship; rather, it controlled the amount of power the motor developed. "The diesel runs at constant revolutions," Erlenwanger said, "with the output delivered through a torque converter."

"I don't understand."

"Oh." The Professor blinked. "Well, you know how a block and tackle work," he began. At the end of half an hour's discussion, Carl *did* understand a torque converter, because he had seen the one in the engine compartment. The diesel squatted there, hot and oily but as silent as heat lightning. The humming of the prop drew up and down the scale as the Professor adjusted its pitch to demonstrate. They went forward again, through

the central compartment with its three fold-down
bunks and a tiny but marvelously-equipped lavatory. Carl was conscious (as he had not been before) of the *machineness* of what they were riding.
Flying had been like drifting in a cloud or—better—
floating on his back in the stock pond with water-
wings at his ankles and neck. Now . . . the diesel
made no sound, but the gondola trembled to its
power; and the linkage of control to power to
motion had become part of Carl's universe. Amazed
by the concept rather than any single object, Carl
and Molly watched Erlenwanger change their direction by turning the helm on the axis of its
vertical support.

"What do these do?" Carl asked, reaching out a
hand toward the levers in front of the helm.

"Oh, careful—" Molly cried, her own hand catch-
ing Carl's. "These spill the gas out through the
top. As low as we are now, we could—well, it
wouldn't be a pleasant drop."

"I wasn't going to move it," Carl explained; but
the incident reinforced the dangerous reality of
what had initially seemed to be a fairy tale.

They were heading West by South-West—255°
on the compass which somehow flashed onto the
forward window when the Professor thumbed a
button on the helm. The sky darkened with awesome suddeness. Because *The Enterprise* was headed
into a horizon as rich with color as any Carl had
seen since the aftermath of Krakatoa, even that
darkening was not an immediate warning. "I think
we had best find a place for the night," Erlenwanger
was saying. "The land beneath is a good deal more

broken than that in the glaciated portion of the state, isn't—"

The first gust of the storm racing down from the north caught *The Enterprise*. The gondola rotated twenty degrees around the axis of the buoyancy chamber.

Carl had youthful reflexes and a farmer's familiarity with shifting footing. His left hand caught the edge of the diesel control panel, firmly enough to twist the light metal. His right hand caught Molly as she rebounded from the starboard bulkhead when the gondola swung back. Professor Erlenwanger was slower and in a worse position to act. A leather strap hung from the roof above him, but instead of snatching for it the older man froze on the helm. The helm simultaneously turned and pivoted, and the airship nosed into the squall with its prop idled and unable to keep a way on. *The Enterprise* tumbled in a horizontal plane, swapping ends twice and shuddering as updrafts sucked it toward the thunderheads invisible above.

Erlenwanger got his footing and thumbed a button. Lime-colored lights brightened the cabin. They were dim, but in contrast to the storm's sudden blackness they felt as warm as the kitchen stove in winter. The craft steadied, the motor giving them enough headway for control despite the buffeting of the wind. Rain slashed *The Enterprise* with a sound like tearing canvas, and the interior lights reflected in surreal nightmares from water-rippled windows.

Then the lightning bolt hit them.

Carl had heard the boiler blow at the Star Brewery in 1893. Perhaps that was louder than the thunderclap—but Carl had been half a mile from the brewery, not inside the boiler at the time. Now the thunder was only a stunning physical counterpart to the blinding dazzle of the lightning. Carl's flesh tingled. Molly's hair was standing out straight from her head like the fuzz on a dandelion, crackling with tiny blue discharges from the tip of each tendril. Rubber was smouldering everywhere. It did not occur to Carl to marvel that the direct voltage of the lightning had been insulated from the occupants of the gondola.

"I have to land," Erlenwanger cried, his voice tinny in the aftermath of the thunderclap. "Molly, can you—?"

The girl nodded. The emergency lights were gone but St Elmo's Fire frosted all the external metal surfaces and illuminated the cabin through the glass. Molly's mouth was open as she struggled to her feet, but the muscles of her cheeks were set in a rictus, not a scream. A fat blue spark popped to her finger tip. Her gasp was a soft echo of the spark, but she grasped her controls without hesitation and slid two of the levers down to their bottom positions.

They were presumably dropping, but with the darkness and the wind's hammering it was impossible to tell. The altimeter column was invisible; it would have been uselessly erratic even if Erlenwanger had had enough light to read it. The Professor was leaning over the helm, peering helplessly at the black countryside. Carl wondered why the older man did not use the spotlight. Then he noticed that Erlenwanger was ceaselessly flipping a switch in the center of the helm, back and forth, back and forth, though he must have realized minutes ago that the lightning bolt had put the spot out of commission until repairs could be made.

Erlenwanger slid the gondola door open. Droplets slung from the doorframe eddied and spattered within the compartment. The tendrils of St Elmo's Fire were growing longer and brighter. They blunted the night vision of those in the gondola without helping to illuminate the ground beneath. Carl hung from the door jamb, his head and shoulders out in the onrushing night. Big, wind-flung raindrops bit his cheeks like horseflies. Molly sat at her controls, feet locked on the bench against the hammering gusts. Her face was pale but prepared.

"There's a level field beneath us!" the Professor cried over a roll of thunder from half a mile away. "I'm going to void a tank to set us down quickly." He reached for one of the levers beside the helm. A landing leg extended across Carl's field of vision like the arm of a mantis. The boy peered forward, blinded by a lightning flash and trying to superimpose what its instant had showed him over the yellow after-image on his retinas.

"Trees a hundred yards ahead," Carl shouted.

The Enterprise lurched. In the same moment there was light, a great blue flare reflecting from the cloud ceiling as static ignited the hydrogen released from tank nine. Carl screamed, "Jesus Christ, we're over water! Get up, *get up!*"

Even as Carl spoke, Molly was thrusting her levers to the top, a help but too slow a help. The silent fire still blazed above them, mirrored by clouds and the storm-tossed Missouri River beneath. It was a huge sheet of illumination a mile in diameter. The Professor slammed his throttle forward, to and through the gate that blocked it with an inch of potential travel. The diesel roared, racketing even against the storm as yard-long flames spurted rearward from exhaust cut-outs. *The Enterprise* wallowed like a bogged wagon. A landing leg touched a wave top and dragged a line of spray to tilt the gondola. They were over mudflats, the wind swinging them as they struggled to rise above the line of willows that fringed the Kansas shore. The storm whipped a willow-frond up at them, the tendril snaking in through the open door and stripping off its leaves on the trailing corner as they pulled past. But that was the last touch of the storm and itself more a love-pat than a threat.

They were skimming a pasture, the six-foot heads of bull thistles throwing sharp silhouettes against the cropped grass as lightning flared again. Erlenwanger throttled back and swung the airship into the wind. Molly's fingers played on the controls. They sank, brushing the ground as they drifted back toward the dark bulk of the far hedgerow. The Professor edged his throttle a half point open and the ship steadied, bumped, and settled solidly onto the field. The pumps whined to empty the tanks into the hydrogen reservoir. Lightning skipped across the sky to the south of them, but the thunder was half a minute coming.

The Professor looked at his companions, like him exhausted. He beamed. "I think we all owe ourselves a vote of thanks for able action under difficult circumstances. Now, who would care to

join me in a supper of ham, fresh corn, and . . .
cider, I think, from New Hampshire?"

Carl looked away from the sparse vegetation
below them. "Are you trying to set a record time
crossing the country?" he asked Professor Erlenwanger.

"Goodness no," said the older man, squinting a
little in surprise. "That's for the railway barons,
cleared track and fifty miles an hour. I will reach
San Francisco in—a matter of time. But for me,
the . . . well, the journey is itself the destination."

Carl nodded. "I just wondered," he said, "from
the way we spent a day there at the river."

"Oh, well," Erlenwanger said, gesturing down
at the alkaline landscape. "We needed to replen-
ish our hydrogen, and I thought it best to do so
before we got much farther west. As we have.
Besides, the peddler we met was a fascinating
person."

"He was just a peddler, wasn't he?" Molly asked.
"I wouldn't of thought you would want a picture of
him in particular."

The Professor bobbed his head, animated by the
discussion though he disagreed with the implica-
tions of the statement. "Yes," he said, "an ordinary peddler. But have you ever considered for
how brief a time a peddler may be normal?" He
spread his hands, palms upward. "With growing
centralization, with the better communications that
metalled roads will bring, there will no longer be a
need for goods to be trucked from door to door,
from farm to farm. That man with his mule and his
wagon and his . . . little bit of everything civilized—

he is on the end of a chain stretching back ten millenia. And he really is the end of it."

Erlenwanger smiled at Molly to show there was no hostility in his disagreement. "He is very much worth—photographing—you see. Very much worth preserving for another age."

From the air, western Kansas was a waste of chalk gullies and buffalo grass. *The Enterprise* had sailed over cattle too scattered to be called herds; there had been no other signs of human habitation for forty miles.

"That's a campfire," Carl said, pointing out the forward window.

"Why yes, I believe it is," agreed the Professor. He tilted the helm a point, centering the tendril of gray on the pale evening sky. Molly sat quickly at her bench, waiting for instructions.

In the fading sunlight, the airship must have been a drop of blood to the slouch-hatted man who saw it as he tossed another buffalo chip on the fire. He yelped. The younger man across from him, turning the antelope haunch, spun around. He jumped to the rifle leaning against the wagon box and levered a cartridge into the chamber. The gondola door was already open. Neither the Professor nor Molly could leave their stations. Carl leaned far out into the air, clinging to the jamb as he had two nights before in the storm. He shouted, "Hey, what's the matter with you? We don't mean you no harm!"

"Great god, there's men in it!" the rifleman blurted.

Behind him, the tent flap quivered to pass a third man wearing dungarees over a set of combinations. He was older than either of the others, balding and burly with a gray moustache drooping to either side of his bearded mouth. "Of course there's men in it, Jimmy," he thundered. "Did you think it was alive?" He glanced down at the meat and added to the slouch-hatted man, "Watch the roast, Corley, or it's back to rice and beans."

The airship had drifted very close to the campsite. The landing legs creaked out. Carl picked up the grapnel and a handful of its coiled line. He had learned that the hooks were not a necessity but that they made a landing easier by keeping the vessel headed into the wind. "Can you set this solid?" he shouted and hurled the grapnel to the ground. The burly man took the idea at once. He nodded and wedged the hooks just down-wind of the camp between a pair of the boulders that dotted the surface of more friable rock. A moment later they were down, the airship wheezing to itself as it resettled its hydrogen.

Carl stepped to the ground and shook the great, calloused hand which the eldest of the campers thrust at him. "Carl Gudeint," he muttered.

"Claudius Bjornholm," the other said. "And these are my assistants Mr. James Beadle, and Mr. Corley whom I hired to drive and to cook for us."

Carl found himself spokesman from his location. "Ah," he said, "Professor Erlenwanger and Molly, ah, Molly Erlenwanger. The Professor built this bal—airship."

There was mutual murmuring and shaking of hands, though Carl noticed that Corley was hanging back. Apparently he was afraid to step beneath the looming buoyancy chamber of *The Enterprise*.

Most of the light now came from the campfire.
Carl eyed the array of digging implements stacked
near the wagon and asked, "You, you're . . .
prospecting?"

"You mean, 'You're crazy?'" Bjornholm replied
good-naturedly. "No gold in this chalk, of course.
But it could be that I'm madder still, you know.
I'm here—we're here—hunting for bones. It's been
my life now for thirty-seven years, and I expect to
carry on so long as the Lord gives me the strength
to do so."

Carl and Molly exchanged blank glances. The
youngest of the campers, Jimmy—he must have
been Carl's age though he was much more lightly
built—knuckled his jaw in some embarrassment.
Professor Erlenwanger, however, said, "Yes, of
course; searching for the fossils of the Great Ne-
braska Sea. Have you had much success?"

"Very little this far," Bjornholm admitted, "though
Jimmy believes he spotted something in a gully
wall while bringing back our supper here—" he
nodded at the antelope haunch. "We'll see to it as
soon as there's enough light to work without chanc-
ing damage to the finds." The big man looked at
Erlenwanger appraisingly. "You're a learned man,
sir," he said, "as one would have expected from
your—" he nodded—"creation. It seems far too
huge to be so silent."

The Professor smiled. "People accuse machinery
of being a curse when their real problems are with
the side effects rather than the machines themselves. Noise is one of the most unpleasant side
effects, I have found; but it can be cured." Waving
at the fire from which Corley had just removed

the meat, Erlenwanger added, "Perhaps you'd be willing to share your fire? We can of course provide our share of the supplies. And—if possible—I would greatly appreciate it if we might accompany you in the morning on your search."

Bjornholm straightened. With the glow of the fire behind him and the power of his stance and broad shoulders, he was no longer a part-dressed figure of fun. "Sir," he said, "we would be honored by your presence—tonight and whenever else."

Fresh vegetables from the airship were well received by the bone-hunters, but the greatest delicacy Erlenwanger provided was fresh water. Bjornholm savored his first sip, tonguing it around within his mouth until he finally swallowed. "You don't know what it's like," he said slowly, looking at each of the visitors in turn, "to have nothing to drink for months at a time but water so alkaline that even a handful of coffee beans can't kill the taste. Every mug is a dose of salts—literally, I'm sorry to say." He nodded solemnly at Carl, who was farthest around the circle from Molly. "You waste away during a dig, and the good lord help the poor fools who try to live here and farm."

"But why do you stay?" asked Molly, handling her plate ably on her knees as she squatted on the ground with the men.

"You see, it's not really like this," said Jimmy unexpectedly, lowering the dainty antelope femur at which he had been gnawing. He waved out at the endless, gullied night. "This was a great bay, ten times the Gulf of Mexico and more. Still water, hiding monsters the like of none on Earth today; still air with gliding reptiles greater than any birds. It's—" He stopped, his lips still working as he decided what words to frame. More than the fire lighted his narrow face. He continued, "I'm at Haverford. Last year I heard Professor Cope lecture and . . . it wasn't a new world opening, it was a thousand new worlds, as many new worlds as there had been past ages of our Earth. Can you imagine that? Can you—see tarpons sixteen feet long, flashing just under the surface as the mackerel they chase make the sea foam? Or the tylosaur, the *real* sea serpent, lifting itself long enough to take a sighting before it slides through the depths toward the disturbance?

"Can you see it?"

Bjornholm was nodding. "I've worked for Professor Cope—God rest his soul—on several occasions in the past. He sent Mr. Beadle to me with a letter of introduction; and Mr. Beadle has proven a splendid and trustworthy companion in my search of the world of two million years ago."

"Two million?" Erlenwanger repeated. "Oh, yes; of course. Lord Kelvin proved from the temperature of the Earth that it could be no more than—twenty to forty million years old, wasn't that the figure? I am sometimes amazed at the conclusions a great scientist can draw from data which a man of more—common—understanding would have found hopelessly inadequate for the purpose." He smiled.

"Yes indeed," agreed Bjornholm heavily. "I have always envied men like Professor Cope the understanding which I can only draw on second hand. I grew up in Cincinnati, where every building stone is marked by a crinoid or a clam preserved eternally from a past age. When I was fifteen, I determined that I would have some part in bringing that past to light, whatever it might cost me personally."

He looked around the circuit of firelight, the tent and wagon, both of them worn; the tools and the brutal labor they implied; the faces of his companions, like his unshaven for the waste of water shaving would entail. "It has a cost. But though I've done things besides digging for fossils, nothing else will really matter after I'm dead except the part of the past I leave to the future."

Corley spit into the fire. "Bones," he said without looking up. "Bones and stones and durned fools."

"And yet you're here too, Jake," Beadle said sharply. "A dollar a day, all found, and corn for your horses. Well, maybe those're better reasons than ours, but—you're here too."

The fire popped back in emphasis, and the dark moved a little closer.

Leaving the tent and the great, hollow bulk of the airship behind, Professor Erlenwanger's party climbed into the wagon with Corley and the equipment. There was barely light enough to see by. Carl was not surprised to notice that Professor Erlenwanger carried his camera cases. Bjornholm and his assistant rode their own horses, the burly man displaying a quiet mastery of his beast that belied his apparent clumsiness.

"Too much for the team to draw," Corley grumbled as he harnessed the horses.

"With three months of my feed in their bellies,

they'll draw this load better than they did the empty wagon when I hired you," retorted Bjornholm.

Jimmy Beadle directed them, scowling under his hatbrim as he searched for landmarks in a country of ruts and scrub grass. He looked older by daylight than he had seemed around the fire. Far on the horizon they could see a pair of pronghorns. Beadle laid a hand on his saddle-scabbard, but Bjornholm noted curtly, "We've better ways to spend our time today."

They skirted one gully and crossed a second, the wagon passengers dismounting as the iron-bound wheels crumbled the rock of the far rim. The sun rose higher and the wind picked up with a burden of dust so finely divided that it looked like yellow fog. At last, as they approached a gully that almost deserved the name of canyon, Jimmy pointed and said, "There—on the far wall. See where the speck of white is?"

They halted at the rim, squinting across the hundred feet or so at a brighter splash against the yellowish chalk. "We can't get across that," Corley said suddenly. "It's sixty feet down and durned near straight up and down on t'other side."

"Be easier to hang down from the rim, wouldn't it?" Beadle suggested. "It's about half-way up the wall, and I'd sure rather swing down than climb up."

"We'd have to climb that wall to be able to hang over," Bjornholm said. "Unless you've found a way around this arroyo that I haven't. We can get down this side easy enough—"

"Not the wagon!" Corley interjected.

"Not the wagon," Bjornholm agreed, "but on foot. We'll figure a way then to get up the other side."

They used their hands to descend the draw, and Carl made the last ten feet in an uncontrolled rush besides; but they all made it. Molly had less evident trouble than Carl did, picking her footing and getting to the gully floor with no more than a smear of chalk dust on her linen wrapper. But the wall that loomed above them was nearly as straight as a building's, though there was enough batter from the middle upwards to hide the fleck of bone from their eyes.

Bjornholm absently worried a twig from one of the mesquite bushes that pocked the arroyo. "We'll have to cut steps," he said. He set the blade of the shovel he carried against the wall and twisted with his weight on it. Flecks of chalk spat and the steel rang. "Have to use the hatchet, I guess," he said disgustedly.

"I can get to it if you give me a boost," Jimmy said, eying the stone.

Bjornholm frowned. He laid down his shovel, leaned on the arroyo wall, and looked upward. "It's still too high," he observed.

Corley said, "Bjornholm, if you can take the weight, I'll stand on your shoulders and tug the kid up."

The burly man turned his head to stare. Corley seemed to shrink inward, but he did not lower his eyes. "Climb up, then," Bjornholm rumbled. He braced himself against the chalk. Corley gripped Bjornholm's shoulder and raised a cracked boot to the bigger man's jutting right hip.

"Here!" Carl said, springing to Bjornholm's side and gripping a handful of Corley's dungarees to haul him upward. The gangling teamster balanced bent-over for a moment, then straightened with a boot on the shoulder of each of the bigger men beneath him. "All right," Corley grunted, reaching one hand back and down for Jimmy while his other hand clamped a knob of rock. "Come if you're coming, boy."

Jimmy caught Corley's hand, his boot a brief agony on Carl's out-thrust hip as the student pushed off. Then there was only the doubled weight being transmitted through Corley. Carl locked hands with Bjornholm, less for mutual support than for commiseration of the sharp leather soles cutting to their collar bones. Then Jimmy cried, "Okay, okay, I'm getting there," and half the weight was gone. In relief as if he were wholly unburdened, Carl flexed his shoulders.

"Hold on, I'm coming down," said Corley. He jumped, falling to hands and knees on the hard soil. Carl backed away, rubbing his muscles and staring up at Jimmy. The student was using minute projections and the slight tilt of the rock to climb steadily toward the exposed bone. From beneath, the watchers tensed as the student's increasingly-greater deliberation showed that he was nearing the prize.

"I've got it," Jimmy said, the chalk muffling his voice. Then, "Oh. . . . Oh."

"What is it, Jimmy?" Bjornholm demanded hoarsely.

The younger man half-turned, no longer particularly interested in keeping his position. "It's a buffalo thigh, Mr. Bjornholm," he said flatly. "It must have rolled over the lip of the draw and caught here in a little crevice. I doubt it's as old as I am."

Bjornholm nodded silently, his great shoulders suddenly stooped. "Another time, then," he said. "I've searched longer and found less at other times." But the last words were spoken so softly as to be almost inaudible.

"Look out," Beadle said. He dropped the buffalo femur. It clattered twice on the gully wall before raising a puff of dust on the ground. Bjornholm's assistant eased one foot onto a lower projection, then the other. His boot soles slipped. Jimmy skidded down the side of the arroyo, boots and hips grinding away a shower of pebbles as they slowed him. Carl took a half-step to catch the sliding man, realized that the student was in control of everything but his speed, and got out of the way lest interference cripple both of them. Beadle hit the ground with his legs bent at the knees. His feet flew out from under him at the shock and he sprawled. Bjornholm and Carl both reached out to help the slender man up. "Well, that's it for this pair," Jimmy said glumly, sticking his hand through the hole the rock had abraded in his trousers. "The others haven't been washed in six weeks, neither."

Claudius Bjornholm was not listening to him. The burly man had knelt, his mouth open and his tongue absently exploring his cracked lips. He brushed his left hand over the surface of the ground where Beadle's boots had scarred it. After a moment he slipped a reground oyster knife from his hip pocket and began scraping. Jimmy looked down and his own jaw dropped. "Oh, oh . . . ," he whispered, kneeling as if joining the older man in prayer.

Corley thrust his narrow shoulders between his two companions. "God damn," he said, "that sure's hell *is* a skull!"

"It's more than a skull," Bjornholm said, his big index finger pointing along the gully floor. Regular projections were visible against the chalk, now that they had been pointed out. They were bony knobs running for twenty feet in a straight line. It was as if the tips of a huge saw blade were sticking up above the gully floor. "I think we have—everything here. Just below the surface. Those are the upper processes of the vertebrae of a mosasaur, unless I mistake what I can see of this skull. If none of it has been lost by weathering, it will be as perfect . . . more perfect than anything I've—I've—" The big man paused, blinking back tears. "As anything I've found in thirty-seven years of searching."

"Gentlemen," Professor Erlenwanger said, "would you object to my taking a photograph?"

Carl looked around in surprise and saw that Erlenwanger really had set up his camera. How he had brought the cases down the slope without disaster was more than the boy could imagine.

"Of the find in place?" said Bjornholm, edging back so as not to block the field of view. "Of course, of course."

"No," said the Professor sharply. He gestured the three bone-hunters closer together with both hands. "These bones have been in the ground a hundred million years. Others like them will still be there to be found in another hundred million years. But your like, with the whole of the past fresh under your fingertips—that will pass with your generation."

"But you don't want *us*, then," Jimmy Beadle said with a puzzled frown. He was still kneeling. "You want a picture of the real greats. . . . Well, Dr. Cope is gone now, but Dr. Osborne or Milius of Tubingen."

Erlenwanger flicked his eyebrows back a millimeter in utter denial. "Did you shoot that antelope yesterday in the chest?" he asked.

"Huh?" said Jimmy. "No, it wasn't but fifty yards away, so I shot it through the head."

"That ruined the trophy, didn't it?"

"Trophy?" repeated the student. "I don't understand. I didn't want a trophy, I wanted meat."

The Professor's smile was beatific. "So do I," he said, and he bent back over the camera. The rim of the arroyo still hid the morning sun. The three oddly-assorted bone-hunters linked arms and stared back at Erlenwanger, the triumph bright in their faces.

"I don't know why anybody'd want to live like those cowboys in the line camp yesterday," Carl said, staring through the side windows at the increasingly rugged terrain below.

Molly was at the helm while Professor Erlenwanger sent what he said was a "wireless message" back to his associates in Boston. She said, "It's not that they want to, I think . . . any more than I wanted to be in service with the O'Neills. But I was willing—for a while. And those fellows were willing to live their lives in a little hut, ride fences while the weather lets them and spend three months of the winter reading the catalog pages pasted to the walls. Someday they won't do that. They'll get a few cows of their own and marry, or they'll move in town and work at a feed store. But for now, they're willing."

Carl looked over at the Professor. Erlenwanger's eyes were open but unfocused. His thumb and index finger made a muted tapping on the brass key he had set on the ledge in front of the buoyancy controls. "Did he take a picture of you too?" Carl asked quietly, still looking at the older man.

"Oh, yes—right there on the street before he bought me a meal," the girl replied. "He—oh! Carl! Look at this!"

Both the men jumped to their feet, their eyes following Molly's pointing finger down to the gullied foothills below. The scale was deceptive. The beast could have been a dun-colored hog rooting through mesquite until Carl took his thousand feet of altitude into account. "My goodness!" gasped Professor Erlenwanger, his wireless gear forgotten, "It's a grizzly bear. I *must* get it!"

The Professor threw open the dunnage locker in the rear bulkhead. Carl expected him to draw out an express rifle, but instead it was the pair of camera cases again. "Carl," he said as he unlatched the equipment, "will you take the helm and bring us up to the bear dead slow? And Molly, since you're more experienced with altitude correction, can you drop us to twenty feet and hold us there?"

Molly throttled back and handed the wheel to Carl. "You're going to take a picture from the doorway, Professor?" she asked in some concern. Her fingers began playing with the gas chamber controls.

"Well, from this instead, I think," Erlenwanger said. He lifted a ladder of ropes and wooden battens from the locker and fastened the ends to staples set in the floor for that purpose. Then he slid the door open and tossed the ladder out to twist and dangle, blown sternward despite their present slow speed. "I think I will need the greater field of view, since the bear may have its own notions about being photographed. And—well, this keeps *The Enterprise* herself a little further from the ground in case something . . . untoward happens." His tongue touched his lips. Molly, keeping a close watch on the terrain which they now had approached so closely, blinked but said nothing.

The Professor fitted the strap of the bulky camera over his left shoulder. He looked down at the dangling ladder. "Well . . . ," he said, and paused. He turned and opened a drawer beneath the engine control panel which Carl had not noticed before. From it he took an angular handgun. He stuck the weapon into his hip pocket where the tails of his tweed coat hid it. "Well," he repeated, and he began to climb carefully down the ladder.

They were barely moving forward now. The bear was a hundred feet ahead, ambling between dwarf cedars with an odd, sidelong gait. It looked very large. Molly bit her lip and made an infinitesimal adjustment to a pair of her controls. The airship dipped. Carl thought the girl had overcorrected, but they recovered and stabilized with the ground just twenty feet below them as the Professor had directed. Carl eased on a little more throttle and started his final approach.

The only sound *The Enterprise* made was the minute whistle of the air curling around it, and that was lost in the rustle of the trees. When their sharp-edged shadow fell across the grizzly, however, the brute paused and turned with its snout raised. Erlenwanger was steadying himself with his arms through the loop of the ladder as if it were the sling of a rifle. His camera was ready. The bear coughed and charged without hesitation.

Carl's heart leaped as he saw through the port in the gondola floor that the grizzly was rearing onto its hind legs. The beast slashed the air with its claws, black and worn by use to chisel edges instead of points. The gondola lurched as the Professor jerked his knees up to his chest, supporting his whole weight on his arms. Then they were safely past. Carl turned to call something to Erlenwanger, and five thousand feet above them a cloud passed before the sun. The hydrogen cooled and shrank. The airship lost buoyancy almost as suddenly as if Carl had dumped a tank. *The Enterprise* dropped ten feet to a new equilibrium. The end of the rope ladder clattered on the ground. The gondola itself was well within the range of claws that could rip open trees to get at the honey within.

The grizzly coughed again and charged, as quickly as a cat sighting prey. Professor Erlenwanger had pulled his torso into the gondola. Carl leaped from the controls to drag him the rest of the way to safety. The older man, gripping the jamb with his left hand, drew his pistol. The shots rattled like a

dozen lathes cracking, sharp but overwhelmed by
the blasts of the bullets themselves bursting on
the ground beneath. Shards of rock sang off the
underside of the gondola. One bit hummed through
the doorway to sting Carl's outstretched hand. The
snarl deep in the bear's throat *whuffed*! out instead as a startled bleat. The Professor laid his
pistol on the gondola floor. "Now, Carl," he gasped.
"If you would."

Carl grasped the older man under both armpits
and hefted him aboard. Molly had slammed all her
levers upward when she realized what was happening. The airship was soaring and already near
its normal cruising altitude. Beneath them the
grizzly sat back on its haunches, washing its face
with both paws.

Professor Erlenwanger unstrapped his camera
and slid the door shut. He was breathing heavily.
Carl had returned to the helm but kept only steer-
age way, uncertain of what the Professor would
want to do. Molly had leveled them off at a thousand feet again. She was beginning to regain some
of her normal color. "I think we can resume course,"
Erlenwanger said at last. He picked up the little
handgun and extracted the magazine from its grip.

"You shot the bear?" Carl asked, watching the
older man. He was thumbing brass cartridges into
the magazine from a box that had shared the drawer
with the pistol.

Professor Erlenwanger looked up sharply. "I fired
into the ground in front of the bear," he said.
"That was sufficient." He slid the reloaded magazine back into the butt of the pistol, his lips silently working as he considered whether or not to

continue. "I dare say it is sometimes necessary to kill," he said finally. "In order to stay alive, or sometimes for better reasons. But it isn't a decision to be taken lightly or as anything but a last resort."

Erlenwanger shook his head as if to clear it of his present mood. He set the weapon and the box of ammunition back into the drawer and closed it. Smiling he added, "It's an automatic pocket pistol of European manufacture. And I suppose you're familiar with the use of explosive bullets in hunting dangerous game?"

Carl nodded. "I've heard of that."

"Well," the Professor said, "I had a—Belgian gunsmith of great ability make up some explosive rounds for the pistol. On stony soil they produced quite a startling effect, don't you think?"

Molly took a deep, thankful breath. "More to the point," she said, "the bear thought it was startling."

"Goodness," said the Professor, noticing that his wireless apparatus still sat out on the ledge, "I'd best complete my report, hadn't I? Especially now that I've had a real adventure!" Chuckling, he sat down at the key again as the airship swept steadily westward through the calm air.

Professor Erlenwanger looked at the altimeter, frowned, and glanced over at Molly's bank of controls. They were all uncomfortably close to the top. Despite that, *The Enterprise* was within five hundred feet of the ground. The dry snow blew like fog around the trunks of the conifers marching up the slopes. "Between the thin air at this altitude and the film of ice we're gathering," the Professor said, "we need maximum lift. And I'm afraid that there's enough condensate in several of the chambers that we aren't getting the lift we should be."

Carl frowned back. "Are we in danger?" he asked, carefully controlling his voice. He did not want to sound as though he were on the edge of panic—but five hundred feet was a long way to fall, and the ground beneath looked as hard as a millstone.

"Oh, goodness," the Professor said, blinking in concern at the impression he had given. "Oh, not at all. I just propose to land in a suitable location— I'm sure there must be one." He squinted through the forward windows. The cabin heat kept the center of each pane clear. The edges, where the aluminum frames conveyed the warmth to the outside more swiftly, were blind with frost. "I'll vent and dry Tanks Three and Seven—they seem to be the wettest—and recharge them. It may not be the most attractive country on which to set down, but I think I can promise you that we will do so gently."

"There's a clear hill over there," Molly said, pointing so that her finger left a smudge on the glass. "But you'll need water to refill the tanks, won't you?"

"Oh, that's quite all right," Erlenwanger explained, already swinging the helm. "We can melt the snow for electrolysis, and goodness knows there's enough snow. See if you can bring us down just a little above the tallest trees, my dear."

Despite the gusty winds and the lack of anyone

on the ground to set their grapnel for them, Professor Erlenwanger brought them to the smooth landing he had promised. Twigs, poking through the crust of snow which had come early even for the mountains, snapped beneath the weight of *The Enterprise*. "Well," said the Professor, "I think the first order of business is to clear the chambers, don't you?" He gripped one of the vent levers and tried to slide it to the side. It did not move. All three people looked momentarily blank. "Of course," Erlenwanger said, "the ice! The valve mechanism must be frozen shut."

"Something we can fix?" asked Carl, frowning again but without the immediate concern that the prospect of crashing into the ground had raised in him.

"Well, yes," agreed the older man, "but it means climbing up to chip the valve loose, and I'm afraid it's really too near dusk to do that now. I had hoped to have the chambers refilling overnight."

Carl shrugged. "No problem," he said. "I'll take a lantern up with me and do it now."

Erlenwanger frowned. Then he, too, shrugged and said, "Well, that's all right, I suppose. But don't even think of getting above any other airship with an open flame. Blocking the percolation of hydrogen through the very atoms of the skin was perhaps the greatest of the advances incorporated into *The Enterprise*—" his grin flashed—"though it isn't one I would expect an investigator of the present time to note."

Carl drew on the sheepskin jacket and cowhide work gloves the Professor had bought him at a rail siding the night before. Molly handed him the kerosine lamp she had just lighted. It whispered deep in its throat, and the yellow glow it cast was friendlier and more human than that of the chilly electrical elements. Carl stepped outside, bracing himself against the expected eddy of wind-blown snow. The lantern rocked in his hand but did not go out. He slammed the door and began to climb the open ladder just astern of it, up the side of the gas compartment. There was a slick of ice crackling on the rungs, and the lamp in his left hand made climbing harder; but Carl had carried shingles to the roof of the barn in a drizzle, and this was nothing beyond his capacity.

The snow and the twilight made the evening seem bright, but the vents were deep in a shadowed recess. A catwalk ran along the airship's spine. Without the lantern the trip would have been vain, though the yellow light paled everywhere but where it was needed. Carl set the lamp down on the walk and rapped the valve with the bolster of his clasp knife. He took the glove off his left hand and opened the blade to scrape the joints in the brass.

Movement at the woodline caught the corner of Carl's eye. A pair of steers bolted into the open. One had horns which had been cropped to stumps shorter than its ears. Carl stared, squinting into the failing light. "Professor!" he called, just as the light on the gondola's prow spread its broad fan down the hillside. The floodlight glared red from the eyes of the cattle and the three horses following them. The nearest of the three riders was wrapped in a dark-colored blanket. Even his hands, gripping a long-barreled rifle across the saddle-

bow, were hidden. Trotting his pinto just behind
the first rider was a second whose straight black
hair fell to his shoulders. A youthful whoop died in
his throat at the blaze of light. His left arm, up-
raised with an unstrung bow, jerked down as his
right hand sawed the pinto's reins back.

The third Indian was far the oldest, though his
twin braids were still so black as to give the lie to a
face wrinkled like walnut burl. He wore a buffalo
robe—as old, perhaps, as he was—pinned at the
shoulder but open down the front to display a
buckskin shirt. The old cap-and-ball revolver thrust
through his waistband was nickeled. It sparkled
like a faceted mirror in the instant before the rider
slid it out and down into the shadow of his horse's
neck.

The gondola door rumbled open, thumping
against its stop. Carl peered over the side. The
curve of the buoyancy chamber hid the Professor
until the older man stepped out in front of his
floodlight. His shadow flashed suddenly toward
the Indians. Its outline was misshapen with the
angles of camera and tripod.

"Professor!" Carl called, "those aren't reserva-
tion cows!" If the older man heard Carl, he did not
understand. He continued to walk downhill toward
the Indians, calling to them in a language unfamiliar
to Carl. Carl swung down the ladder, leaving skin
from the palm of his left hand frozen to the top
rung. He was muttering an unconscious prayer.

The steers had shied from the light, disappearing again into the trees. The eldest of the riders
spoke. The rifleman swung his weapon clear of the
blanket. The knob of its bolt handle, polished by

decades of wear, winked. As Carl jumped into the gondola, a trick of the breeze brought Erlenwanger's words up the hill: "Why, my goodness, a Dreyse needle gun here!"

"Where's the lantern!" Molly cried.

"Jesus Christ, I left it!" Carl shouted, slamming open the pistol drawer. The cartridge box flew out, spilling the deadly brass to roll in a shifting pattern on the floor. Carl leaned out the doorway, leveling the unfamiliar pistol.

Molly vented Tank Three. The hydrogen bathed the lantern and ignited in a blue glare spraying a hundred feet in the air. The pinto reared, spilling its young rider. The rifle muzzle wavered from Erlenwanger to the airship, then back into the woods as the leading rider wheeled his mount. Molly opened Tank Seven. The eldest Indian fought his horse for an instant, the flare from his revolver no harsher than that of his eyes. Then he gave the beast its head to gallop into the forest, followed by the pinto and the third of the cattle thieves. That last Indian was holding the pinto's reins with both hands and running along beside it. A steer bawled from a distance. Then the night was silent again, leaving the Professor poised awkwardly in the light of his own airship.

Erlenwanger turned and began trudging up the hill. Molly cut the floodlight. Carl lowered the pistol which he had not fired. It apparently had a safety catch somewhere, like a hammerless shotgun. His left palm was burning and he noticed the blood for the first time.

Professor Erlenwanger slid the door shut behind him and set down his camera carefully. "One

can get carried away and make mistakes," he said
softly. "They were doing something illegal; and of
course we frightened them." He looked from Carl
to Molly and back again. "When one does something foolish, as I just did, it's important that one
have friends with better sense and quick minds.
Thank you both, for my life and for much more."

Carl set the pistol down to take and squeeze one
of the hands the older man stretched to both of
them.

"Less than fifty years old," the Professor said,
apparently to himself, "and look at it even now."

Molly leaned forward for a better look. She had
stared down on Boston, however, and the skeletal
mass of lights in the pre-dawn did not impress
her. Carl had never seen anything like San Francisco in his life. "Oh, if Dad could only be here,"
he said. "He wouldn't brag on his trip to Kansas
City ever again."

"You can follow the veins of the city out beyond
the lighted heart," Professor Erlenwanger said.
"Every one of those blue sparks in the collector
arm of a trolley, bringing the late shifts home,
carrying the earliest workers in to their jobs. Some
times I think that cities live too, and that one day
they will send travellers back in time to record
their own births."

The airship had met a mass of cool air over the
bay and dropped to about five hundred feet. Molly
started to nudge a pair of levers up, but the Professor's hand stayed her. "No," he said. "I'm going
to land here."

"Are we staying in San Francisco?" asked Carl,

a little surprised because of the Professor's previous avoidance of populous areas. But after all, they were on the West Coast, now; there was nowhere further to go.

The Professor cocked the helm slightly, searching the terrain below so that he did not have to look at his companions. The sky beyond the hills was metallically lighter. "I'm going to land you here and go on," he said. "I've enjoyed your company more than I can tell you; but it is time for me to leave. I am not—" he swallowed—"simply abandoning you; I will leave you with five hundred dollars in gold pieces—"

"Professor, *no*!" Molly cried, her hand shooting out to touch but not grip his elbow. "We didn't come with you for the money—but don't leave us!"

Erlenwanger's fingers squeezed the girl's hand to his tweed sleeve briefly, then detached it. "You didn't come with me to save my life, either; but you saved it," he said firmly. "The money is something for which I have no further use anyway." he touched his lips with his tongue. "Please believe me when I say that you cannot accompany me further. It is not something I say lightly. We will meet again, I promise; though that lies still in the future."

Very quietly, Carl said, "I'm not going back to the farm. Not now."

"Bring us down to one hundred feet, please, Molly," Professor Erlenwanger said. He half-turned from the view forward. "You needn't go back, you know," he said. "Kummel and Son, the meat canners on Market Street, will have openings for a stock clerk and a receptionist this morning."

Carl frowned. "I'm not a stock clerk," he said.

The Professor shook his head abruptly. "You're a strong young man who has worked with cattle all his life. You're bright and you're honest—and you will remind Mr. Kummel of his only son, who died last week of influenza." Erlenwanger tongued his lips again. "Kummel's is a very small firm now— only a few years ago it was a butcher shop. But if gold should be discovered on the coasts of Alaska and Canada, the inevitable rush will be supplied from San Francisco. A firm with a solid reputation will be able to expand greatly; and employees who have been trustworthy in small things . . . will be entrusted with great ones. You may live to endow your grandson's education at . . . the California Institute of Technology, for instance."

Erlenwanger trimmed his prop pitch fine. "Set us down gently, now," he said as the landing legs squealed and extended. Molly was blinking back tears, but her fingers worked the controls with practiced delicacy. The spotlight of *The Enterprise* stabbed narrowly, then flooded a barren area at a touch of the Professor's wrist. Gas standards reached up forlornly, installed but unlighted along a three-block line of vacant lots. The older man coarsened the prop to give him a touch more helm and bring the airship's nose around. Carl swallowed and slid the door open. "I don't think we will need the grapnel," Erlenwanger said. They were barely moving forward, sinking as slowly as bodies in a still, cold lake. A moment before they touched, Molly eased back on a lever. The nose tilted up minusculy and the rear landing leg cut the rank grass before the front did. They were down with less jolt than a man got stepping out of bed.

The Professor opened the sleeping compartment and handed out the two small suitcases that were all Carl's and Molly's possessions. They took them silently, Molly holding the grip with both hands and her lower lip with her teeth. Even the cases had been the Professor's gift. Erlenwanger slipped a heavy purse into the side pocket of the girl's coat. He kissed her very gently on the cheek, just forward of her ear. "There'll be a trolley in two minutes," he said without pulling his watch from his vest pocket. "One thing," he added. "There is both good and bad in every life, every age. But always remember what—relatives of mine told me when I was very young: you must never give up on Mankind. Because Mankind never quite gives up on itself." He shook Carl's hand and turned him to the open door.

Carl stepped down. Molly followed, her head bent over. Neither of them spoke. From the gondola behind them they heard the Professor call, "Goodby, Pops. Goodby, Mama Gudeint. I'm proud to have known you."

Air billowed sluggishly as *The Enterprise* rose. Carl and Molly raised their faces to watch the airship. The great cylinder was climbing very swiftly on an even keel. A few hundred feet up it caught the sunrise over the hills and blazed like a plow-share in God's forge. The suitcases were forgotten on the ground. Molly's fingers squeezed Carl's in fear. "What's happening to it?" she demanded.

The blur of light was higher, now, and farther

west, but it was growing fainter more quickly than it rose. It seemed to merge with the sky or something beyond the sky. Carl licked his lips. "Goodby," he whispered. He squeezed Molly's hand in return.

Still staring at the empty sky, he said, "It's all right. Wherever he's going, he'll get there. And so will we . . . and it'll be all right."

I love dinosaurs. The first book I bought—at age 6—was Science Guide #70: Dinosaurs, by Edwin H. Colbert, ordered from the American Museum of Natural History (and on my shelves today in its original mailing envelope).

My interest was tweaked back to full life in the '70s by the new data and theories about dinosaurs— that they were warm-blooded, active, and reasonably intelligent. But "Time Safari" was less about dinosaurs than it was about men and women hunting the beasts; and hunters are something of an exotic group themselves.

I did a little hunting when I was younger, but I gave it up when I decided that I really didn't like to kill things. That's a personal statement, not a moral judgment; and my friends include a man who has done a considerable amount of trophy hunting. (His Schultz and Larsen rifle appears in the story; he doesn't.)

I have also read—for pleasure, but again as research—all the memoirs I could lay my hands on by big-game hunters and hunting guides. Such works don't tell you any more about animals than a line infantryman can tell you about strategy— but they (and line soldiers) can give you a lot of insight into human beings.

My affection for "Time Safari" goes beyond the fun I had in writing it. My editor asked me to turn the idea into a novel by writing another pair of novellas to link with the original one. (The result, also titled Time Safari, *is still in print as of this writing.)*

And on the basis of that novel, I got the first of

the multi-book contracts that permitted me to be-
come a full-time freelance writer.

I always knew a love for dinosaurs would stand
me in good stead.

TIME SAFARI

The tyrannosaur's bellow made everyone jump except Vickers, the guide. The beast's nostrils flared, sucking in the odor of the light helicopter and the humans aboard it. It stalked forward.

"The largest land predator that ever lived," whispered one of the clients.

"A lot of people think that," said Vickers in what most of the rest thought was agreement.

There was nothing in the graceful advance of the tyrannosaur to suggest its ten ton mass, until its tail side-swiped a flower-trunked cycad. The tree was six inches thick at the point of impact, and it sheared at that point without time to bend.

"Oh dear," the female photographer said. Her brother's grip on the chair arms was giving him leverage to push its cushion against the steel backplate.

The tyrannosaur's strides shifted the weight of its deep torso, counterbalanced by the swinging of its neck and tail. At each end of the head's arcs, the beast's eyes glared alternately at its prey. Except for the size, the watchers could have been observing a grackle on the lawn; but it was a grackle seen from a june-bug's perspective.

"Goddam, he won't hold still!" snarled Salmes, the old-money client, the know-it-all. Vickers smiled. The tyrannosaur chose that moment to pause and bellow again. It was now a dozen feet from the helicopter, a single claw-tipped stride. If the blasting sound left one able, it was an ideal time to admire the beauty of the beast's four-foot head. Its teeth were irregular in length and placement, providing in sum a pair of yellowish, four-inch deep, saws. They fit together too loosely to shear; but with the power of the tyrannosaur's jaw muscles driving them, they could tear the flesh from any creature on Earth—in any age.

The beast's tongue was like a crocodile's, attached for its full length to the floor of its mouth. Deep blue with purple veins, it had a floral appearance. The tongue was without sensory purpose and existed only to help by rhythmic flexions to ram chunks of meat down the predator's throat. The beast's head scales were the size of little fingernails, somewhat finer than those of the torso. Their coloration was consistent—a base of green nearing black, blurred by rosettes of a much lighter, yellowish, hue. Against that background, the tyrannosaur's eyes stood out like needlepoints dripping blood.

"They don't always give you that pause," Vickers said aloud. "Sometimes they come—"

The tyrannosaur lunged forward. Its lower jaw, half-opened during its bugling challenge, dropped to full gape. Someone shouted. The action blurred as the hologram dissolved a foot or two from the arc of clients.

Vickers thumbed up the molding lights. He walked to the front of the conference room, holding the remote control with which the hotel had provided him. The six clients viewed him with varied expressions. The brother and sister photographers, dentists named McPherson, whispered in obvious delight. They were best able to appreciate the quality of the hologram and to judge their own ability to duplicate it. Any fear they had felt during the presentation was buried in their technical enthusiasm afterward.

The two individual gunners were a general contractor named Mears and Brewer, a meat-packing magnate. Brewer was a short man whose full moustache and balding head made him a caricature of a Victorian industrialist. He loosened his collar and massaged his flushed throat with his thumb and index finger. Mears, built like an All-Pro linebacker after twenty years of retirement, was frowning. He still gripped the chair arms in a way that threatened the plastic. Those were normal reactions to one of Vickers' pre-hunt presentations. It meant the clients had learned the necessity of care in a way no words or still photos could have taught them. Conversely, that familiarity made them less likely to freeze when they faced the real thing.

The presentations unfortunately did not have

any useful effect on people like the Salmes. Or at least on Jonathan Salmes, blond and big but with the look of a movie star, not a football player. Money and leisure could not make Salmes younger, but they made him look considerably less than his real age of forty years. His face was now set in its habitual pattern of affected boredom. As not infrequently happens, the affectation created its own reality and robbed Salmes of whatever pleasure three generations of oil money might otherwise have brought him.

Adrienne Salmes was as blond and as perfectly preserved as her husband, but she had absorbed the presentation with obvious interest. Time safaris were the property of wealth alone, and she had all the trapping of that wealth. Re-emitted light made her dress—and its wearer—the magnet of all eyes in a dim room, and her silver lame wristlet responded to voice commands with a digital display. That sort of money could buy beauty like Adrienne Salmes'; but it could not buy the inbred assurance with which she wore that beauty. She forestalled any tendency the guide might have had to think that her personality stopped with the skin by asking, "Mr. Vickers, would you have waited to see if the tyrannosaurus would stop, or would you have shot while it was still at some distance from the helicopter?"

"Umm?" said Vickers in surprise. "Oh, wait, I suppose. If he doesn't stop, there's still time for a shot; and your guide, whether that's me or Dieter, will be backing you. That's a good question." He cleared his throat. "And that brings up an important point," he went on. "We don't shoot large carnivores on foot. Mostly, the shooting platform—the helicopter—won't be dropping as low as it was for the pictures, either. For these holos I was sitting beside the photographer, sweating blood the whole time that nothing would go wrong. If the bird had stuttered or the pilot hadn't timed it just right, I'd have had just about enough time to try for a brain shot. Anywhere else and we'd have been in that fellow's gut faster'n you could swallow a sardine." He smiled. It made him look less like a bank clerk, more like a bank robber. "Three sardines," he corrected himself.

"If you used a man-sized rifle, you'd have been a damned sight better off," offered Jonathan Salmes. He had one ankle crossed on the other knee, and his chair reclined at a 45° angle.

Vickers looked at the client. They were about of an age, though the guide was several inches shorter and not as heavily built. "Yes, well," he said. "That's a thing I need to talk about. Rifles." He ran a hand through his light brown hair.

"Yeah, I couldn't figure that either," said Mears. "I mean, I read the stuff you sent, about big-bores not being important." The contractor frowned. "I don't figure that. I mean, God almighty, as big as one of those mothers is, I wouldn't feel overgunned with a one-oh-five howitzer . . . and I sure don't think my .458 Magnum's any too big."

"Right, right," Vickers said, nodding his head. His discomfort at facing a group of humans was obvious. "A .458's fine if you can handle it—and I'm sure you can. I'm sure any of you can," he added, raising his eyes and sweeping the group again. "What I said, what I meant, was that size isn't important, penetration and bullet placement are what's important. The .458 penetrates fine—with solids—I hope to God all of you know to bring solids, not soft-nosed bullets. If you're not comfortable with that much recoil, though, you're liable to flinch. And that means you'll miss, even at the ranges we shoot dinos at. A wounded dino running around, anywhere up to a hundred tons of him, and that's when things get messy. You and everybody around is better off with you with a gun that doesn't make you flinch."

"That's all balls, you know," Salmes remarked conversationally. He glanced around at the other clients. "If you're man enough, I'll tell you what to carry." He looked at Vickers, apparently expecting an attempt to silence him. The guide eyed him with a somewhat bemused expression. "A .500 Salmes, that's what," the big client asserted loudly. "It was designed for me specially by Marquart and Wells, gun and bullets both. It uses shortened fifty-caliber machinegun cases, loaded to give twelve thousand foot-pounds of energy. That's enough to knock a tyrannosaurus right flat on his ass. It's the only gun that you'll be safe with on a hunt like this." He nodded toward Vickers to put a period to his statement.

"Yes, well," Vickers repeated. His expression shifted, hardening. He suddenly wore the visage that an animal might have glimpsed over the sights of his rifle. "Does anybody else feel that they need a—a *gun* like that to bring down anything they'll see on this safari?"

No one nodded to the question when it was put

that way. Adrienne Salmes smiled. She was a tall
woman, as tall as Vickers himself was.

"Okay, then," the guide said. "I guess I can skip
the lesson in basic physics. Mr. Salmes, if you can
handle your rifle, that's all that matters to me. If
you can't handle it, you've still got time to get
something useful instead. Now—"

"Now wait a goddamned minute!" Salmes said,
his foot thumping to the floor. His face had flushed
under its even tan. "Just what do you mean by
that crack? You're going to teach *me* physics?"

"I don't think Mr. Vickers—" began Miss McPherson.

"I want an explanation!" Salmes demanded.

"All right, no problem," said Vickers. He rubbed
his forehead and winced in concentration. "What
you're talking about," he said to the floor, "is
kinetic energy. That's a function of the square of
the velocity. Well and good, but it won't knock
anything down. What knocks things down is momentum, that's weight times velocity, not velocity
squared. Anything that the bullet knocks down,
the butt of the rifle would knock down by recoiling—
which is why I encourage clients to carry something they can handle." He raised his eyes and
pinned Salmes with them. "I've never yet had a
client who weighed twelve thousand pounds, Mr.
Salmes. And so I'm always tempted to tell people
who talk about 'knock-down power' that they're
full to the eyes."

Mrs. Salmes giggled. The other clients did not,
but all the faces save Salmes' own bore more-than-
hinted smiles. Vickers suspected that the hand-
some blond man had gotten on everyone else's

nerves in the bar before the guide had opened the conference suite.

Salmes purpled to the point of an explosion. The guide glanced down again and raised his hand before saying, "Look, all other things being equal, I'd sooner hit a dino—or a man—with a big bullet than a little one. But if you put the bullet in the brain or the heart, it really doesn't matter much how big it is. And especially with a dino, if you put the bullet anywhere else, it's not going to do much good at all."

"Look," said Brewer, hunching forward and spreading his hands palms down, "I don't flinch, and I got a .378 Weatherby that's got penetration up the ass. But—" he turned his hands over and over again as he looked at them—"I'm not Annie Oakley, you know. If I have to hit a brain the size of a walnut with a four-foot skull around it—well, I may as well take a camera myself instead of the gun. I'll have *something* to show people that way."

Salmes snorted—which could have gotten him one of Brewer's big, capable fists in the face, Vickers thought. "That's another good question," the guide said. "Very good. Well. Brain shots are great if you know where to put them. I attached charts of a lot of the common dinos with the material I sent out, look them over and decide if you want to try.

"Thing is," he continued, "taking the top off a dino's heart'll drop it in a couple hundred yards. They don't charge when they're heart-shot, they just run till they fall. And we shoot from up close, as close as ten yards. They don't take any notice of you, the big ones, you could touch them if you wanted. You just need enough distance to be able to pick your shot. You see—" he gestured toward Brewer with both index fingers—"you won't have any problem hitting a heart the size of a bushel basket from thirty feet away. Brains—well, skin hunters have been killing crocs with brain shots for a century. Crocodile brains are just as small as a tyrannosaur's, and the skulls are just as big. Back where we're going, there were some that were a damn sight bigger than tyrannosaurs'. But don't feel you have to. And anyway, it'd spoil your trophy if you brain-shot some of the small-headed kind."

Brewer cleared his throat. "Hey," he said, "I'd like to go back to something you said before. About using the helicopter."

"Right, the shooting platform," Vickers agreed.

"Look," said the meat-packer, "I mean . . . well, that's sort of like shooting wolves from a plane, isn't it? I mean, no, well, Christ . . . not sporting, is it?"

Vickers shrugged. "I won't argue with you," he said, "and you don't have to use the platform if you don't want to. But it's the only way you can be allowed to shoot the big carnosaurs. I'm sorry, that's just how it is." He leaned forward and spoke more intensely, popping the fingers of his left hand against his right palm. "It's as sporting as shooting tigers from elephant-back, I guess, or shooting lions over a butchered cow. The head looks just as big over your mantle. And there's no sport at all for me to tell my bosses how one of my clients was eaten. They aren't bad, the big dinos, people aren't in their scale so they'll pretty much ignore you. Wound one and it's kitty bar the door. These aren't

plant eaters, primed to run if there's trouble. These
are carnivores we're talking about, animals that
spend most of their waking lives killing or looking
for something to kill. They *will* connect the noise
of a shot with the pain, and they *will* go after
whoever made the noise."

The guide paused and drew back. More calmly
he concluded, "So carnosaurs you'll hunt from the
platform. Or not at all."

"Well, what happens if they come to us?" Salmes
demanded with recovered belligerance. "Right up
to the camp, say? You can't keep us from shooting
then."

"I guess this is a good time to discuss arrangements for the camp," Vickers said, approaching
the question indirectly. "There's four of us staff
with the safari, two guides—that's me and Dieter
Jost—and two pilots. One pilot, one guide, and
one client—one of you—go up in the platform
every day. You'll each have two chances to bag a
big carnosaur. They're territorial and not too thick
on the ground, but there's almost certain to be at
least one tyrannosaur and a pack of gorgosaurs in
practical range. The other guide takes out the rest
of the clients on foot, well, on motorized wagons
you could say, ponies we call them. And the pilot
who isn't flying the platform doubles as camp guard.
He's got a heavy machinegun—" the guide smiled—
"a Russian .51 cal. Courtesy of your hosts for the
tour, the Israeli government. It'll stop dinos and
light tanks without a bit of bother."

Vickers' face lost its crinkling of humor. "If there's
any shooting to be done from the camp," he continued, "that's what does it. Unless Dieter or me

specifically tell you otherwise. We're not going to
have the intrusion vehicle trampled by a herd of
dinos that somebody spooked right into it. If something happens to the intrusion vehicle, we don't
go home." Vickers smiled again. "That might be
okay with me, but I don't think any of the rest of
you want to have to explain to the others how you
stuck them in the Cretaceous."

"That would be a paradox, wouldn't it, Mr
Vickers?" Miss McPherson said. "That is, uh, human beings living in the Cretaceous? So it couldn't
happen. Not that I'd want any chances taken with
the vehicle, of course."

Vickers shrugged with genuine disinterest.
"Ma'am, if you want to talk about paradox, you
need Dr. Galil and his team. So far as I understand
it, though, if there's not a change in the future,
then there's no paradox; and if there *is* a change,
then there's no paradox either because the change—
well, the change is reality then."

Mr. McPherson leaned forward with a frown.
"Well, surely two bodies—the same body—can't
exist simultaneously," he insisted. If he and his
sister had been bored with the discussion of fire-
arms, then they had recovered their interest with
mention of the mechanics of time transport.

"Sure they can," the guide said with the asper-
ity of someone who had been asked the same
question too often. He waved his hand back and
forth as if erasing the thought from a chalk board.
"They do. Every person, every gun or can of food,
contains at least some atoms that were around in
the Cretaceous—or the Pre-Cambrian, for that matter. It doesn't matter to the atoms whether they

call themselves Henry Vickers or the third red-
wood from the big rock. . . ." He paused. "There's
just one rule that I've heard for true from people
who know," he continued at last. "If you travel
into the future, you travel as energy. And you
don't come back at all."

Mears paled and looked at the ceiling. People
got squeamish about the damnedest things, thought
Vickers. Being converted into energy . . . or being
eaten . . . or being drowned in dark water lighted
only by the dying radiance of your mind—but he
broke away from that thought, a little sweat on his
forehead with the strain of it. He continued aloud,
"There's no danger for us, heading back into the
far past. But the intrusion vehicle can't be cali-
brated closer than 5,000 years plus or minus so
far. The, the research side—" he had almost said
'the military side,' knowing the two were synony-
mous; knowing also that the Israeli government
disapproved intensely of statements to that effect—
"was trying for the recent past—" 1948, but that
was another thing you didn't admit you knew—
"and they put a man into the future instead. After
Dr. Galil had worked out the math, they moved
the lab and cleared a quarter-mile section of Tel
Aviv around the old site. They figure the poor
bastard will show up sometime in the next few
thousand years . . . and nobody better be sharing
the area when he does."

Vickers frowned at himself. "Well, that's probably more than the, the government wants me to
say about the technical side," he said. "And anyway, I'm not the one to ask. Let's get back to the
business itself—which I do know something about."

"You've said that this presentation and the written material are all yours," Adrienne Salmes said with a wave of her hand. "I'd like to know why."

Vickers blinked at the unexpected question. He looked from Mrs. Salmes to the other clients, all of them but her husband staring back at him with interest. The guide laughed. "I like my job," he said. "A century ago, I'd have been hiking through Africa with a Mauser, selling ivory every year or so when I came in from the bush." He rubbed his left cheekbone where a disk of shiny skin remained from a boil of twenty years before. "that sort of life was gone before I was born," he went on. "What I have is the closest thing there is to it now."

Adrienne Salmes was nodding. Mr. McPherson put his own puzzled frown into words and said, "I don't see what that has to do with, well, you holding these sessions, though."

"It's like this," Vickers said, watching his fingers tent and flatten against each other. "They pay me, the government does, a very good salary that I personally don't have much use for." Jonathan Salmes snorted, but the guide ignored him. "I use it to make my job easier," he went on, "by sending the clients all the data I've found useful in the five years I've been travelling back to the Cretaceous . . . and elsewhere, but mostly the Cretaceous. Because if people go back with only what they hear in the advertising or from folks who need to make a buck or a name with their stories, they'll have problems when they see the real thing. Which means problems for me. So a month before each safari, I rent a suite in New York or Frankfurt or wherever the hell seems reasonable, and I offer to give a presentation to the clients. Nobody has to come, but most people do." He scanned the group. "All of you did, for instance. It makes life easier for me."

He cleared his throat. "Well, in another way, we're here to make life easier for you," he went on. "I've brought along holos of the standard game animals you'll be seeing." He dimmed the lights and stepped toward the back of the room. "First the sauropods, the big long-necks. The most impressive things you'll see in the Cretaceous, but a disappointing trophy because of the small heads. . . ."

"All right, ladies and gentlemen," said Dieter Jost. Vickers always left the junior guide responsible for the social chores when both of them were present. "Please line up here along the wall until the Doctor Galil directs us onto the vehicle."

The members of Cretaceous Safari 87 backed against the hangar wall, their weapons or cameras in their hands. The guides and the two pilots, Washman and Brady, watched the clients rather than the crew preparing the intrusion vehicle. You could never tell what sort of mistake a tensed-up layman would make with a loaded weapon in his or her hands.

In case the clients were not laymen at all, there were four guards seated in a balcony-height alcove in the opposite wall. They wore civilian clothes, but the submachineguns they carried were just as military as their ID cards. The Israelis were, of all people, alert to the chance that a commando raid would be aimed at an intrusion vehicle and its

technical staff. For that reason, the installation was
in an urban setting from which there could be no
quick escape; and its corridors and rooms, including the gaping hangar itself, were better guarded
than the Defense Ministry had been during the
most recent shooting war.

Dr. Galil and his staff were only occasionally
visible to the group on the floor of the hangar. The
intrusion vehicle rested on four braced girders
twenty feet high. On its underside, a cylindrical
probe was repeatedly blurring and reappearing.
The technicians received data from the probe on
instruments plugged into various sockets on the
vehicle. Eighty million years in the past, the
cylinder was sampling its surroundings on a score
of wavelengths. When necessary, Dr. Galil himself changed control settings. Despite that care,
there was no certainty of the surface over which
the travellers would appear—or how far over or
under it they would appear. The long legs gave
the intrusion vehicle a margin that might otherwise have been achieved by a longer drop than
anything aboard would have survived.

"Well, this is it, hey?" said Jonathan Salmes,
speaking to Don Washman. To do so, Salmes had
to talk through his wife, who ignored him in turn.
"A chance to hunt the most dangerous damned
creatures ever to walk the Earth!" Salmes' hands,
evenly tanned like every other inch of exposed
skin on him, tightened still further on the beautiful bolt-action rifle he carried.

Washman's smile went no further than Adrienne Salmes. The pilot was a big man also. The 40
mm grenade launcher he held looked like a sawed-

off shotgun with him for scale. "Gee, Mr. Salmes," he said in false surprise. "People our age all had a chance to learn the most dangerous game on Earth popped out of a spider hole with an AK-47 in its hands. All the *men* did, at least."

Vickers scowled. "Don," he said. But Washman was a pilot, not a PR man. Besides, Salmes had coming anything of the sort he got.

Adrienne Salmes turned to Washman and laughed.

A heavy-set man climbed down from the intrusion vehicle and strolled across the concrete floor toward the waiting group. Like the guards, he wore an ordinary business suit. He kept his hands in his pants pockets. "Good evening, ladies and sirs," he said in accented English. "I am Mr. Stern; you might say, the company manager. I trust the preparations for your tour have been satisfactory?" He eyed Dieter, then Vickers, his face wearing only a bland smile.

"All present and accounted for," said Dieter in German. At his side, Mears nodded enthusiastically.

"By God," said Jonathan Salmes with recovered vigor, "I just want this gizmo to pop out right in front of a tyrannosaurus rex. Then I'll pop *him*, and I'll double your fees for a bonus!"

Don Washman smirked, but Vickers' scowl was for better reason than that. "Ah, Mr. Salmes," the guide said, "I believe Mr. Brewer drew first shot of the insertion. Fire discipline is something we *do* have to insist on."

"Naw, that's okay," said Brewer unexpectedly. He looked sheepishly at Vickers, then looked away. "We made an agreement on that," he added. "I don't mind paying for something I want; but I don't mind selling something I don't need, either, you see?"

"In any case," said Stern, "even the genius of Dr. Galil cannot guarantee to place you in front of a suitable dinosaur. I must admit to some apprehension, in fact, that some day we will land an intrusion vehicle in mid-ocean." He gestured both elbows outward, like wings flapping. "Ah, this is a magnificent machine; but not, I fear, very precise." He smiled.

"Not precise enough to . . . put a battalion of paratroops in the courtyard of the Temple in 70 AD, you mean?" suggested Adrienne Salmes with a trace of a smile herself.

Vickers' gut sucked in. Stern's first glance was to check the position of the guards. The slightly seedy good-fellowship he had projected was gone. "Ah, you Americans," Stern said in a voice that was itself a warning. "Always making jokes about the impossible. But you must understand that in a small and threatened country like ours, there are some jokes one does not make." His smile now had no humor. Adrienne Salmes returned it with a wintry one of her own. If anyone had believed her question was chance rather than a deliberate goad, the smile disabused them.

Atop the intrusion vehicle, an indicator began buzzing in a continuous rhythm. It was not a loud sound. The high ceiling of the hangar drank it almost completely. The staff personnel looked up sharply. Stern nodded again to Vickers and began to walk toward a ground-level exit. He was whistling under his breath. After a moment, a pudgy man stepped to the edge of the vehicle and looked down. He had a white moustache and a fringe of hair as crinkled as rock wool. "I believe we are ready, gentlemen," he said.

Dieter nodded. "We're on the way, then, Dr. Galil," he replied to the older man. Turning back to the safari group, he went on, "Stay in line, please. Hold the handrail with one hand as you mount the steps, and do be very careful to keep your weapons vertical. Accidents happen, you know." Dieter gave a brief nod of emphasis and led the way. The flight of metal steps stretched in a steep diagonal between two of the vehicle's legs. Vickers brought up the rear of the line, unhurried but feeling the tingle at the base of the neck which always preceded time travel with him. It amused Vickers to find himself trying to look past the two men directly in front of him to watch Adrienne Salmes as she mounted the stairs. the woman wore a baggy suit like the rest of them, rip-stopped Kelprin which would shed water and still breathe with 80% efficiency. On her the mottled coveralls had an interest which time safari clients, male or female, could rarely bring to such garments.

The floor of the intrusion vehicle was perforated steel from which much of the antislip coating had been worn. Where the metal was bare, it had a delicate patina of rust. In the center of the twenty-foot square, the safari's gear was neatly piled. The largest single item was the 500-gallon bladder of kerosene, fuel both for the turbine of the shooting platform and the diesel engines of the ponies. There was some dehydrated food, though the bulk of the group's diet would be the meat they shot. Vickers had warned the clients that anyone who could not stomach the idea of eating dinosaur should bring his own alternative. It was the idea that caused some people problems—the meat itself was fine. Each client was allowed a half-cubic meter chest for personal possessions. Ultimately they would either be abandoned in the Cretaceous or count against the owners' volume for trophies.

The intrusion vehicle was surrounded by a waist-high railing, hinged to flop down out of the way during loading and unloading. The space between the rail and the gear in the center was the passenger area. This open walkway was a comfortable four feet wide at the moment. On return, with the vehicle packed with trophies, there would be only standing room. Ceratopsian skulls, easily the most impressive of the High Cretaceous trophies, could run eight feet long with a height and width in proportion.

On insertion, it was quite conceivable that the vehicle would indeed appear in the midst of a pack of gorgosaurs. That was not something the staff talked about; but the care they took positioning themselves and the other gunners before insertion was not mere form. "Mr. McPherson," Dieter said, "Mr. Mears, if you will kindly come around with me to Side Three—that's across from the stairs here. Do not please touch the red control panel as you pass it."

"Ah, can't Charles and I stay together?" Mary McPherson asked. Both of the dentists carried motion cameras with the lenses set at the 50 mm minimum separation. A wider spread could improve hologram quality; but it might prove impossibly awkward under the conditions obtaining just after insertion.

"For the moment," Vickers said, "I'd like you on Side One with me, Miss McPherson. That puts two guns on each side; and it's just during insertion."

Boots clanking on the metal stairs, the safari group mounted the vehicle. Four members of Dr. Galil's team had climbed down already. They stood in a row beside the steps like a guard of honor in lab smocks. Galil himself waited beside the vertical control panel at the head of the stairs. The red panel was the only portion of the vehicle which looked more in keeping with a laboratory than a mineshaft. Even so, its armored casing was a far cry from the festooned breadboards that typically marked experimental machinery.

Not that anyone suggested to the clients that the machinery was as surely experimental as a 1940 radar set.

Dr. Galil shook hands with each member of the group, staff and clients alike. Vickers shifted his modified Garand rifle into the crook of his left arm and took the scientist's hand. "Henry, I pray you God-speed and a safe return," Galil said in English. His grip was firm.

"God's for afterwards, Shlomo," the guide said. "You'll bring us back, you and your boys. That's what I have faith in."

Dr. Galil squeezed Vickers' hand again. He walked quickly down the steps. The hangar lights dimmed as the big room emptied of everything but the intrusion vehicle and its cargo. Vickers took a deep breath and unlocked the T-handled switch in the center of the control panel. He glanced to either side. Miss McPherson was to his left, Mrs. Salmes to his right.

Adrienne Salmes smiled back. "Did you put me with you because you think you can't trust a woman's shooting?" she asked.

Vickers cleared his throat. "No," he lied. More loudly, he added, "We are about to make our insertion. Everyone please grip the rail with your free hand. Don't let your rifles or cameras project more than two feet beyond the railing, though." He threw the switch. A blue light on the hangar ceiling began to pulse slowly, one beat per second. Vickers' belly drew in again. At the tenth pulse, the light and the hangar disappeared together. There was an instant of sensory blurring. Some compared the sensation of time travel to falling, others to immersion in vacuum. To Vickers, it was always a blast of heat. Then the heat was real and the sun glared down through a haze thick enough to shift the orb far into the red. The intrusion vehicle lurched in a walloping spray. Ooze and reeds sloshed sideways to replace those scalloped out of the slough and transported to the hangar in Tel Aviv. The vehicle settled almost to the full depth of its legs.

"Christ on a crutch!" snarled Don Washman, hidden from Vickers by the piled gear. "Tell us its a grassy clearing and drop us in a pissing swamp! Next time it'll be a kelp bed!" In a different voice he added, "Target."

All of Vickers' muscles had frozen when he thought they were about to drown. They were safe after all, though, and he turned to see the first dinosaur of the safari.

It was a duckbill—though the head looked more like that of a sheep than a duck. Jaw muscles and nasal passages filled the hollows of the snout which early restorations had left bare. The dinosaur had been dashing through the low pines fringing the slough when the crash and slap of the insertion caused it to rear up and attempt to stop. Reeds and water sprayed in a miniature echo of the commotion the vehicle itself had made.

The firm soil of the shore was only ten feet from the vehicle, roughly parallel to Side Four. The duckbill halted, almost in front of Washman and Jonathan Salmes. Scrabbling for traction in muck covered by two feet of water, the beast tried to reverse direction. The pilot leveled his grenade launcher but did not fire. Vickers stepped to the corner where he could see the target. It lacked the crests that made many similar species excellent trophies, but it was still two tons at point-blank range and the first dino the clients had seen in the flesh. "Go ahead," he said to Salmes. "It's yours."

The duckbill lunged back toward the shore, swinging the splayed toes of its right foot onto solid ground. Salmes' rifle slammed. It had an integral muzzle brake to help reduce recoil by redirecting muzzle gases sideways. The muzzle blast was redirected as well, a palpable shock in the thick air. The duckbill lurched, skidding nose-first through a tree. Its long hind legs bunched under it while the stubby forelegs braced to help the beast rise. If it could get to the well-beaten trail by which it had approached the slough, it would disappear.

"Good, good," said Vickers. His voice was tinny

in his own ears because of the muzzle blast. "Now finish it with another one at the base of the tail." Fired from such short range, Salmes' bullet could be expected to range through the duckbill's body. It was certain to rip enough blood vessels to let the beast's life out quickly, and it might also break the spine.

The second shot did not come. The duckbill regained its feet. There was a rusty splotch of blood against the brown-patterned hide of its left shoulder. Vickers risked a look away from the shore to see what was the matter with Salmes. The client had a glazed expression on his face. His big rifle was raised, but its butt did not appear to be solidly resting on his shoulder. Don Washman wore a disgusted look. Beyond both gunners, Mr. McPherson knelt and shot holo tape of the beast leaping back toward the trees.

"Shoot, for Chrissake!" Vickers shouted.

Salmes' rifle boomed again. A triple jet of smoke flashed from the bore and muzzle brake. Salmes cried out as the stock hit him. The bullet missed even the fringe of ten-foot pine trees. The duckbill disappeared into them.

Vickers carefully did not look at Salmes—or Adrienne Salmes, standing immediately behind the guide with her rifle ready to shoot if directed. She had snickered after her husband's second shot. "First we'll find a dry campsite and move the gear," Vickers started to say.

The forest edge exploded as the duckbill burst back through it in the midst of a pack of dromaeosaurs.

In the first flaring confusion, there seemed to be

a score of the smaller carnivores. In fact, there
were only five—but that was quite enough. One
had the duckbill by the throat and was wrapping
forelegs around the herbivore's torso to keep from
being shaken loose. The rest of the pack circled
the central pair with the avidity of participants in a
gang rape. Though the carnivores were bipedal,
they bore a talon on each hind foot that was a
sickle in size and lethality. Kicking from one leg,
the hooting dromaeosaurs slashed through the duckbill's belly hide. Soft, pink coils of intestine spilled
out into the water.

One of the half-ton carnivores cocked its head at
the group on the intrusion vehicle. The men on
Side Four were already spattered with the duckbill's blood. "Take'em," Vickers said. He punched
a steel-cored bullet through the nearest dromaeosaur's skull, just behind its eyes.

Washman and Adrienne Salmes fired while
Vickers' cartridge case was still in the air. The
pilot's grenade launcher chugged rather than banging, but the explosion of its projectile against the
chest of a carnivore was loud even to ears numbed
by the muzzle blasts of Salmes' rifle. The grenade
was a caseless shaped charge which could be used
point-blank without endangering the firer with frag-
ments. Even so, the concussion from less than
twenty feet rocked everyone on the near side of
the vehicle. There was a red flash and a mist of
pureed dinosaur. A foreleg, torn off at the shoulder, sailed straight into the air. Two of the
dromaeosaurs bolted away from the blast, disappearing among the trees in flat arcs and sprays of
dirt and pine straw.

Vickers' target had fallen where it stood. All four limbs jerked like those of a pithed frog. The dromaeosaur Adrienne Salmes had shot dropped momentarily, then sprang to its feet again. The tall woman worked the bolt of her rifle smoothly without taking the butt from her shoulder. The grenade explosion did not appear to have disconcerted her. The guide, poised to finish the beast, hesitated. Adrienne shot again and the dino's limbs splayed. Its dark green hide showed clearly the red and white rosette between the shoulders where the second bullet had broken its spine.

Dieter Jost leaned past Mr. McPherson and put a uranium penetrator through the brain of the duckbill, ending its pain. All four of the downed dinosaurs continued to twitch.

"Jesus," said Don Washman quietly as he closed the breech on a grenade cartridge.

Although he had only fired once, Henry Vickers replaced the 20-round magazine of his Garand with a fresh one from his belt pouch. "Mr. McPherson," he said, "I hope you got good pictures, because I swear that's the most excitement I've had in a long time in this business."

Dieter had moved back to watch the slough with Steve Brady. Most of the clients crowded to Side Four to get a better view of the Cretaceous and its denizens. Adrienne Salmes had not moved from where she stood beside Vickers. She thumbed a second cartridge into the magazine of her rifle and closed the breech. "Still doubt I can shoot?" she asked with a smile.

"Heart and spine," the guide said. "No, I guess you can back me up any day of the week. I tell you, dromaeosaurs aren't as impressive as some of the larger carnivores, but they're just as dangerous." He looked more carefully at her rifle, a Schultz and Larsen with no ornamentation but the superb craftsmanship that had gone into its production. "Say, nice," Vickers said. "In .358 Norma?"

The blonde woman smiled with pleasure. "It's the same rifle I've used for everything from whitetails to elephant," she said. "I'd planned to bring something bigger, but after what you said, I had five hundred bullets cast from bronze and loaded at the factory for me. Johnnie—" she glanced at her husband, now loudly describing how he had shot the duckbill to the other clients. "Well," Adrienne continued quietly, "I'm the hunter in the household, not him. I told him he was crazy to have a cannon like that built, but he listens to me as badly as he listens to everyone else."

"That may be a problem," Vickers muttered. More loudly, he said, "All right, I think it's time to start setting up camp on top of this ridge. Around now, it's asking for trouble to be any closer than a hundred yards to the water, especially with this much meat nearby. After Steve and I get the ponies assembled, we'll need everybody's help to load them. Until then, just try not to get in the way."

Sometimes working with his hands helped Vickers solve problems caused by the human side of his safaris. It did not seem to do so on this occasion. Of course, a client who was both arrogant and gun-shy was a particularly nasty problem.

But Vickers was irritated to realize that it also

bothered him that Don Washman and Mrs. Salmes seemed to be getting along very well together.

The campfire that evening provided an aura of human existence more important than the light of its banked coals. The clients had gone to sleep—or at least to their tents. That the Salmes at least were not asleep was evident from the sound of an argument. The double walls of the tents cut sound penetration considerably, but there were limits. Steve Brady shoved another log on the fire and said, "Damn, but I swear that chainsaw gets heavier every time I use it. Do you suppose the Israelis designed them to be air-dropped without parachutes?"

"You want a high horsepower-to-weight ratio, you don't use a diesel," agreed Dieter Jost with a shrug. "If you want a common fuel supply for everything and need diesel efficiency for the ponies, though—well, you get a heavy chainsaw."

"Can't imagine why she ever married him," Don Washman said. "Beef like that's a dime a dozen. Why, you know he didn't even have balls enough to chamber a third round? He's scared to death of that gun, scared almost to touch it now."

"Yeah," agreed Vickers, working a patch into the slot of his cleaning rod, "but the question's what to do about it. I don't have any good answers, God knows."

"Do?" Washman repeated. "Well, hell, leave him, of course. She's got money of her own—"

Brady broke into snorting laughter. Dieter grimaced and said, "Don, I do not think it is any business of ours how our clients live. The Salmes

are adults and can no doubt solve their own problems." He pursed his lips. The fire threw the shadow
of his bushy moustache misshapenly against his
cheeks. "As for our problem, Henry, why don't we
offer him the use of the camp gun? The .375? I
think Mr Salmes' difficulty is in precisely the same
category as the more usual forms of mechanical
breakdown or guns falling into the river."

"Fine with me if you can talk him into it,"
Vickers said dubiously, "but I wouldn't say Salmes
is the sort to take a well-meant suggestion." He
nodded toward the tent. The couple within seemed
to be shouting simultaneously. "Or any other kind
of suggestion," he added.

"Things would sure be simpler if they didn't
allow booze on safaris," Brady said.

"Things would be simpler for us if our employers paid us to sleep all day and drink schnapps,"
said Dieter Jost. He tugged a lock of hair absently.
"That does not comport well with economic realities, however. And so long as each of our clients
has paid fifty thousand American dollars for the
privilege of spending two weeks in the Cretaceous, it is unrealistic to assume that the staff will
be treated as anything but the hired help. If
drunken clients make the job more difficult, then
that is simply one of the discomforts of the job.
Like loading gear in the heat, or tracking down an
animal that a client has wounded. It is easier for
our employers, Mr. Stern and those above him, to
hire new staff members than it would be to impose
their underlings' view on persons of the sort who
take time safaris."

"Moshe Cohn was head guide when I made my

first insertion," said Vickers aloud. His cleaning rod rested on his lap beside the Garand, but he had not run it through the bore yet. "He told a client—a Texan, it was a US safari that time too—that he'd be better off to slack up a little on his drinking while he was in the field. The client was generally too stiff to see a dino, much less shoot one." The guide's forefinger tapped the breech of his rifle as he recalled the scene. "He said to Moshe, 'Jew-boy, you sound just like my third wife. One more word and I'll whip you with my belt, just like I did her.' Moshe broke his hand on the Texan's jaw. When we got back, the government—the Israeli but very pragmatic government—fired Moshe and denied him compensation for his hand. Ten days in the field with broken bones, remember." Vickers paused, then went on, "That taught me the rules. So far, I've been willing to live by them."

Don Washman laughed. "Right, when you hit a client, use your gunstock," he said and opened another beer.

Technically Steve Brady had the first watch, even though all four staff members were up. The alarm panel was facing Steve when it beeped, therefore. "Jesus!" the stubby, long-haired pilot blurted when he saw the magnitude of the signal fluorescing on the display. "Down the trail—must be a herd of something!"

Don Washman upset his fresh beer as he ran to the spade grips of the heavy machine-gun. It was in the center of the camp, on ground slightly higher than its immediate surroundings but by no means high enough to give the weapon an unbro-

ken field of fire. The staff had sawed clear a campsite along the game trail leading down to the
intrusion vehicle two hundred yards away. Assuming that animals were most likely to enter the
area by the trail, Dieter had sited the tents on the
other side of the gun. The next day they could
assemble the six-foot high tower for the gun, but
time had been too short to finish that the first
night.

While the other staff members crouched over
weapons, Vickers darted to the three occupied
tents. The sensor loop that encircled the camp 100
yards out could pick up very delicate impacts and
relay them to the display screen. This signal, however, was already shaking the ground. Miss Mc-
Pherson poked her head out of the tent she shared
with her brother. "What—" the dentist began.

The file of huge ceratopsians rumbled into sight
on their way to the water to drink. They were
torosaurs or a species equally large. In the dim
glow of the fire, they looked more like machines
than anything alive. Their beaks and the tips of
their triple horns had a black glint like raku ware,
and they averaged twice the size of elephants.

The tent that Mears and Brewer shared shuddered as both clients tried to force their way through
the opening simultaneously. Vickers lifted the muz-
zles of their rifles skyward as he had been waiting
to do. "No shooting now," he cried over the thunder of the dinosaurs. "In the morning we'll follow
them up."

Adrienne Salmes slipped out of her tent before
Vickers could reach over and take her rifle. It was
pointed safely upward anyway. Despite the hour-

long argument she had been engaged in, the blonde woman looked calm and alert. She looked breathtakingly beautiful as well—and wore only her rifle. "If you can wait a moment for my firepower," she said to Vickers without embarrassment, "I'll throw some clothes on." The guide nodded.

The bony frills at the back of the ceratopsians' skulls extended their heads to well over the height of a man. Less for protection than for muscle attachment, the frills locked the beasts' heads firmly to their shoulders. The bulging jaw muscles that they anchored enabled the ceratopsians to literally shear hardwood the thickness of a man's thigh. The last thing a safari needed was a herd of such monsters being stampeded through the camp. A beast wounded by a shot ill-aimed in the darkness could lead to just that result.

Mears and Brewer were staring at the rapid procession in wonder. The left eye of each torosaur glinted in the firelight. "Mother o' God, what a trophy!" Brewer said.

"Best in the world," Vickers agreed. "You'll go back with one, never fear." He looked at the McPhersons to his other side. The dentists were clutching their holo cameras, which were almost useless under the light conditions. "And you'll get your fill too," Vickers said. "The trip isn't cheap, but I've never yet guided a client who didn't think he'd gotten more than he bargained for." Though a drunken SOB like Jonathan Salmes might spoil that record, he added silently.

Adrienne Salmes re-emerged from her tent, wearing her coveralls and boots. Mears and Brewer had been so focused on the herd of torosaurs that the guide doubted the men had noticed her previous display. She was carrying a sleeping bag in addition to her rifle. Vickers raised an eyebrow. Adrienne nodded back at the tent. "Screaming beauty seems to have passed out," she said, "but I'm damned if I'll stay in the tent with him. Going on about his shoulder, for God's sake, and expecting sympathy from *me*. Is it all right if I doss down in the open?"

The ceratopsians were sporting in the water, making as much noise as the Waikiki surf. Vickers smiled. "They could eat tree trunks and drink mud," he said, as if he had not heard the client's question. "And I still meet people who think mammals are better adapted for survival than dinos were." He turned to Adrienne Salmes. "It's all right, so long as you stay out of the gun's way," he said, "but you'll wash away if it rains. And we're bound to get at least one real gully-washer while we're here."

"Hell, there's an easy answer to that," said Don Washman. He had strolled over to the tents when it became clear no predators had followed the torosaurs. "One of us is on watch all night, right? So there's always a slot open in the staff tents. Let noble hunter there sleep by himself, Hank. And she shoots well enough to be a pro, so let her stay dry with us too." He gave his engaging smile.

The other clients were listening with interest. "Maybe if Mr. McPherson wants to trade—" Vickers began in a neutral voice.

Adrienne Salmes hushed him with a grimace. "I'm a big girl now, Mr. Vickers," she snapped, "and I think I'm paying enough to make my own decisions. Don, if you'll show me the tent, I'll resume getting the sleep I've been assured I'll need in the morning."

Washman beamed. "Let's see," he said, "Steve's got watch at the moment, so I suppose you're my tentmate till I go on at four in the morning. . . ."

They walked toward the tent. Dieter, standing near the fire with his rifle cradled, looked from them to Vickers. Vickers shrugged. He was thinking about Moshe Cohn again.

"Platform to Mobile One," crackled the speaker of the unit clipped to Vickers' epaulet. Vickers threw the last of the clamps that locked the two ponies into a single, articulated vehicle. "Go ahead, Dieter," he said.

"Henry, the torosaurs must have run all night after they left the water," the other guide announced through the heavy static. "They're a good fifteen klicks west of camp. But there's a sauropod burn just three klicks south and close to the river. Do you want me to drop a marker?"

Vickers frowned. "Yeah, go ahead," he decided. He glanced at but did not really see the four clients, festooned with gear, who awaited his order to board the ponies. "Any sign of carnosaurs?"

"Negative," Dieter replied, "but we're still looking. I spotted what looked like a fresh kill when we were tracking the torosaurs. If we don't get any action here, I'll carry Miss McPherson back to that and see what we can stir up."

"Good hunting, Dieter," Vickers said. "We'll go take a look at your sauropods. Mobile One out." Again his eyes touched the clients. He appeared startled to see them intent on him. "All right," he said, "if you'll all board the lead pony. The other's along for trophies—sauropods this time, we'll get you the ceratopsians another day. Just pull down the jump seats."

The guide seated himself behind the tiller bar and clipped his rifle into its brackets. His clients stepped over the pony's low sides. The vehicle was the shape of an aluminum casket, scaled up by a half. A small diesel engine rode over the rear axle. Though the engine was heavily muffled, the valves sang trills which blended with the natural sounds of the landscape. Awnings were pleated into trays at either end of the vehicle, but for today the trees would be sun-screen enough.

Don Washman waved. He had strung a tarp from four trees at the edge of the clearing. In that shade he was pinning together the steel framework of the gun tower. The alarm and his grenade launcher sat beside him.

"Take care," Vickers called.

"You take care," the pilot responded with a broad grin. "Maybe I can lose the yo-yo and then we're all better off." He jerked his head toward the tent which still held Jonathan Salmes. Dieter had tried to arouse Salmes for breakfast. Because Vickers was sawing at the time, no one but Dieter himself heard what the client shouted. Dieter, who had served in at least three armies and was used to being cursed, had backed out of the tent with a white face. Vickers had shut down the saw, but the other guide had shaken his head. "Best to let him sleep, I think," he said.

Remembering the night before, Vickers wished

that it was Brady and not Washman who had the guard that day. Oh, well. "Hold on," he said aloud. He put the pony into gear.

Just west of the crest on which they had set up camp, the height and separation of the trees increased markedly. Small pines and cycads were replaced by conifers that shot over one hundred feet in the air. Everything east of the ridgeline was in the floodplain, where the river drowned tree roots with a regularity that limited survival to the smaller, faster-growing varieties. The thick-barked monsters through which Vickers now guided the ponies were centuries old already. Barring lightning or tornado, they would not change appreciably over further centuries. They were the food of the great sauropods.

The forest was open enough to permit the pony to run at over 15 mph, close to its top speed with the load. The saplings and pale, broad-leafed ferns which competed for the dim light were easily brushed aside. Animal life was sparse, but as the pony skirted a fallen log, a turkey-sized coelurosaur sprang up with a large beetle in its jaws. Mears' .458 boomed. There was an echo-chamber effect from the log which boosted the muzzle blast to a near equal for that of the .500 Salmes. Everyone on the pony jumped—Vickers more than the rest because he had not seen the client level his rifle. The dinosaur darted away, giving a flick of its gray-feathered tail as it disappeared around a trunk.

"Ah, don't shoot without warning," the guide said, loudly but without looking around. "It's too easy to wound something that you should have had backup for. Besides, we should be pretty close to the sauropods—and they make much better targets."

Even as Vickers spoke, the forest ahead of them brightened. The upper branches still remained, but all the limbs had been stripped below the level of sixty feet. One tree had been pushed over. It had fallen to a 45° angle before being caught and supported by the branches of neighboring giants. The matted needles were strewn with fresh blankets of sauropod droppings. They had a green, faintly Christmasy scent. Vickers stopped the vehicle and turned to his clients. "We're getting very close," he said, "and there'll be plenty of shooting for everybody in just a moment. But there's also a chance of a pack of carnosaurs nearby for the same reason that we are. Keep your eyes open as we approach—and for *God's* sake don't shoot until I've said to." His eyes scanned the forest again and returned to Adrienne Salmes. A momentary remembrance of her the night before, a nude Artemis with rifle instead of bow, made him smile. "Mrs. Salmes," he said, "would you watch behind us, please? Carnivores are likely to strike up a burn as we did . . . and I can't watch behind us myself."

Adrienne grinned. "Why Mr. Vickers, I think you've just apologized for doubting I could shoot," she said. She turned and faced back over the towed pony, left arm through the sling of her rifle in order to brace the weapon firmly when she shot.

Vickers eased forward the hand throttle. They were past the marker beacon Dieter had dropped from the shooting platform. The responder tab on the guide's wrist had pulsed from green to red and was now lapsing back into fire orange; he cut it off absently. The sounds of the dinosaurs were audible to him now: the rumble of their huge intestines; the slow crackle of branches being stripped of their needles, cones, and bark by the sauropods' teeth; and occasional cooing calls which the clients, if they heard them over the ringing of the diesel, probably mistook for those of unseen forest birds.

The others did not see the sauropods even when Vickers cut the motor off. They were titanosaurs or a similar species, only middling huge for their suborder. Vickers pointed. Mears, Brewer, and McPherson followed the line of the guide's arm, frowning. "It's all right now, Mrs. Salmes," Vickers said softly. "The dinos will warn us if predators get near." Adrienne Salmes faced around as well.

"Oh, Jesus Christ," someone whispered as he realized what Vickers was pointing out. It was incredible, even to the guide, how completely a score or more of thirty-ton animals could blend into an open forest. In part, it may have been that human minds were not used to interpreting as animals objects which weighed as much as loaded semis. Once recognized, the vast expanses of russet and black hide were as obvious as inkblot pictures which someone else has described.

Silently and without direction, McPherson stepped from the pony and spread the lenses of his camera. Vickers nodded to the others. "They won't pay attention to a normal voice," he said—in a quieter than normal voice. "Try to avoid sudden movements, though. They may think its a warning signal of some kind." He cleared his throat. "I want each of you to mark a target—"

"That one!" whispered Mears urgently, a boy in

the toystore, afraid his aunt will reneg on her promise of a gift unless he acts at once. The big contractor was pointing at the nearest of the sauropods, a moderate-sized female only thirty feet away.

"Fine, but wait," the guide said firmly. "I'll position each of you. When I call 'fire', go ahead— but only then. They won't attack anything our size, but they might step on one of us if they were startled at the wrong time. That big, they don't have to be hostile to be dangerous."

The nearby female, which had been browsing on limbs twenty feet high, suddenly stepped closer to a tree and reared up on her hind legs. She anchored herself to the trunk with her forefeet, each armed with a single long claw. It shredded bark as it gripped. With the grace and power of a derrick, the titanosaur's head swung to a high branch, closed, and dragged along it for several yards. It left only bare wood behind.

With his left hand, Vickers aimed a pen-sized laser pointer. A red dot sprang out on the chest of the oblivious titanosaur. "There's your aiming point," the guide said. "If she settles back down before I give the signal, just hit her at the top of the shoulder."

Mears nodded, his eyes intent on the dinosaur.

Vickers moved Brewer five yards away, with a broadside shot at a large male. McPherson stood beside him, using a pan-head still camera on the six sauropods visible within a stone's throw. The dentist's hands were trembling with excitement.

Vickers took Adrienne Salmes slightly to the side, to within twenty yards of another male. He chose the location with an eye on the rest of the herd. Sauropods had a tendency to bolt straight ahead if aroused.

"Why does this one have bright red markings behind its eyes?" Adrienne asked.

"First time I ever saw it," the guide said with a shrug. "Maybe some professor can tell you when you get back with the head." He did not bother to gesture with the laser. "Ready?" he asked.

She nodded and aimed.

"Fire!"

The three gunners volleyed raggedly. The thick tree trunks acted as baffles, blurring the sharpness of the reports. The gunfire had the same feeling of muffled desecration as farts echoing in a cathedral. The red-flashed titanosaur began striding forward. Adrienne Salmes worked her bolt and fired again. A wounded animal gave a warning call, so loud and low-pitched that the humans' bowels trembled. Mrs. Salmes fired again. The titanosaur was a flickering picture in a magic lantern formed by open patches between six-foot tree boles. The huntress began to run after her disappearing prey.

Vickers grabbed her shoulder, halting her with an ease that belied his slender build. She turned on him in fury. "I won't let a wounded animal go!" she screamed.

"It won't go far," Vickers said. He released her. "We'll follow as soon as it's safe." He gestured, taking in the bellowing, mountainous forms padding in all directions among the even larger trees. "They'll circle in a moment. Then it'll be safe for things our size to move," he said.

Russet motion ceased, though the tidal bellowing of over a dozen sauropods continued. Mears was still firing in the near distance. Brewer had lowered his rifle and was rubbing his shoulder with his left hand. "Let's get everybody together," the guide suggested, "and go finish off some trophies."

Brewer's expression was awed as they approached. "It really did fall," he said. "It was so big, I couldn't believe. . . . But I shot it where you said and it just ran into the tree." He waved. "And I kept shooting and it fell."

The haunches of the titanosaur were twice the height of a man, even with the beast belly-down in the loam. McPherson pointed at the great scars in the earth beneath the sauropod's tail. "It kept trying to move," he said in amazement. "Even though there was a tree in the way. It was kicking away, trying to get a purchase, and I thought the *tree* was going to go over. But it did. The, the dinosaur. And I have a tape of all of it!"

Mears, closest to the bellowing giants, was just as enthusiastic. "Like a shooting gallery!" he said, "but the tin ducks're the size of houses. God Almighty! I only brought one box of ammo with me. I shot off every last slug! God Almighty!"

The titanosaurs had quieted somewhat, but they were still making an odd series of sounds. The noises ranged from bird calls as before, to something like the venting of high-pressure steam. Vickers nodded and began walking toward the sounds. He had caught Adrienne Salmes' scowl of distaste at the contractor's recital. If the guide agreed, it was still not his business to say so.

The herd was larger than Vickers had estimated. Fully forty of the sauropods were circled, facing

outward around a forest giant enough bigger than
its neighbors to have cleared a considerable area.
Several of the beasts were rearing up. They flailed
the air with clawed forefeet and emitted the pene-
trating steam-jet hiss that seemed so incongruous
from a living being. Mears raised his rifle with a
convulsed look on his face before he remembered
that he had no ammunition left.

McPherson was already rolling tape. "Have you
reloaded?" the guide asked, looking from Salmes
to Brewer. The blonde woman nodded curtly while
the meat packer fumbled in the side pocket of his
coveralls.

"I don't see the one I hit," Adrienne Salmes
said. Her face was tight.

"Don't worry," the guide said quietly. "It's down,
it couldn't have made it this far the way you hit it.
It's the ones that weren't heart-shot that we're
dealing with now."

"That's not my responsibility," she snapped.

"It's no duty you owe to me," Vickers agreed,
"or to anything human."

Brewer snicked his bolt home. Vickers' laser
touched the center of the chest of a roaring titanosaur. Orange pulmonary blood splashed its tiny
head like a shroud. "On the word, Mr. Brewer,"
he said, "if you would."

Adrienne said, "All right." She did not look at
Vickers.

Across the circle, eighty yards away, a large male
was trying to lick its belly. Its long neck strained,
but it was not flexible enough to reach the wound.
The laser pointer touched below the left eye.
"There?" the guide asked.

Adrienne nodded and braced herself, legs splayed. Her arms, sling, and upper body made a web of interlocking triangles.

The guide swung his own weapon onto the third of the wounded animals. "All right," he said.

Adrienne's Schultz and Larsen cracked. The light went out of the gut-shot sauropod's eye. Undirected, the rest of the great living machine began slowly to collapse where it stood. Brewer was firing, oblivious of his bruised shoulder in the excitement. Vickers put three rounds into the base of his own target's throat. Its head and neck were weaving too randomly to trust a shot at them.

Either the muzzle blasts or the sight of three more of their number sagging to the ground routed the herd. Their necks swung around like compass needles to iron. With near simultaneity, all the surviving titanosaurs drifted away from the guns. Their tails were held high off the ground.

Adrienne Salmes lowered her rifle. "God Almighty, let me use that!" Mears begged, reaching out for the weapon. "I'll pay you—"

"Touch me and I'll shove this up your bum, you bloody butcher!" the blonde woman snarled.

The contractor's fist balled. He caught himself, however, even before he realized that the muzzle of the .358 had tilted in line with his throat.

"The river isn't that far away," said Vickers, pointing in the direction the sauropods had run. "We'll follow in the pony—it's a sight worth seeing. And taping," he added.

The undergrowth slowed the hunters after they recrossed the ridgeline, but the titanosaurs were still clearly evident. Their heads and even hips

rocked above the lower vegetation that sloped
toward the river. The herd, despite its size and
numbers, had done surprisingly little damage in
its rush to the water. The pony repeatedly had to
swing aside from three-inch saplings which had
sprung back when the last of the titanosaurs had
passed.

But the beasts themselves were slowed by the
very mechanics of their size. Their twelve-foot strides
were ponderously slow even under the goad of
panic. The tensile strength of the sauropods' thigh
bones simply was not equal to the acceleration of
the beasts' mass to more than what would be a fast
walk in a man. The hunters reached a rocky spur
over the mudflats fringing the water just as the
leading titanosaurs splashed into the stream 150
yards away. The far bank of the river was lost in
haze. The sauropods continued to advance without
reference to the change in medium. Where a moment before they had been belly-deep in reeds,
now they were belly-deep in brown water that was
calm except for the wakes of their passage. When
the water grew deeper, the procession sank slowly.
The beasts farthest away, in mid-stream over a
quarter mile out, were floating necks and tails
while the forefeet propelled them by kicking down
into the bottom muck.

"Don't they hide underwater and snorkel through
their necks?" Brewer asked. Then he yipped in
surprise as his hand touched the barrel of his
Weatherby. The metal was hot enough to burn
from strings of rapid fire and the Cretaceous
sunlight.

Vickers nodded. He had heard the question often before. "Submarines breathe through tubes because the tubes are steel and the water pressure doesn't crush them," he explained. "Sauropods don't have armored gullets, and their lungs aren't diesel engines inside a steel pressure hull. Physics again. Besides, they float—the only way they could sink would be to grab a rock."

As Vickers spoke, the last titanosaur in the line sank.

"Well, I'll be damned!" the guide blurted.

The sauropod surfaced again a moment later. It blew water from its lungs as it gave the distress cry that had followed the shooting earlier.

The mild current of the river had bent the line of titanosaurs into a slight curve. The leaders were already disappearing into the haze. None of the other beasts even bothered to look back to see the cause of the bellowing. No doubt they already knew.

The stricken titanosaur sank again. It rolled partly onto its left side as it went under the surface this time. It was still bellowing, wreathing its head in a golden spray as it disappeared.

"I think," said Adrienne Salmes dryly, "that this time the rock grabbed the dinosaur."

Vickers grunted in reply. He was focusing his binoculars on the struggle.

Instead of rising vertically, the sauropod rolled completely over sideways. Clinging to the herbivore's left foreleg as it broke surface was something black and huge and as foul as a tumor. The linked beasts submerged again in an explosion of spray. Vickers lowered the binoculars, shivering. They were not common, even less commonly seen.

Great and terrible as they were, they were also widely hated. For them to sun themselves on mudbanks as their descendants did would have been to court death by the horns and claws of land animals equally large. But in their own element, in the still, murky waters, they were lords without peer.

"Christ Almighty," Mears said, "was that a whale?"

"A crocodile," the guide replied, staring at the roiling water. "Enough like what you'd find in the Nile or the Congo that you couldn't tell the difference by a picture. Except for the size." He paused, then continued, "The science staff will be glad to hear about this. They always wondered if they preyed on the big sauropods too. It seems that they prey on *any* goddam thing in the water."

"I'd swear it was bigger than the tyrannosaurus you showed us," Adrienne Salmes observed, lowering her own binoculars.

Vickers shrugged. "As long, at least. Probably heavier. I looked at a skull, a fossil in London . . . I don't know how I'd get one back as a trophy. . . . It was six feet long, which was impressive; and three feet wide, which was incredible, a carnivore with jaws three feet *wide*. Tyrannosaurs don't compare, no. Maybe whales do, Mr Mears. But nothing else I know of."

There were no longer any titanosaurs visible. The herd had curved off down-stream, past the intrusion vehicle and the hunting camp. They were lost against the haze and the distant shoreline by now. The water still stirred where the last of them had gone down, but by now the struggles must have been the thrashings of the sauropod's autonomic nervous system. The teeth of the crocodile were six inches long; but they were meant only to hold, not to kill. The water killed, drowning a thirty-ton sauropod as implacably as it would any lesser creature anchored to the bottom by the crocodile's weight.

"We'd best take our trophies," Vickers said at last. No one in the world knew his fear of drowning, no one but himself. "The smell'll bring a pack of gorgosaurs soon, maybe even a tyrannosaur. I don't want that now, not with us on the ground."

The guide rubbed his forehead with the back of his left hand, setting his bush hat back in place carefully. "The ponies convert to boats," he said, patting the aluminum side. "The tread blocks can be rotated so they work like little paddle wheels." He paused as he swung the tiller bar into a tight circle. "I guess you see why we don't use them for boats in the Cretaceous," he added at last. "And why we didn't keep our camp down on the intrusion vehicle."

Vickers was even quieter than his wont for the rest of the morning.

The shooting platform had returned before the ponies did, the second of them dripping with blood from the titanosaur heads. Two heads had Mears' tags on them, though the contractor had finished none of the beasts he had wounded. The best head among those he had sprayed would have been the one the guide had directed Adrienne Salmes to kill—with a bullet through the skull that destroyed all trophy value.

There were no game laws in the Cretaceous,
but the line between hunters and butchers was
the same as in every other age.

The McPhersons greeted each other with mutual enthusiasm. Their conversation was technical
and as unintelligible to non-photographers as the
conversation of any other specialists. Jonathan
Salmes was sitting on a camp stool, surly but alert.
He did not greet the returning party, but he
watched the unloading of the trophies with undis-
guised interest. The right side of his face was
puffy.

"We've found a tyrannosaur," Dieter called as
he and the pilots joined Vickers. That was good
news, but there was obvious tension among the
other members of the staff. Brady carried a spray
gun loaded with antiseptic sealer. A thorough coating would prevent decay for almost a month, ample time to get the heads to proper taxidermists.

When Dieter was sure that all the clients were
out of earshot, he said in a low voice, "Don has
something to tell you, Henry."

"Eh?" prompted Vickers. He set one of the
sauropod heads on the spraying frame instead of
looking at the pilot.

"I had to clobber Salmes," Washman said, lifting out the red-flashed trophy. "He was off his
head—I'm not sure he even remembers. There
was a mixed herd of duckbills came down the trail.
He came haring out of his tent with that gun of
his. He didn't shoot, though, he started chasing
them down the trail." The pilot straightened and
shrugged. Steve Brady began pumping the spray
gun. The pungent mist drifted down wind beyond

the gaping heads. "I grabbed him. I mean, who knows what might be following a duckbill? When he swung that rifle at me, I had to knock him out for his own good. Like a drowning man." Washman shrugged again. "His gun wasn't even loaded, you know?"

"Don, run the ponies down to the water and mop them out, will you?" Vickers said. The pilot jumped onto the leading vehicle and spun them off down the trail. The two guides walked a little to the side, their rifles slung, while Brady finished sealing the torphies. "It's going to have to be reported, you know," Vickers said. "Whether Salmes does or not."

"You or I might have done the same thing," Dieter replied.

"I'm not denying that," the senior guide snapped. "But it has to be reported."

The two men stood in silence, looking out at a forest filled with sounds that were subtly wrong. At last Dieter said, "Salmes goes up in the platform with you and Don tomorrow, doesn't he?"

Vickers agreed noncommittally.

"Maybe you ought to go with Steve instead," Dieter suggested. He looked at Vickers. "Just for the day, you know."

"Washman just flies us," Vickers said with a shake of his head. "I'm the one that's in contact with the client. And Don's as good as pilots come."

"That he is," the other guide agreed, "that he is. But he is not a piece of furniture. You are treating him as a piece of furniture."

Vickers clapped his companion on the shoulder. "Come on," he said, "Salmes'll be fine when he gets his tyrannosaur. What we ought to be worrying about is three more for the others. If Salmes goes home with a big boy and the rest have to settle for less—well, it says no guarantees in the contracts, but you know the kind of complaints the company gets. That's the kind of problem we're paid to deal with. If they wanted shrinks instead of guides, they'd have hired somebody else."

Dieter laughed half-heartedly. "Let us see what we can arrange for lunch," he said. "At the moment, I am more interested in sauropod steak than I am in the carnivores that we compete with."

"Damn, the beacon cut out again!" Washman snarled. There was no need of an intercom system; the shooting platform operated with only an intake whine which was no impediment to normal speech. The silence was both a boon to coordination and a help in not alarming the prey. It did, however, mean that the client was necessarily aware of any technical glitches. When the client was Jonathan Salmes—

"God damn, you're not going to put *me* on that way!" the big man blazed. He had his color back and with it all his previous temper. Not that the bruise over his right cheekbone would have helped. "One of the others paid you to save the big one for them, didn't they?" he demanded. "By God, I'll bet it was my wife! And I'll bet it wasn't money either, the—"

"Take us up to a thousand feet," Vickers said sharply. "We'll locate the kill visually if the marker isn't working. Eighty tons of sauropod shouldn't be hard to spot."

"Hang on, there it's on again," said the pilot. The shooting platform veered slightly as he corrected their course. Vickers and Salmes stood clutching the rail of the suspended lower deck which served as landing gear as well. Don Washman was seated above them at the controls, with the fuel tank balancing his mass behind. The air intake and exhaust extended far beyond the turbine itself to permit the baffling required for silent running. The shooting platform was as fragile as a dragonfly; and it was, in its way, just as efficient a predator.

By good luck, the tyrannosaur had made its kill on the edge of a large area of brush rather than high forest. The platform's concentric-shaft rotors kept blade length short. Still, though it was possible to maneuver beneath the forest canopy, it was a dangerous and nerve-wracking business to do so. Washman circled the kill at 200 feet, high enough that he did not need to allow for trees beneath him. Though the primary airflow from the rotors was downward, the odor of tens of tons of meat dead in the sun still reached the men above. The guide tried to ignore it with his usual partial success. Salmes only wrinkled his nose and said, "Whew, what a pong." Then, "Where is it? The tyrannosaurus?"

That the big killer was still nearby was obvious from the types of scavengers on the sauropod. Several varieties of the smaller coelurosaurs scrambled over the corpse like harbor rats on a drowned man. None of the species weighed more than a few hundred pounds. A considerable flock of pterosaurs joined and squabbled with the coelurosaurs, wings tented and toothless beaks stabbing out like shears. There were none of the large carnivores around the kill—and that implied that something was keeping them away.

"Want me to go down close to wake him up?" Washman asked.

The guide licked his lips. "I guess you'll have to," he said. There was always a chance that a pterodactyl would be sucked into the turbine when you hovered over a kill. The thought of dropping into a big carnosaur's lap that way kept some guides awake at night. Vickers looked at his client and added, "Mr. Salmes, we're just going to bring the tyrannosaur out of wherever it's lying up in the forest. After we get it into the open, we'll maneuver to give you the best shot. All right?"

Salmes grunted. His hands were tight on his beautifully-finished rifle. He had refused Dieter's offer of the less-bruising camp gun with a scorn that was no less grating for being what all the staff had expected.

Washman dropped them vertically instead of falling in a less wrenching spiral. He flared the blades with a gentle hand, however, feathering the platform's descent into a hover without jarring the gunners. They were less than thirty feet in the air. Pterosaurs, more sensitive to moving air than the earth-bound scavengers, squealed and hunched their wings. The ones on the ground could not take off because the down-draft anchored them. The pilot watched carefully the few still circling above them.

"He's—" Vickers began, and with his word the tyrannosaur strode into the sunlight. Its bellow was intended to chase away the shooting platform.

The machine trembled as the sound induced sympathetic vibrations in its rotor blades. Coelurosaurs scattered. The cries of the pterosaurs turned to blind panic as the downdraft continued to frustrate their attempts to rise. The huge predator took another step forward. Salmes raised his rifle. The guide cursed under his breath but did not attempt to stop him.

At that, it should have been an easy shot. The tyrannosaur was within thirty feet of the platform and less than ten feet below them. All it required was that Salmes aim past the large head as it swung to counterweight a stride and rake down through the thorax. Perhaps the angle caused him to shoot high, perhaps he flinched. Vickers, watching the carnosaur over his own sights, heard the big rifle crash. The tyrannosaur strode forward untouched, halving the distance between it and the platform.

"Take us up!" the guide shouted. If it had not been a rare trophy, he might have fired himself and announced that he had "put in a bullet to finish the beast". There were three other gunners who wanted a tyrannosaur, though; if Salmes took this one back, it would be after he had shot it or everyone else had an equal prize.

Salmes was livid. He gripped the bolt handle, but he had not extracted the empty case. "God damn you!" he screamed. "You made it wobble to throw me off! You son of a bitch, you robbed me!"

"Mr. Salmes—" Vickers said. The tyrannosaur was now astride the body of its prey, cocking its head to see the shooting platform fifty feet above it.

"By God, you want another chance?" Washman demanded in a loud voice. The platform plunged down at a steep angle. The floor grating blurred the sight of the carnosaur's mottled hide. Its upturned eye gleamed like a strobe-lit ruby.

"Jesus *Christ!*" Vickers shouted. "Take us the hell up, Washman!"

The platform steadied, pillow soft, with its floor fifteen feet from the ground and less than twenty from the tyrannosaur. Standing on the sauropod's corpse, the great predator was eye to eye with Vickers and his client. The beast bellowed again as it lunged. The impulse of its clawed left leg rolled the sauropod's torso.

Salmes screamed and threw his rifle to the grating. The guide leveled his Garand. He was no longer cursing Washman. All of his being was focused on what would be his last shot if he missed it. Before he could fire, however, the shooting platform slewed sideways. Then they were out of the path of the charging dinosaur and beginning to circle with a safe thirty feet of altitude. Below them, the tyrannosaur clawed dirt as it tried to follow.

Salmes was crying uncontrollably.

"Ah, want me to hold it here for a shot?" Washman asked nervously.

"We'll go on back to the camp, Don," the guide said. "We'll talk there, all right?"

"Whatever you say."

Halfway back, Vickers remembered he had not dropped another marker to replace the one that was malfunctioning. God knew, that was the least of his problems.

*   *   *

"You know," Brewer said as he forked torosaur steaks onto the platter, "it tastes more like buffalo than beef; but if we could get some breeding stock back, I'd by God find a market for it!"

Everyone seemed to be concentrating on their meat—good, if pale and lean in comparison with feed-lot steer. "Ah," Vickers said, keeping his voice nonchalant. He looked down at the table instead of the people sitting around it. "Ah, Dieter and I were talking. . . . We'll bunk outside tonight. The, ah, the rest of that pack of dromaeosaurs chased some duckbills through the camp this morning, Steve thinks. So just for safety's sake, we'll both be out of the tent. . . . So, ah, Mrs. Salmes—"

Everyone froze. Jonathan Salmes was turning red. His wife had a forkful of steak poised halfway to her mouth and her eyebrows were rising. The guide swallowed, his eyes still fixed on his plate, and plowed on. "That is, you can have your own tent. Ah, to sleep in."

"Thank you," Adrienne Salmes said cooly, "but I'm quite satisfied with the present arrangements."

Dieter had refused to become involved in this, saying that interfering in the domestic affairs of the Salmes was useless at best. Vickers was sweating now, wishing that there was something to shoot instead of nine pairs of human eyes fixed on him. "Ah," he repeated, "Mrs. Salmes—"

"Mr. Vickers," she overrode him, "who I choose to sleep with—in any sense of the term—is none of your business. Anyone's business," she added with a sharp glance across the table at her husband.

Jonathan Salmes stood up, spilling his coffee

cup. His hand closed on his fork. Each of the four staff members made unobtrusive preparations. Cursing, Salmes flung the fork down and stalked back to his tent.

The others eased. Vickers muttered, "Christ." Then, "Sorry, Dieter, I. . . ." the thing that bothered him most about the whole incident was that he was unsure whether he would have said anything at all had it been Miss McPherson in Don's bed instead of someone he himself found attractive. Christ. . . .

"Mr. Vickers?" Adrienne Salmes said in a mild voice.

"Umm?" His steak had gotten cold. With Brewer cutting and broiling the meat, the insertion group was eating better than Vickers could ever remember.

"I believe Mr. Brady is scheduled to take me up in the platform tomorrow?"

"Yeah, that's right," Vickers agreed, chewing very slowly.

"I doubt my—husband—will be going out again tomorrow," the blonde woman continued with a nod toward his tent. "Under the circumstances, I think it might be better if Mr. Brady were left behind here at the camp. Instead of Don."

"Steve?" Dieter asked.

Brady shrugged. "Sure, I don't need the flying time. But say—I'm not going to finish ditching around the tents by myself. I've got blisters from today."

"All right," said Dieter. "Henry, you and Don—" no one was looking directly at Washman, who was blushing in embarrassment he had damned well brought on himself—"will take Mrs. Salmes up after the tyrannosaur tomorrow." Vickers and Brady both nodded. "The rest of us will wait here to see if the duckbills come through again as they have become accustomed. Steve, I will help you dig. And if the duckbills have become coy, we will ride down the river margin a little later in the morning and find them. Perhaps Mr. Salmes will feel like going with us by then."

Thank God for Dieter, Vickers thought as he munched another bite of his steak. He could always be counted on to turn an impossible social situation into a smoothly functioning one. There would be no trouble tomorrow after all.

The bulging heads of three torosaurs lay between the gun tower and the fire. There the flames and the guard's presence would keep away the small mammals that foraged in the night. As Miss McPherson followed her brother to their tent, she paused and fingered one of the brow horns of the largest trophy. The tip of the horn was on a level with the dentist's eyes, even though the skull lay on the ground. "They're so huge, so . . . powerful," she said. "And for them to fall when you shoot at them, so many of them falling and running. . . . I could never understand men who, well, who shot animals. But with so many of them everywhere—it's as if you were throwing rocks at the windows of an abandoned house, isn't it? It doesn't seem to hurt anything, and it's . . . an attractive feeling."

"Mary!" objected her brother, shadowed by the great heads.

"Oh, I don't mean I'm sorry that I didn't bring a

gun," continued Mary McPherson calmly, her fingers continuing to stroke the smooth black horn. "No, I'm glad I didn't. Because if I had had a gun available this morning, I'm quite sure I would have used it. And after we return, I suppose I would regret that. I suppose." She walked off toward the tent. The rhythms of her low-voiced argument with her brother could be heard until the flaps were zipped.

"Dieter tells me they bagged sixteen torosaurs today," Vickers said. "Even though the intrusion vehicle hasn't room for more than one per client." Only Washman, who had the watch, and Adrienne Salmes were still at the campfire with him.

"*I* bagged one," the woman said with an emphatic flick of her cigar. "Jack Brewer shot six; and I sincerely hope that idiot Mears hit no more than ten, because that's all Dieter and I managed to finish off for him." She had unpinned her hair as soon as she came in from the field. In the firelight it rolled across her shoulders like molten amber.

"Dieter said that too," Vickers agreed. He stood, feeling older than usual. "That's why I said 'they'." He turned and began to walk back to the tent where Dieter was already asleep. There had been no point in going through with the charade of sleeping under the stars—overcast, actually—since the dromaeosaurs were daylight predators. They were as unlikely to appear in the camp after dark as the Pope was to speak at a KKK rally.

To the guide's surprise—and to Don Washman's—Adrienne rustled to her feet and followed. "Mr. Vickers," she said, "might I speak to you for a moment, please?"

Vickers looked at her. As the staff members did, and unlike the other clients, the blonde woman carried her weapon with her at all times. "All right," he said. They walked by instinct to the shooting platform, standing thirty feet away at the end of the arc of tents. The torosaur heads were monstrous silhouettes against the fire's orange glow. "Would it bother you as much if I were a man?" she asked bluntly.

"Anything that makes my job harder bothers me," Vickers said in half-truth. "You and Don are making my job harder. That's all."

Adrienne stubbed out her small cigar on the platform's rail. She scattered the remnants of the tobacco on the rocky soil. "Balls," she said distinctly. "Mr. Vickers—Henry, for Christ's sake—my husband was going to be impossible no matter what. He's here because I was going on a time safari and he was afraid to look less of a man than his wife was. Which he is. But he was going to be terrified of his rifle, he was going to pack his trunk with Scotch, and he was going to be a complete prick because that's the way he is."

"Mrs. Salmes—"

"Adrienne, and let me finish. I didn't marry Jonathan for his money—my family has just as much as his does. I won't claim it was a love match, but we . . . we seemed to make a good pair. A matched set, if you will. He won't divorce me—" her dimly-glimpsed index finger forestalled another attempt by the guide to break in—"because he correctly believes I'd tell the judge and the world that he couldn't get it up on our wedding night. Among other things. I haven't divorced him because I've never felt a need to. There are times that it's been marvelously useful to point out that 'I *do* after all have a husband, dearest. . . .' "

"This is none of my business, Mrs. Salmes—"

"Adrienne!"

"Adrienne, dammit!" Vickers burst out. "It's none of my business, but I'm going to say it anyway. You don't have anything to prove. That's fine, we all should be that way. But most of my clients have a lot to prove, to themselves and to the world. Or they wouldn't be down here in the Cretaceous. It makes them dangerous, because they're out of normal society and they may not be the men they hoped they were after all. And your husband is very God damned dangerous, Adrienne. Take my word for it."

"Well, it's not *my* fault," the woman said.

"Fault?" the guide snapped. "Fault? Is it a pusher's fault that kids OD on skag? You're goddamn right it's your fault! It's the fault of everybody involved who doesn't make it better, and you're sure not making it better. Look, you wouldn't treat a gun that way—and your husband is a human being!"

Adrienne frowned in surprise. There was none of the anger Vickers had expected in her voice when she said, "So are you, Henry. You shouldn't try so hard to hide the fact."

Abruptly, the guide strode toward his tent. Adrienne Salmes watched him go. She took out another cigar, paused, and walked carefully back to the fire where Washman waited with the alarm panel. The pilot looked up with concern. Adrienne sat beside him and shook her hair loose. "Here you go, Don sweetest," she said, extending her cigar. "Why don't you light it for me? It's one of the things you do so well."

Washman kissed her. She returned it, tonguing his lips; but when his hand moved to the zipper of her coveralls, she forced it away. "That's enough until you go off guard duty, dearest," she said. She giggled. "Well—almost enough."

Jonathan Salmes hunched in the shadow of the nearest torosaur head. He listened, pressing his fists to his temples. After several more minutes, he moved in a half-crouch to the shooting platform. In his pocket was a six-inch wooden peg, smooth and close-grained. It was whittled from a root he had worried from the ground with his fingers. Stepping carefully so that his boots did not scrunch on the metal rungs, Salmes mounted the ladder to the pilot's seat. He paused there, his khaki coveralls and strained, white face reflecting the flames. The couple near the fire did not look up. The pilot was murmuring something, but his voice was pitched too low to hear . . . and the words might have been unintelligible anyway, given the circumstances.

Jonathan Salmes shuddered also. He moved with a slick grace that belied the terror and disgust frozen on his face. He slipped the dense peg from his pocket. Stretching his right arm out full length while he gripped the rotor shaft left-handed, Salmes forced the peg down between two of the angled blades of the stator. When he was finished, he scrambled back down the ladder. He did not look

at his wife and the pilot again, but his ears could
not escape Adrienne's contented giggle.

"Hank, she just isn't handling right this morning," Don Washman said. "I'm going to have to
blow the fuel lines out when we get back. Must've
gotten some trash in the fuel transferring from the
bladder to the cans to the tank. Wish to hell we
could fuel the bird directly, but I'm damned if I'm
going to set down on the intrusion vehicle where
it's sitting now."

Vickers glanced down at the treetops and scowled.
"Do you think we ought to abort?" he asked. He
had not noticed any difference in the flight to that
point. Now he imagined they were moving slower
and nearer the ground than was usual, and both
the rush of air and the muted turbine whine took
on sinister notes.

"Oh . . . ," the pilot said. "Well, she's a lot more
likely to clear herself than get worse—the crud
sinks to the bottom of the tank and gets sucked up
first. It'll be okay. I mean, she's just a little sluggish, is all."

The guide nodded. "M—" he began. After his
outburst of the night before, he was as embarrassed around Adrienne Salmes as a boy at his first
dance. "Ah, Adrienne, what do you think?"

The blonde woman smiled brightly, both for the
question and the way it was framed. "Oh, if Don's
willing to go on, there's no question," she said.
"You know I'd gladly walk if it were the only way
to get a tyrannosaurus, Henry—if you'd let me, I
mean. We both know that when we go back in
today, I've had my last chance at a big carnosaur

until you've rotated through all your clients again. Including my husband."

"We'll get you a tyrannosaur," Vickers said.

Adrienne edged slightly closer to the guide. She said softly, "Henry, I want you to know that when we get back I'm going to give Johnnie a divorce."

Vickers turned away as if slapped. "That's none of my business," he said. "I—I'm sorry for what I said last night."

"Sorry?" the woman repeated in a voice that barely carried over the wind noise. "For making me see that I shouldn't make a doormat of . . . someone who used to be important to me? Don't be sorry." After a pause, she continued, "When I ran for Congress . . . God I was young! I offended it must have been everybody in the world, much less the district. But Johnnie was fantastic. I owe what votes I got to hands he shook for me."

"I had no right to talk," Vickers said. By forcing himself, he managed to look the blonde woman in the eyes.

Adrienne smiled and touched his hand where it lay on the forestock of his rifle. "Henry," she said, "I'm not perfect, and the world's not going to be perfect either. But I can stop trying to make it actively worse."

Vickers looked at the woman's hand. After a moment, he rotated his own to hold it. "You've spent your life being the best man around," he said, as calm as he would be in the instant of shooting. "I think you've got it in you to be the best person around instead. I'm not the one to talk . . . but I think I'd be more comfortable around people if more of them were the way you could be."

With a final squeeze, Vickers released Adrienne's hand. During the remainder of the fifteen-minute flight, he concentrated on the ground below. He almost forgot Washman's concern about the engine.

Dieter Jost flicked a last spadeful of gritty soil from the drainage ditch and paused. Steve Brady gave him a thumbs-up signal from the gun tower where he sat. "Another six inches, peon," he called to the guide. "You need to sweat some."

"Fah," said Dieter, laughing. "If it needs to be deeper, the rain will wash it deeper—not so?" He dug the spade into the ground and began walking over to the table. They had found a cache of sauropod eggs the day before. With the aid of torosaur loin and freeze-dried spices from his kit, Brewer had turned one of them into a delicious omelet. Brewer, Mears, and the McPhersons were just finishing. Dieter, who had risen early to finish ditching the tents, had worked up quite an appetite.

"Hey!" Brady called. Then, louder, "Hey! Mr. Salmes, that's not safe! Come back here, please!"

The guide's automatic rifle leaned against the gun tower. He picked it up. Jonathan Salmes was carrying his own rifle and walking at a deliberate pace down the trail to the water. He did not look around when the guard shouted. The other clients were staring in various stages of concern. Cradling his weapon, Dieter trotted after Salmes. Brady, standing on the six-foot tower, began to rotate the heavy machinegun. He stopped when he realized what he was doing.

The guide reached Salmes only fifty yards from the center of the camp, still in sight of the others. He put a hand on the blond man's shoulder and said, "Now, Mr. Salmes—"

Salmes spun like a mousetrap snapping. His face was white. He rang his heavy rifle off Dieter's skull with enough force to tear the stock out of his hands. The guide dropped as if brainshot. Salmes backed away from the fallen man. Then he turned and shambled out of sight among the trees.

"God damn!" Steve Brady said, blinking in surprise. Then he thought of something even more frightening. He unslung his grenade launcher and jumped to the ground without bothering to use the ladder. "If that bastard gets to the intrusion vehicle—" he said aloud, and there was no need for him to finish the statement.

Brady vaulted the guide's body without bothering to look at the injury. The best thing he could do for Dieter now was to keep him from being stranded in the Cretaceous. Brady's hobnails skidded where pine needles overlay rock, but he kept his footing. As the trail twisted around an exceptionally large tree, Brady caught sight of the client again. Salmes was not really running; or rather, he was moving like a man who had run almost to the point of death.

"Salmes, God damn you!" Brady called. He raised the grenade launcher. Two dromaeosaurs burst from opposite sides of the trail where they lay in ambush. Their attention had been on Salmes;

but when the guard shouted, they converged on him.

The leftward dromaeosaur launched itself toward its prey in a flat, twenty-foot leap. Only the fact that Brady had his weapon aimed permitted him to disintegrate the beast's head with a point-blank shot. Death did nothing to prevent the beast from disemboweling Brady reflexively. The two mutilated bodies were thrashing in a tangle of blood and intestines as the remaining clients hurtled around the tree. They skidded to a halt. Mr. McPherson, who held Salmes' rifle—his sister had snatched up Dieter's FN a step ahead of him—began to vomit. Neither Salmes nor the other dromaeosaur were visible.

Jonathan Salmes had in fact squelched across the mud and up the ramp of the intrusion vehicle. He had unscrewed the safety cage from the return switch and had his hand poised on the lever. Something clanged on the ramp behind him.

Salmes turned. The dromaeosaur, panicked by the grenade blast that pulped its companion's head, was already in the air. Salmes screamed and threw the switch. The dromaeosaur flung him back against the fuel bladder. As everything around it blurred, the predator picked Salmes up with its forelegs and began methodically to kick him to pieces with its right hind foot. The dinosaur was still in the process of doing so when the submachineguns of the startled guards raked it to death with equal thoroughness.

The broad ribs of the sauropod thrust up from a body cavity that had been cleared of most of its flesh. There was probably another meal on the haunches, even for a beast of the tyrannosaur's voracity. If Adrienne missed the trophy this morning, however, Vickers would have to shoot another herbivore in the vicinity in order to anchor the prize for the next client.

Not that there was much chance that the blonde woman was going to miss.

Adrienne held her rifle with both hands, slanted across her chest. Her hip was braced against the guardrail as she scanned the forest edge. If she had any concern for her balance, it was not evident.

"Okay, down to sixty," Don Washman said, barely enough height to clear the scrub oaks that humped over lower brush in the clearing. The lack of grasses gave the unforested areas of the Cretaceous an open aspect from high altitude. Lower down, the spikes and wooden fingers reached out like a hedge of spears.

The tyrannosaur strode from the pines with a hacking challenge.

"Christ, he's looking for us," the pilot said. The carnosaur slammed aside the ribs of its kill like bowling pins. Its nostrils were flared, and the sound it made was strikingly different from the familiar bellow of earlier occasions.

"Yeah, that's its territorial call," Vickers agreed. "It seems to have decided that we're another tyrannosaur. It's not just talking, it wants our blood."

"S'pose Salmes really hit it yesterday?" Washman asked.

Vickers shook his head absently. "No," he said, "but the way you put the platform in its face after it'd warned us off. . . . Only a tyrannosaur would

challenge another tyrannosaur that way. They don't
have much brain, but they've got lots of instinctive
responses; and the response we've triggered is,
well . . . a good one to give us a shot. You ready,
Adrienne?"

"Tell me when," the blonde woman said curtly.
Washman was swinging the platform in loose
figure-8s about 150 yards distant from the carnosaur.
They could not circle at their present altitude
because they were too low to clear the conifer
backdrop. Adrienne aimed the Schultz and Larsen
when the beast was on her side of the platform,
raising the muzzle again each time the pilot swung
onto the rear loop of the figure.

"Don, see if you can draw him out from the
woods a little farther," the guide said, squinting
past the barrel of his Garand. "I'd like us to have
plenty of time to nail him before he can go to
ground in the trees."

"Ah, Hank . . . ," the pilot began. Then he went
on, "Oh, hell, just don't blow your shots. That's all
I ask." He put the controls over and wicked up.
There was a noticeable lag before the turbine responded to the demand for increased power. The
section of root slapped as it vibrated from the
stator and shot into the rotors spinning at near-
maximum velocity.

"If you'll stand over here, Mis—Adrienne,"
Vickers said, stepping to the back rail of the platform. The client followed with brittle quickness.
"When I say shoot," Vickers continued, "aim at
the middle of the chest."

Washman had put the platform in an arc toward
the tyrannosaur. The big carnivore lunged forward

with a series of choppy grunts like an automatic cannon. The pilot rotated the platform on its axis, a maneuver he had carried out a thousand times before. This time the vehicle dipped. It was a sickening, falling-elevator feeling to the two gunners and a heart-stopping terror to the man at the controls who realized it was not caused by clumsiness. The platform began to stagger away from the dinosaur, following the planned hyperbola but lower and slower than intended.

"Nail him," Vickers said calmly, sighting his rifle on the green-mottled sternum for the backup shot.

Partial disintegration of the turbine preceded the shot by so little that the two seemed a single event. Both gunners were thrown back from the rail. Something whizzed through the side of the turbine and left a jagged rent in the housing. Adrienne Salmes' bullet struck the tyrannosaur in the lower belly.

"Hang on!" Don Washman shouted needlessly. "I'm going to try—"

He pulled the platform into another arc, clawing for altitude. To get back to camp they had to climb over the pine forest that lay between. No one knew better than the pilot how hopeless that chance was. Several of the turbine blades had separated from the hub. Most of the rest were brushes of boron fiber now, their casing matrices destroyed by the peg or harmonics induced by the imbalance. But Washman had to try, and in any case they were curving around the wounded tyrannosaur while it was still—

The whole drive unit tore itself free of the rest

of the shooting platform. Part of it spun for a
moment with the rotor shafts before sailing off in a
direction of its own. Had it not been for the oak
tree in their path, the vehicle might have smashed
into the ground from fifty feet and killed everyone
aboard. On the other hand, Don Washman just
might have been able to get enough lift from the
auto-rotating blades to set them down on an even
keel. Branches snagged the mesh floor of the platform and the vehicle nosed over into the treetop.

They were all shouting, but the din of bursting
metal and branches overwhelmed mere human
noise. Vickers held the railing with one hand and
the collar of his client's garment with the other.
Both of the rifles were gone. The platform continued to tilt until the floor would have been vertical
had it not been so crumpled. Adrienne Salmes was
supported entirely by the guide. "For God's sake!"
she screamed. "Let go or we'll go over *with* it!"

Vickers' face was red with the impossible strain.
He forced his eyes down, feeling as if even that
minuscule added effort would cause his body to
tear. Adrienne was right. They were better off
dropping onto a lower branch—or even to the
ground forty feet below—than they would be
somersaulting down in the midst of jagged metal.
The platform was continuing to settle as branches
popped. Vickers let go of the blonde woman.
Screaming at the sudden release of half the load,
he loosed his other hand from the rail.

The guide's eyes were shut in a pain reflex. His
chest hit a branch at an angle that saved his ribs
but took off a plate-sized swatch of skin without
harming his tunic's tough fabric. He snatched con-

vulsively at the limb. Adrienne, further out on the
same branch, seized him by the collar and armpit.
Both her feet were locked around the branch. She
took the strain until the guide's overstressed muscles allowed him to get a leg up. The branch
swayed, but the tough oak held.

Don Washman was strapped into his seat. Now
he was staring straight down and struggling with
the jammed release catch. Vickers reached for the
folding knife he carried in a belt pouch. He could
not reach the pilot, though. "Don, cut the strap!"
he shouted.

A large branch split. The platform tumbled outward and down, striking on the top of the rotor
shafts. The impact smashed the lightly-built aircraft into a tangle reeking of kerosene. Don
Washman was still caught in the middle of it.

The limb on which Vickers and Adrienne Salmes
balanced was swaying in harmony with the whole
tree. When the thrashing stopped, the guide sat
up and eyed the trunk. He held his arms crossed
tightly over his chest, each hand squeezing the
opposite shoulder as if to reknit muscles which felt
as if they had been pulled apart. Nothing was
moving in the wreckage below. Vickers crawled to
the crotch. He held on firmly while he stepped to
a branch three feet lower down.

"Henry," Adrienne Salmes said.

"Just wait, I've got to get him out," Vickers
said. He swung down to a limb directly beneath
him, trying not to wince when his shoulders fell
below the level of his supporting hands.

"Henry!" the blonde woman repeated more urgently. "The tyrannosaur!"

Vickers jerked his head around. He could see nothing but patterns of light and the leaves that surrounded him. He realized that the woman had been speaking from fear, not because she actually saw anything. There was no likelihood that the carnosaur would wander away from its kill, even to pursue a rival. Adrienne, who did not understand the beast's instincts, in her fear imagined it charging toward them. The guide let himself down from the branch on which he sat, falling the last five feet to the ground.

Adrienne thought Vickers must have struck his head during the crash. From her vantage point, thirty feet in the air and well outboard on the limb that supported her, she had an excellent view of the tyrannosaur. Only low brush separated it from the tree in which they had crashed. The beast had stood for a moment at the point Washman lifted the platform in his effort to escape. Now it was ramping like a creature from heraldry, balanced on one leg with its torso high and the other hind leg kicking out at nothing. At first she did not understand; then she saw that each time the foot drew back, it caressed the wounded belly.

Suddenly the big carnivore stopped rubbing itself. It had been facing away from the tree at a 30° angle. Now it turned toward the woman, awesome even at three hundred yards. It began to stalk forward. Its head swung low as usual, but after each few strides the beast paused. The back raised, the neck stretched upward, and now Adrienne could see that the nostrils were spreading. A leaf, dislodged when Vickers scrambled to the ground, was drifting down. The light breeze angled it toward the oncoming dinosaur.

Vickers cut through one of the lower cross-straps holding Washman five feet in the air with his seat above him. The pilot was alive but unconscious. The guide reached up for the remaining strap, his free hand and forearm braced against the pilot's chest to keep him from dropping on his face.

"Henry, for God's sake!" the woman above him shouted. "It's only a hundred yards away!"

Vickers stared at the wall of brush, his lips drawn back in a snarl. "Where are the guns? Can you see the guns?"

"I can't see them! Get back, for God's sake!"

The guide cursed and slashed through the strap. To take Washman's weight, he dropped his knife and bent. Grunting, Vickers manhandled the pilot into position for a fireman's carry.

The tyrannosaur had lowered its head again. Adrienne Salmes stared at the predator, then down at Vickers staggering under the pilot's weight. She fumbled out one of her small cigars, lit it, and dropped the gold-chased lighter back into her pocket. Then she scrambled to the bole and began to descend. The bark tore the skin beneath her coveralls and from the palms of both hands.

From the lowest branch, head-height for the stooping Vickers, Adrienne cried, "Here!" and tried to snatch Washman from the guide's back. The pilot was too heavy. Vickers thrust his shoulders upward. Between them, they slung Washman onto the branch. His arms and legs hung down to either side and his face was pressed cruelly into the bark.

The tyrannosaur crashed through the woody undergrowth twenty feet away. It stank of death, even against the mild breeze. The dead sauropod, of course, rotting between the four-inch teeth and smeared greasily over the killer's head and breast . . . but beyond the carrion odor was a tangible sharpness filling the mouths of guide and client as the brush parted.

Vickers had no chance of getting higher into the oak than the jaws could pick him off. Instead he turned, wishing that he had been able to keep at least his knife for this moment. Adrienne Salmes dragged on her cigar, stood, and flung the glowing cylinder into the wreckage of the platform. "Henry!" she cried, and she bent back down with her hand out to Vickers.

One stride put the tyrannosaur into the midst of the up-ended platform. As flimsy as the metal was, its edges were sharp and they clung instead of springing back the way splintered branches would. The beast's powerful legs had pistoned it through dense brush without slowing. It could still have dragged the wreckage forward through the one remaining step that would have ended the three humans. Instead, it drew back with a startled snort and tried to nuzzle its feet clear.

The kerosene bloomed into a sluggish red blaze. The tyrannosaur's distended nostrils *whuffed* in a double lungful of the soot-laden smoke that rolled from the peaks of the flames. The beast squealed and kicked in berserk fury, scattering fire-wrapped metal. Its rigid tail slashed the brush, fanning the flames toward the oak. Deeply-indented leaves shrivelled like hands closing. Vickers forgot about trying to climb. He rolled Don Washman off the branch again, holding him by the armpits. The pilot's feet fell as they would. "While we've got a chance!" the guide cried, knowing that the brush fire would suffocate them in the treetop even if the flames themselves did not climb so high.

Adrienne Salmes jumped down. Each of them wrapped one of the pilot's arms around their shoulders. They began to stumble through the brush, the backs of their necks prickling with the heat of the fire.

The tyrannosaur was snarling in unexampled rage. Fire was familiar to a creature which had lived a century among forests and lightning. Being caught in the midst of a blaze was something else again. The beast would not run while the platform still tangled its feet, and the powerful kicks that shredded the binding metal also scattered the flames. When at last the great killer broke free, it did so from the heart of an amoeba a hundred yards in diameter crackling in the brush. Adrienne and the guide were struggling into the forest when they heard the tyrannosaur give its challenge again. It sounded far away.

"I don't suppose there's any way we could retrieve the rifles," Adrienne said as Vickers put another stick on their fire. It was a human touch in the Cretaceous night. Besides, the guide was chilly. They had used his coveralls to improvise a stretcher for Washman, thrusting a pruned sapling up each leg and out the corresponding sleeve. They had not used the pilot's own garment for fear that being stripped would accelerate the effects of shock.

Washman was breathing stertorously and had not regained consciousness since the crash.

"Well, I couldn't tell about yours," Vickers said with a wry smile, "but even with the brush popping I'm pretty sure I heard the magazine of mine go off. I'd feel happier if we had it along, that's for sure."

"I'm going to miss that Schultz and Larsen," the woman said. She took out a cigar, looked at it, and slipped it back into her pocket. "Slickest action they ever put on a rifle. Well, I suppose I can find another when we get back."

They had found the saplings growing in a sauropod burn. Fortunately, Adrienne had retained her sheath knife, a monster with a saw-backed, eight-inch blade that Vickers had thought a joke—until it became their only tool. The knife and the cigaret lighter, he reminded himself. Resiny wood cracked, pitching sparks beyond the circle they had cleared in the fallen needles. The woman immediately stood and kicked the spreading flames back in toward the center.

"You saved my life," Vickers said, looking into the fire. "With that cigar. You were thinking a lot better than I was, and that's the only reason I'm not in a carnosaur's belly."

Adrienne sat down beside the guide. After a moment, he met her eyes. She said, "You could have left Don and gotten back safely yourself."

"I could have been a goddam politician!" Vickers snapped, "but that wasn't a way I wanted to live my life." He relaxed and shook his head. "Sorry," he said. She laughed and squeezed his bare knee above the abrasion. "Besides," Vickers went on,

"I'm not sure it would have worked. The damned tyrannosaur was obviously tracking us by scent. Most of what we know about the big carnivores started a minute or two before they were killed. They . . . I don't mean dinos're smart. But their instincts are a lot more efficient than you'd think if you hadn't watched them."

Adrienne Salmes nodded. "A computer isn't smart either, but that doesn't keep it from solving problems."

"Exactly," Vickers said, "exactly. And if the problem that tyrannosaur was trying to solve was us— well, I'm just as glad the fire wiped out our scent. We've got a long hike tomorrow lugging Don."

"What bothers me," the blonde woman said carefully, "Is the fact it could find us easily enough if it tried. Look, we can't be very far from the camp, not at the platform's speed. Why don't we push on now instead of waiting for daylight?"

Vickers glanced down at the responder on his wrist, tuned to the beacon in the center of the camp. "Five or six miles," he said. "Not too bad, even with Don. But I think we're better off here than stumbling into camp in the dark. The smell of the trophies is going to keep packs of the smaller predators around it. They're active in the dark, and they've got damned sharp teeth."

Adrienne chuckled, startling away some of the red eyes ringing their fire. Vickers had whittled a branch into a whippy cudgel with an eye toward bagging a mammal or two for dinner, but both he and his client were too thirsty to feel much hunger as yet. "Well," she said, "we have to find something else to do till daybreak, then—and I'm too keyed up to sleep." She touched Vickers' thigh again.

All the surrounding eyes vanished when a dinosaur grunted.

It could have been a smaller creature, even a herbivore; but that would not have made it harmless. In the event, it was precisely what they feared it was when the savage noise filled the forest: the tyrannosaur hunting them and very close.

The fire was of branches and four-foot lengths of sapling they had broken after notching with the knife. Vickers' face lost all expression. He grabbed the unburned end of a billet and turned toward the sound. "No!" Adrienne cried. "Spread the fire in a line—it won't follow us through a fire again!"

It was the difference between no good chance and no chance at all. Vickers scuffed a bootload of coals out into the heaped pine needles and ran into the night with his brand. The lowest branches of the pines were dead and dry, light-starved by the foliage nearer the sky. The resin-sizzling torch caught them and they flared up behind the guide. Half-burned twigs that fell to the forest floor flickered among the matted needles. Vickers already was twenty yards from their original campfire when he remembered that Don Washman still lay helpless beside it.

The dozen little fires Vickers had set, and the similar line Adrienne Salmes had ignited on the other side of the campfire, were already beginning to grow and merge. The guide turned and saw the flames nearing Washman's feet, though not—thank God—his head. That was when the tyrannosaur stepped into view. In the firelight it was hard to tell the mottled camouflage natural to its hide from the cracked and blistered areas left by the earlier blaze. Vickers cursed and hurled his torch. It spun end over end, falling short of its intended target.

The tyrannosaur had been advancing with its head hung low. It was still fifteen feet high at the hips. In the flickering light, it bulked even larger than the ten tons it objectively weighed. Adrienne looked absurd and tiny as she leaped forward to meet the creature with a pine torch. Behind her the flames were spreading, but they were unlikely to form a barrier to the beast until they formed a continuous line. That was seconds or a minute away, despite the fact that the fuel was either dry or soaking with pitch.

Adrienne slashed her brand in a figure-8 like a child with a sparkler. Confused by the glare and stench of the resinous flames, the carnosaur reared back and took only a half step forward—onto the torch Vickers had thrown.

The guide grabbed up the poles at Washman's head. He dragged the pilot away from the fire like a pony hauling a travois. When the tyrannosaur screeched, Vickers dropped the stretcher again and turned, certain he would see the beast striding easily through the curtain of fire. Instead it was backing away, its great head slashing out to either side as if expecting to find a tangible opponent there. The blonde woman threw her torch at the dinosaur. Then, with her arms shielding her face, she leaped across the fire. She would have run into the bole of a tree had Vickers not caught her as she blundered past. "It's all right!" he shouted. "It's turned! Get the other end of the stretcher."

Spattering pitch had pocked but not fully ignited Adrienne's garments. The tears furrowing the soot on her cheeks were partly the result of irritants in the flames. "It'll be back," she said. "You know it will."

"I'll have a rifle in my hands the next time I see it," the guide said. "This is one dino that won't be a matter of business to shoot."

The alarm awakened the camp. Then muzzle flashes lit the white faces of the clients when the first dinosaur trotted down the trail. Even the grenade launcher could not divert the monsters. After a long time, the gunfire slackened. Then Miss McPherson returned with additional ammunition.

Somewhat later, the shooting stopped for good.

If he had not been moving in a stupor, the noise of the scavengers would have warned Vickers. As it was, he pushed out of the trees and into a slaughteryard teeming with vermin on a scale with the carcasses they gorged on. Only when Mears cried out did the guide realize they were back in the camp. The four clients were squeezed together on top of the machinegun tower.

Vickers was too shocked to curse. He set down his end of the stretcher abruptly. The other end was already on the ground. "Henry, do you want the knife?" Adrienne asked. He shook his head without turning around.

There were at least a dozen torosaurs sprawled

on the northern quadrant of the camp, along the
trail. They were more like hills than anything that
had been alive, but explosive bullets from the 12.7
mm machinegun had opened them up like chain-
saws. The clients were shouting and waving rifles
in the air from the low tower. Vickers, only fifty
feet away, could not hear them because of the
clatter of the scavengers. There were well over
one hundred tons of carrion in the clearing. Literally thousands of lesser creatures had swarmed out
of the skies and the forest to take advantage.

"Lesser" did not mean "little" in the Cretaceous.

Vickers swallowed. "Can you carry Don alone if
I lead the way?" he asked. "We've got to get to
the others to find out what happened."

"I'll manage," the woman said. Then, "You know,
they must have fired off all their ammunition.
That's why they're huddled there beside—"

"I know what they goddam did!" the guide
snarled. "I also know that if there's one goddam
round left, we've got a chance to sort things out!"
Neither of them voiced the corollary. They had
heard the tyrannosaur challenge the dawn an hour
earlier. Just before they burst into the clearing,
they had heard a second call; and it was much
closer.

Adrienne knelt, locking one of the pilot's arms
over her shoulders. She straightened at the knees,
lifting her burden with her. Washman's muscles
were slack. "That's something I owe my husband
for," Adrienne gasped. "Practice moving drunks.
When I was young and a fool."

Vickers held one of the stretcher poles like a
quarterstaff. He knew how he must look in his

underwear. That bothered him obscurely almost
as much as the coming gauntlet of carrion-eaters
did.

A white-furred pterosaur with folded, twenty-
foot wings struck at the humans as they maneu-
vered between two looming carcasses. Vickers
slapped away the red, chisel-like beak with his
staff. Then he prodded the great carrion-eater again
for good measure as Adrienne staggered around it.
The guide began to laugh.

"What the hell's so funny?" she demanded.

"If there's an intrusion vehicle back there,"
Vickers said, "which there probably isn't or these
sheep wouldn't be here now, maybe I'll send everybody home without me. That way I don't have
to explain to Stern what went wrong."

"That's a hell of a joke!" Adrienne snapped.

"Who's joking?"

Because of the huge quantity of food, the scavengers were feeding without much squabbling. The
three humans slipped through the mass, challenged
only by the long-necked pterosaur. Fragile despite
its size, the great gliding creature defended its
personal space with an intensity that was its only
road to survival. Met with equal force, it backed
away of necessity.

Dieter Jost lay under the gun tower, slightly
protected by the legs and cross-braces. He was
mumbling in German and his eyes did not focus.
Vickers took the pilot's weight to set him by the
ladder. Mears hopped down and began shrieking
at Adrienne Salmes, "God damn you your crazy
husband took the time machine back without us,
you bitch!"

Vickers straightened and slapped the contractor with a blow that released all the frustrations that had been building. Mears stumbled against the tower, turned back with his fists bunched, and stopped. The blonde woman's knife was almost touching his ribs.

"Where's Steve?" the guide asked loudly. He was massaging his right palm with his left as if working a piece of clay between them.

Miss McPherson jumped to the ground. In the darkness the tower had drawn them. Since both boxes of 12.7 mm ammunition had been sluiced out into the night, it was obviously irrational to stay on a platform that would not reach a tyrannosaur's knee . . . but human reason is in short supply in a darkened forest. "One of the dinosaurs killed him," the older woman blurted. "We, we tried to keep Mr. Jost safe with us, but we ran out of bullets and, and, the last hour has been—"

Brewer had a cut above his right eyebrow. He looked shell-shocked but not on the edge of hysteria as his three companions were. "When it was light enough to search," he said, "I got your ammo out. I thought it might work in his—" he gestured toward Dieter beneath him—"rifle. Close but no cigar." The meat packer's fingers traced the line which a piece of bursting cartridge case had drawn across his scalp.

"Well, we put the fear of God into'em," Mears asserted sullenly. "They've been afraid to come close even though we're out of ammo now. But how d'we get *out* of here, I want to know!"

"We don't," Vickers said flatly. "If the intrusion vehicle's gone, we are well and truly screwed.

Because there's never yet been an insertion within a hundred years of another insertion. But we've got a closer problem than that, because—"

The tyrannosaur drowned all other sounds with its roar.

Vickers stepped into the nearer of the ponies without changing expression. The engine caught when he pushed the starter. "Adrienne," he said, "get the rest of them down to the slough—Don and Dieter in the pony. Fast. If I don't come back, you're on your own."

Adrienne jumped in front of the vehicle. "We'll both go."

"God damn it, *move!*" the guide shouted. "We don't have time!"

"We don't know which of us it's tracking!" the woman shouted back. "I've got to come along!"

Vickers nodded curtly. "Brewer," he called over his shoulder, "get everybody else out of here before a pack of carnosaurs arrives and you're in the middle of it." He engaged the pony's torque converter while the blonde woman was barely over the side. As they spun out southward from the camp, the guide shouted, "Don't leave Don and Dieter behind, or so help me—"

"How fast can it charge?" Adrienne asked as they bounced over a root to avoid a tangle of berry bushes.

"Fast," Vickers said bluntly. "I figure if we can reach the sauropods we killed the other day, we've got a chance, though."

They were jouncing too badly for Adrienne to stay in a seat. She squatted behind Vickers and hung onto the sides. "If you think the meat's going to draw it off, won't it stop in the camp?" she asked.

"Not that," said the guide, slamming over the tiller to skirt a ravine jeweled with flecks of quartz. "I'm betting there'll be gorgosaurs there by now, feeding. That's how we'd have gotten carnosaur heads for the other gunners, you see. The best chance I can see is half a dozen gorgosaurs'll take care of even *our* problem."

"They'll take care of us too, won't they?" the woman objected.

"Got a better idea?"

The smell of the rotting corpses would have guided them the last quarter mile even without the marker. The tyrannosaur's own kill had been several days riper, but the sheer mass of the five titanosaurs together more than equalled the effect. The nearest of the bodies lay with its spine toward the approaching pony in a shaft of sunlight through the browsed-away top cover. Vickers throttled back with a curse. "If there's nothing here," he said, "then we may as well bend over and kiss our asses goo— "

A carnosaur raised its gory head over the carrion. It had been buried to its withers in the sauropod's chest, bolting bucket-loads of lung tissue. Its original color would have been in doubt had not a second killer stalked into sight. The gorgosaurs wore black stripes over fields of dirty sand color, and their tongues were as red as their bloody teeth. Each of the pair was as heavy as a large automobile, and they were as viciously lethal as leopards, pound for pound.

"All right," Vickers said quietly. He steered to

the side of the waiting pair, giving the diesel a little more fuel. Three more gorgosaurs strode watchfully out of the forest. They were in an arc facing the pony. The nearest of them was only thirty feet away. Their breath rasped like leather pistons. The guide slowed again, almost to a stop. He swung the tiller away.

One of the gorgosaurs snarled and charged. Both humans shouted, but the killer's target was the tyrannosaur that burst out of the forest behind the pony. Vickers rolled the throttle wide open, sending the vehicle between two of the lesser carnivores. Instead of snapping or bluffing, the tyrannosaur strode through the gorgosaur that had tried to meet it. The striped carnosaur spun to the ground with its legs flailing. Pine straw sprayed as it hit.

"It's still coming!" Adrienne warned. Vickers hunched as if that could coax more speed out of the little engine. The four gorgosaurs still able to run had scattered to either side. The fifth threshed on the ground, its back broken by an impact the tyrannosaur had scarcely noted. At another time the pack might have faced down their single opponent. Now the wounded tyrannosaur was infuriated beyond questions of challenge and territory.

"Henry, the river," the woman said. Vickers did not change direction, running parallel to the unseen bank. "Henry," she said again, trying to steady herself close to his ear because she did not want to shout, not for this, "we've done everything else we could. We have to try this."

A branch lashed Vickers across the face. His tears streamed across the red brand it left on his cheek. He turned as abruptly as the pony's narrow axles allowed. They plunged to the right, over the ridgeline and into the thick-set younger trees that bordered the water. Then they were through that belt, both of them bleeding from the whipping branches. Reeds and mud were roostering up from all four wheels. The pony's aluminum belly began to lift. Their speed dropped as the treads started to act as paddles automatically.

"Oh dear God, he's stopping, he's stopping," Adrienne whimpered. Vickers looked over his shoulder. There was nothing to dodge now that they were afloat, only the mile of haze and water that they would never manage to cross. The tyrannosaur had paused where the pines gave way to reeds, laterite soil to mud. It stood splay-legged, turning first one eye, then the other, to the escaping humans. The bloody sun jeweled its pupils.

"If he doesn't follow—" Vickers said.

The tyrannosaur stepped forward inexorably. The muddy water slapped as the feet slashed through it. Then the narrow keel of the breastbone cut the water as well. The tyrannosaur's back sank to a line of knobs on the surface, kinking horizontally as the hind legs thrust the beast toward its prey. The carnosaur moved much more quickly in the water than did the vehicle it pursued. The beast was fifty yards away, now, and there was no way to evade it.

They were far enough out into the stream that Vickers could see the other pony winking on the bank a half mile distant. Brewer had managed to get them out of the charnel house they had made of the camp, at least. "Give me your knife," Vickers said. Twenty feet away, the ruby eye of the carnosaur glazed and cleared as its nictitating membrane wiped away the spray.

"Get your own damned knife!" Adrienne said. She half-rose, estimating that if she jumped straight over the stern she would not overset the pony.

Vickers saw the water beneath them darken, blacken. The pony quivered. There was no wake, but the tons of death slanting up from beneath raised a slick on the surface. They were still above the crocodile's vast haunches when its teeth closed on the tyrannosaur.

The suction of the tyrannosaur going under halted the pony as if it had struck a wall. Then the water rose and slapped them forward. Vickers' hand kept Adrienne from pitching out an instant after she had lost the need to do so. They drew away from the battle in the silt-golden water, fifty yards, one hundred. Vickers cut off the engine. "The current'll take us to the others," he explained. "And without the paddles we won't attract as much attention."

Adrienne was trying to resheathe her knife. Finally she held the leather with one hand and slipped the knife in with her fingers on the blade as if threading a needle. She looked at Vickers. "I didn't think that would work," she said. "Or it would work a minute after we were . . . gone."

The guide managed to laugh. "Might still happen," he said, nodding at the disturbed water. "Off-hand, though, I'd say the 'largest land predator of all time' just met something bigger." He sobered. "God, I hope we don't meet its mate. I don't want to drown. I really don't."

Water spewed skyward near the other pony. At

first Vickers thought one of the clients had managed to detonate a grenade and blow them all to hell. "My God," Adrienne whispered. "You said they couldn't. . . ."

At the distance they were from it, only the gross lines of the intrusion vehicle could be identified. A pair of machineguns had been welded onto the frame, and there appeared to be a considerable party of uniformed men aboard. "I don't understand it either," Vickers said, "but I know where to ask." He reached for the starter.

Adrienne caught his arm. He looked back in surprise. "If it was safer to drift with the current before, it's still safer," she said. She pointed at the subsiding froth from which the tyrannosaur had never re-emerged. "We're halfway already. And besides, it gives us some time—" she put her hand on Vickers' shoulder—"for what I had in mind last night at the campfire."

"They're watching us with binoculars!" the guide sputtered, trying to break away from the kiss.

"They can all sit in a circle and play with themselves," the blonde woman said. "We've earned this."

Vickers held himself rigid for a moment. Then he reached out and began to spread the pony's front awning with one hand.

The secretary wore a uniform and a pistol. When he nodded, Vickers opened the door. Stern sat at the metal desk. Dr. Galil was to his right and the only other occupant of the room. Vickers sat gingerly on one of the two empty chairs.

"I'm not going to debrief you," Stern said. "Others have done that. Rather, I am going to tell you certain things. They are confidential. Utterly confidential. You understand that."

"Yes," Vickers said. Stern's office was not in the Ministry of Culture and Tourism; but then, Vickers had never expected that it would be.

"Dr. Galil," Stern continued, and the cherubic scientist beamed like a Christmas ornament, "located the insertion party by homing on the alpha waves of one of the members of it. You, to be precise. Frankly, we were all amazed at this breakthrough; it is not a technique we would have tested if there had been any alternative available."

Vickers licked his lips. "I thought you were going to fire me," he said flatly.

"Would it bother you if we did?" Stern riposted.

"Yes." The guide paused. The fear was greater now that he had voiced it. He had slept very little during the week since the curtailed safari had returned. "It—the job . . . suits me. Even dealing with the clients, I can do it. For having the rest."

Stern nodded. Galil whispered to him, then looked back at Vickers. "We wish to experiment with this effect," Stern continued aloud. "Future rescues—or resupplies—may depend on it. There are other reasons as well." He cleared his throat.

"There is the danger that we will not be able to consistently repeat the operation," Dr. Galil broke in. "That the person will be marooned, you see. For there must of course be a brain so that we will have a brain wave to locate. Thus we need a volunteer."

"You want a base line," Vickers said in response to what he had not been told. "You want to refine your calibration so that you can drop a man—or men—or tanks—at a precise time. And if your base line is in the Cretaceous instead of the present, you don't have the problem of closing off another block each time somebody is inserted into the future before you get the technique down pat."

Stern grew very still. "Do you volunteer?" he asked.

Vickers nodded. "Sure. Even if I thought you'd let me leave here alive if I didn't, I'd volunteer. For that, I should have thought of the—the research potential—myself. I'd have blackmailed you into sending me."

The entryway door opened unexpectedly. "I already did that, Henry," said Adrienne Salmes. "Though I wouldn't say their arms had to be twisted very hard." She stepped past Vickers and laid the small receiver on Stern's desk beside the sending unit. "I decided it was time to come in."

"You arranged this for me?" Vickers asked in amazement.

"I arranged it for us," Adrienne replied, seating herself on the empty chair. "I'm not entirely sure that I want to retire to the Cretaceous. But—" she looked sharply at Stern—"I'm quite sure that I don't want to live in the world our friends here will shape if they do gain complete ability to manipulate the past. At least in the Cretaceous, we know what the rules are."

Vickers stood. "Shlomo," he said shaking Dr. Galil's hand, "you haven't failed before, and I don't see you failing now. We won't be marooned. Though it might be better if we were." He turned to the man behind the desk. "Mr. Stern," he said, "you've got your volunteers. I—we—we'll get you a list of the supplies we'll need."

Adrienne touched his arm. "This will work, you know," she said. She took no notice of the others in the room. "Like the crocodile."

"Tell me in a year's time that it *has* worked," Vickers said.

And she did.

FIRST CAME *HAMMER'S SLAMMERS* ...
THEN *AT ANY PRICE* ...

NOW BAEN BOOKS IS PROUD TO PRESENT
DAVID DRAKE'S NEWEST NOVEL OF
ACTION AND HIGH ADVENTURE!

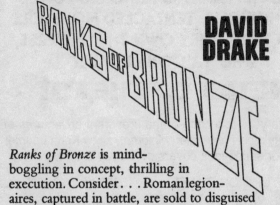

**DAVID
DRAKE**

Ranks of Bronze is mind-
boggling in concept, thrilling in
execution. Consider. . . Roman legionaires, captured in battle, are sold to disguised
alien traders to fight battles with primitive armies on
worlds across the galaxy. The legionaires adapt grudgingly
to their new role, but not out of gratitude for such ameni-
ties as soft billets and regeneration of their wounded
bodies following each campaign. Even the prospect of
near-immortality has no great attraction for them. What
keeps them in line are the strange and powerful weapons of their masters . . .

But Roman legionaires are a proud lot, and "culture
shock" is unknown to them. After being shuttled around
from campaign to campaign, taking it all in stride, they
are ready to go home. This, in spite of the fact that
thousands of years have passed on Earth . . . and in
spite of the fact that the weapons of the new "Com-
mander" and his guard are terrifying in the extreme.
Romans are Romans, and they *will* go home!

Read this masterpiece by the master of military action . . . only from Baen Books!

MAY 1986 • 65568-X • 320 pp. • $3.50

**IF YOUR PLANET IS BEING EXPLOITED
BY CHITINOUS, TENTACLED MONSTERS
WHO THINK THEY OWN THE UNIVERSE,
WHO YA GONNA CALL?**

RETIEF OF THE CDT

Complete your collection of the irreverent adventures of
the galaxy's only two-fisted diplomat, all by Keith Laumer
with super series-look covers by Wayne Barlowe.

THE RETURN OF RETIEF	55903-6	$2.95	____
RETIEF'S WAR	55976-1	$2.95	____
RETIEF OF THE CDT	55990-7	$2.95	____
RETIEF AND THE PANGALACTIC PAGEANT OF PULCHRITUDE	65556-6	$2.95	____
RETIEF AND THE WARLORDS	65575-2	$2.95	____

_____

Please send me the books checked above. I enclose _____
(Please add 75 cents per order for first-class postage and
handling. Mail this form to: Baen Books, 260 Fifth Avenue,
New York, N.Y. 10001.)

Name _____

Address _____

City _____ State _____ Zip _____

WE'RE LOOKING FOR
TROUBLE

Well, feedback, anyway. Baen Books endeavors to publish only the best in science fiction and fantasy—but we need you to tell us whether we're doing it right. Why not let us know? We'll award a Baen Books gift certificate worth $100 (plus a copy of our catalog) to the reader who best tells us what he or she likes about Baen Books—and where we could do better. We reserve the right to quote any or all of you. Contest closes December 31, 1987. All letters should be addressed to Baen Books, 260 Fifth Avenue, New York, N.Y. 10001.

At the same time, ask about the Baen Book Club—buy five books, get another five free! For information, send a self-addressed, stamped envelope. For a copy of our catalog, enclose one dollar as well.

Here is an excerpt from the upcoming novel by Roger MacBride Allen, author of THE TORCH OF HONOR, *coming in September 1986 from Baen Books:*

Hangar Two was the twin of the deck now being used as a ballroom, but where on one side of the bulkhead were gaiety and music, on the other side were gloomy, echoing spaces and the machines of war.

Sir George looked around the space with a distracted look as he sipped at his port.

"Uncle George, will you for God's sake put that stuff away!" Joslyn grabbed the glass and threw it across the deck. "You are the *host* at this party, and the captain of this ship, and I will not let you get to be a sodden drunk before the dancing starts—"

"I'm afraid I'm not the captain any more, my dear," Sir George said, very gently. "Though you are quite right to stop me drinking so soon. It wouldn't do."

Something froze inside Joslyn's gut. "Not the captain?"

"Oh, I suppose I still am, officially. But good old Joe Whitmore just let me know that it might be nice for me to make a toast to my successor—lovely way to tell a fellow, isn't it?"

"Oh, Uncle George, I'm so sorry," Joslyn said, all the anger washing out of her. "It's that doughy little man Thorpe-Peron, isn't it? I should have *known* why he was pumping me for all the information." She threw her arms around her great-uncle and hugged him.

At that moment, a disembodied voice boomed out. "Captain to the bridge. Red Alert. All hands to battle stations. We are under attack. This is not a drill. Captain to the bri—"

The first impact was felt more than heard, a booming, shaking roar that knocked them off their feet. The lights died, and, through the bulkhead that led to Hangar One, they heard the horrible sound of air whistling away into space, of screams and cries and alarm bells dying off when the air that carried them had vanished into space.

"Oh my God, they've hulled Hangar One," Sir George said, his voice deep with shock. They're all dead in there. My God."

Joslyn climbed to her feet—and then got back down on her hands and knees. No sense getting knocked down again, banging around in the dark, waiting for another hit. The gloomy red of the emergency lighting system flickered on, and she saw Sir George striding purposefully across the deck, toward the airlock at the aft end and the nearest way to the bridge. Now that she could see, she got carefully to her feet and kicked off her high heels.

WHANG! A huge noise like the greatest of all bells being run blared out, and the deck shivered. Joslyn fell again and got back up. There came another rending crash, followed by the deep, roaring shout of air rushing out into space. The sound seemed to come from deep inside the ship.

Alarms came on again, pilots and personnel came rushing into the hangar from the aft airlock. Voices began to shout, and a mad tangle of frantic activity tried to sort itself out as hangar crew and pilots readied for combat in the overcrowded space.

Joslyn's fighter, a command SuperWombat, was across the bay. Barefoot, in a ruined evening gown, her hair streaming behind her, she made her way through the confusion to her post.

SEPTEMBER 1986 • 416 pp. • $3.50

To order any Baen Book by mail, send the cover price plus 75 cents for first-class postage and handling to: Baen Books, Dept. BA, 260 Fifth Avenue, New York, N.Y. 10001. To find out how to join the Baen Book Club for fabulous discounts on all Baen Books (you must order at least five), send three first-class stamps or one dollar to the Baen Book Club at the same address.

Here is an excerpt from Charles Sheffield's newest novel, The Nimrod Hunt, *to be published in August 1986 by Baen Books:*

THE·NIMROD·HUNT

CHARLES SHEFFIELD

They were close to a branch point, where the descending shaft divided to continue as a double descent path. He had not seen that before, or heard of it in any of the records left by Team Alpha. It suggested a system of pathways through Travancore's jungles more complicated than they had realized. Chan looked again at S'greela and Shikari. They were both still engrossed in the Angel's efforts. He strolled slowly down along the sloping tunnel and looked out along each branch in turn.

They were not identical. One continued steadily down towards the surface of Travancore, five kilometers below them. The other was narrower and less steep. It curved off slowly to the left with hardly any gradient at all. If it went on like that the narrow corridor would provide a horizontal roadway through the high forest. Chan took just three or four paces along it. He did not intend to lose sight of the other team members.

After three steps he paused, very confused. There seemed to be something like a dark mist obscuring the more distant parts of the corridor. He shone his light, and there was no answering reflection.

Chan hesitated for a moment, then started to move back up the tunnel. Whatever it was in front of him, he was not about to face it alone. He had weapons with him—but more than those he wanted S'greela's strength, Shikari's mobility, and Angel's cool reasoning powers.

As he turned, he heard a whisper behind him. "Chan!"

He looked back. Something had stepped forward from the middle of the dark tunnel. He froze.

It was Leah.

Even as Chan was about to call out to her, he remembered Mondrian's warning. *Leah was dead.* What he was seeing was an illusion, something created in his mind by Nimrod.

As though to confirm his thought, the figure of Leah drifted *upwards* like a pale ghost. It hung unsupported, a couple of feet above the floor of the tunnel. The shape raised one white arm. "Chan," it said again.

"Leah! Is it you—really you?" Chan fought back the sudden urge to run forward and embrace the hovering form in front of him.

It did not seem to have heard him. Chan saw the dark-haired head move slowly from side to side. "Not now, Chan," said Leah's voice. "It would be too dangerous now. Say goodbye—but love me, Chan. Love is the secret."

Ignoring all common sense, Chan found that he had taken another step along the tunnel. He paused, dizzy and irresolute.

The figure held up both arms urgently. "Not now, Chan. Dangerous."

She waved. The slim form stepped sharply backwards, and was swallowed up at once in the dark cloud. The apparition was gone.

Chan stood motionless, too stunned to move. At last a sudden premonition of great danger conquered his inertia. He turned and began to stagger and stumble back towards the others.

A voice inside his head was screaming at him. *"NIMROD. Nimrod is active here. A Morgan Construct can produce delusions within an organic brain—it can change what you see and hear. Get back to the others—NOW!"*

He was suddenly back in the part of the tunnel where he had left the other team members. It was totally deserted.

They were gone! To his horror and dismay, there was no sign of the rest of them. *Where was the team?* Surely they would not have left him behind and gone back up the tunnel without him. Had they fallen victim to Nimrod?

Dizzy with fear, emotion, and unanswerable questions, Chan began to run back up the tunnel, back to the sunlight, back to the doubtful safety of the cetent in the upper vegetation layers. As he did so, the face and form of Leah hovered shimmering before his eyes.

AUGUST 1986 • 65582-6 • 416 pp. • $3.50

To order any Baen Book by mail, send the cover price plus 75¢ to cover first-class postage and handling to: Baen Books, Dept. BA, 260 Fifth Avenue, New York, N.Y. 10001.

Here is an excerpt from the newest novel by Martin Caidin, to be published in September 1986 by Baen Books:

MARTIN
CAIDIN

ZOBOA

The senior officer on duty on the flight line of Guantanamo Air Base on the southern coastline of Cuba checked the time, made a notation on his clipboard, and lifted his head as a buzzer affixed to his ear rattled his skull. He turned. They were right on time. Captain Jeff Baumbach moved his hand more by reflex than directed thought to check the .357 Magnum on his hip. He gestured at the armored vehicle slowing at the gate, its every movement covered by heavy automatic cannon.

"Check 'em *all* out!" Baumbach called. Military Police motioned the truck in between heavy barricades until it was secured. They checked the identity passes of every man, went through, atop and beneath the vehicle, finally sent it through the final barricade to the flight line where two machine gun-armed jeeps rolled alongside as escort. The armored truck stopped by an old Convair 440 twin-engined transport with bright lettering on each side of its fuselage. The cargo doors of the transport of ST. THOMAS OR-CHARD FARMS opened wide. The crew wore Air Force fatigues and all carried sidearms.

A master sergeant studied the truck and the men. "Move it, move it," he said impatiently. "Load 'em up. We're behind schedule."

Four cases moved with exquisite care from the truck to the loading conveyor to the aircraft. Each case carried the same identifying line but differing serial numbers. It didn't really matter. NUCLEAR WEAPON MARK 62 is enough of a grabber without any silly serial number.

The bombs were loaded and secured with steel cabling and heavy webbing tiedowns, men signed their names and exchanged papers, doors slammed closed, and the right engine of the Convair whined as the pilots brought power to the metal bird. . . .

In central Florida, horses moved through the tall morning-wet grass of a remote field. It is an ordinary scene of an ordinary Florida ranch . . . until the trees and the fences begin to move.

Tractors pulled the trees, tugging with steel cables to move the wheeled dollies from the soft ground. Pickup trucks and jeeps latched on to fence ends and moved slowly to swing the fences at enormous hinges. Within minutes a clear path seven thousand feet from north to south had been created, and the whine of machinery sounded over the staccato beating of equine hooves. Men kept the animals clear of field center, where high grass moved as if by magic to reveal an asphalted airstrip beneath. Still invisible to any eye, powerful jet engines rose from a deep-throated whine to ear-twisting shrieks and the cry of acetylene torches. Shouting male voices diminish to feeble cries in the rising crescendo of power, and workers move hastily aside as the front of a hill disappears into the ground and two jet fighters roll forward slowly, bobbing on their nose gear.

"Sir, they're loading now," the controller tells the lead pilot, knowing the second man also listens. "Are you ready to copy? I have their time hack for takeoff and the stages for their route."

The man in the lead jet fighter responds in flawless Arabic. "Quickly; I copy. And do not speak English again." . . .

"Orchard One, you're clear to the active and clear for takeoff. Over."

Captain Jim Mattson pressed his yoke transmit button. "Ah, roger Gitmo Control. Orchard One clear for the active and rolling takeoff. Over."

"Orchard One, it's all yours. Over."

"Roger that, Gitmo. Orchard One is rolling." Mattson advanced the throttles steadily, his copilot, John Latimer, placing his left hand securely atop the knuckles of his pilot. The convair sped toward the ocean, lifted smoothly and began its long climbing turn over open water. . . .

The horses shied nervously with the relentless howl of the jet fighter engines. Everyone on the field waited for the right words to pass between the controller in his underground bunker on the side of the runway and the two men in the fighter cockpits. A headset in the lead fighter hummed.

"Control here."

"Go ahead."

"Your quarry is in the air. Confirm ready."

The pilots glanced at one another. "Allah One ready."

"Allah Two waits."

"Very good, sirs. Three minutes, sirs." . . .

They came out of the sun, silvery streaks trailing the unsuspecting shape of Orchard One. Their presence remained unknown until the instant a powerful electronic jammer in the rear cockpit of the lead T-33 broadcast its signal to overpower any electronics aboard the Convair. The shriek pierced the eardrums of the Convair's radioman and he ripped off his headset. In the cockpit, Captain John Latimer, flying right seat, mirrored the reaction to the icepick scream in their ears. Instinct brought Captain Jim Mattson's hands to the yoke. But the automatic pilot held true, and the Convair did not wave or tremble. Only the radio and electronics systems had seemingly gone mad. The flight engineer rushed to the cockpit, squeezed Mattson's shoulder, and shouted to him. "Sir! To our left! There!"

They looked out to see the all-black fighter with Arabic lettering on the fuselage and tail. The pilot's face was concealed behind an oxygen mask and goldfilm visor. "Who the hell is that?" Mattson wondered aloud, and in the same breath turned to Latimer. "You all right?"

Latimer sat back, shaking his head to clear the battering echoes in his brain. He nodded. "Yeah, sure; fine. What the hell was that?"

The radioman wailed painfully into the flight deck with them, his face furrowed in pain. "Jamming . . . somehow they're jamming us. They must have, God, I don't know . . . but I can't get out on anything."

They exchanged glances. Not a single word was needed to confirm that they were in deep shit. Nobody shows up in a black T-33 jet fighter with Arabic markings and knocks out all radio frequencies unless they're a nasty crowd with killing on their minds. Mattson instantly became the professional military pilot.

"Emergency beacon?"

"No joy, sir. Blocked."

"Anybody see more than one fighter out—"

The answer came in a hammering vibration that blurred their sight. The Convair yawed sharply to the right as metal exploded far out on the right wing. "There's another one out there, all right!" Latimer shouted. "He just shot the hell out of the wing! He's coming alongside—"

They watched the black fighter slide into perfect formation to their right and just above their mangled wingtip. His dive brake extended. The pilot pointed down with his forefinger and then his landing gear extended.

"Jesus Christ!" Latimer exclaimed. "He's ordered us to land!"

"Screw that," Mattson snarled. "Sparks! Get Patrick Control and tell them we're under attack. We need—"

"Sir, goddamnit! I can't get out on any frequency!"

Glowing tracers lashed the air before the Convair. The T-33 on their left had eased back and above to give them another warning burst. They looked out at the fighter to their right. The pilot tapped his left wrist to signify his watch, then drew a finger across his throat.

SEPTEMBER 1986 • 65588-4 • 448 pp. • $3.50

To order any Baen Book by mail, send the cover price plus 75¢ for first-class postage and handling to: Baen Books, Dept. BA, 260 Fifth Avenue, New York, N.Y. 10001.